OMEGA

OMEGA

THE GIRL IN THE BOX
BOOK FIVE

Robert J. Crane

OMEGA

THE GIRL IN THE BOX, BOOK FIVE

Robert J. Crane

AUTHOR'S NOTE

This book is a work of fiction. Names, characters, places and incidents are products of the author's imagination or are used fictitiously. Any resemblance to actual events or locales or persons, living or dead, is entirely coincidental.

Contact Robert J. Crane via email at

cyrusdavidon@gmail.com

Layout and Formatting provided by **Streelight Graphics**

streetlightgraphics.com

Acknowledgments

These are the people who helped me during the writing and publication of this book, in no particular order.

Hated me by the end:

Heather Rodefer, my tireless Editor-in-Chief, fearless wielder of the purple pen and vanquisher of all typographical errors. This is the girl who never cries at the end of sappy movies, nor sheds a single drop from sad books. The fact that I made her cry is probably the greatest achievement of my writing career. She punched me over this. Seriously. In the arm. It hurt.

Damarra Atkins, she of the witty inside-geek jokes, who called me worse than Joss Whedon (Wha?! Every writer is worse than Joss Whedon! How much worse is the question...). But at least she didn't hit me.

Robin McDermott, who fixed many a technical error, and accused me of being far too wordy for my own good and yours, Dear Reader. I trust you all own a dictionary, though, so...

Shannon Garza, whose feelings I rely on to take the emotional temperature of my books. Whose heart I broke, whose tears I stole, whose forgiveness I may never earn. Sorry, Red.

Didn't hate me by the end:

Paul Madsen, who found any number of proofreading oopsies on my part, and who gushed praise about the ending. Well, probably about as gushy as Paul gets, I'm guessing.

Kea Grace, the first to finish, first to render opinion, and whose measured evaluation allowed me to stay the course.

Kari Layman, who berated me for almost an hour on the phone at a moment when I seriously considered changing the ending to something that would be less angst-causing. If you didn't like it, blame her.

Debra Wesley, whose gleeful cackling and constant attention to detail combined to make me worry about her until she told me she loved the story from top to bottom, and not to change a thing, even when Damarra (also) wanted to hit me for it.

Were thankfully neutral about the whole mess:

Sarah Barbour (aeroplanemedia.wordpress.com) who did the final edit and proofread in record time in spite of being hired at the very last minute, still managing to correct for errors great and small, including Russian language (Who does that!? She does!) and a number of suggestions that made the manuscript read much more smoothly. Sarah also did the editing on Untouched, but went unacknowledged due to authorial oversight.

Karri Klawiter of artbykarri.com, whose covers do shine like...uhh...well, they're shiny, in a very «Firefly» sense of the word. Shiny.

To my parents, who raised me, to my wife, who tolerates me, and my kids, who drive me slightly crazy. Love you all.

1.

They're coming for me, he thought, as he hurried down the sidewalk. The wind cut straight through him like a razor as it whipped through the space between the buildings and tore leaves from the trees that protruded from the sidewalk planters. *Downtown Minneapolis is somehow far colder than Dante's last layer of hell*, he thought as he avoided a steady stream of men in suits. *All the worse to know it's coming to an end soon.* The crisp smell of fall permeated the ebb and flow of exhaust fumes from passing cars. He huddled tighter in his coat and pushed his hands in his pockets, stretching the material as he did so.

Downtown was bustling but not too busy. Though you couldn't tell it by the dearth of sunlight, it was afternoon. The lunch rush had subsided and rush hour had yet to begin, so he was able to keep his route without worrying about fighting his way through the crowd. He passed a cafe that extended onto the sidewalk, only a table or two occupied. His hand ran over the cold metal rail that separated the empty tables from traffic passing by. As he caressed it, he felt a pause, a reluctance to go. In summer, on weekends, every table would be full, with a line of people extending out the door, waiting to be seated. It was a good place; he'd eaten there a time or two himself and enjoyed it. He lingered now, each step hesitant, a slow drag, as though the sidewalk were holding him back from the inevitable. *Here, there—either way, they're coming. If only I had more time*, he thought.

He reached the entrance to his apartment building, and as

he stepped into the revolving glass door, he caught a flicker of something in the reflection; eyes. Eyes focused on him. He followed the gaze back to a young man, blondish hair, in his twenties, *unremarkable save for the fact that he's watching me.* The blond man's eyes flickered elsewhere and he disappeared down the street after a moment, almost fading into the minimal crowd.

The revolving door discharged him into the lobby, where bronzed trim and marble floors made for a stunning spectacle. Full—length tapestries hung in four places around the room and a center desk controlled access to the elevators. He ignored the splendor around him, thinking again of the young man on the sidewalk who'd been watching him. He'd seen too many gazes like that lately, eyes following him in the streets as he walked, did his shopping, went to the clubs and talked to women. The tentative feeling gnawed at him again. *They're coming.*

Flashing a smile at the security guard behind the desk, he made his way to the elevator bank. The doors were bronzed, reflective, and fit with the decor in the rest of the lobby. He waited after punching the button for the elevator, his fingers tapping out a rhythm on his pleated khakis. He looked down and saw the faint discoloration of the tan made wet by his fingers and he pushed them against the cloth harder, wiping his sweat there. *Nerves,* he thought. *Just nerves.*

Casting a look and a nod back at the guard, he waited for the elevator. The revolving door in the lobby discharged another man, heavyset, with a balding head. He was big, older, wore a suit, and passed the security guard with a nonchalant wave. The big man came to the elevator as it dinged and followed him in.

"How 'bout them Vikings?" the big man asked. His face bore scars of old acne, and when he smiled, his teeth were yellowed from either coffee or tobacco.

Why does he have to turn this into an awkward moment? Was there something wrong with silence? The younger man returned the smile, weakly, wishing the elevator went faster. "I don't watch football," he said, feeling the distance between them in the elevator and wishing it were considerably more.

"Oh, man, they're off to a great start," the older man said. "I haven't seen a start like this since the year Favre was with them."

The younger man maintained his pleasant smile; he was good at that. "I don't have a clue what you're talking about, but good to hear."

"Ah, you should watch," the older man said, and turned back to the front of the elevator. "Great stuff."

"It's not for me. Too violent." He smiled politely and watched the dial slowly move until the elevator dinged and he sighed in not—too obvious relief. "Well," he said with a nod to the older man, "this is me."

"Oh, yeah, right," the older man said, and squeezed his large frame to the side of the elevator. "Have a good one, okay?"

"You, too." It even sounded sincere.

The elevator opened to a long hallway, and at the end was a window, autumn sun shining through it onto the red carpeting. The walls were done in crimson and beige tones, warm and inviting. He walked, trudging almost, enjoying the heat that came from the radiators on the walls around him after the chill of the street. *Winter is going to be terrible*, he thought. *If I'm even around for it.* Misery settled on him like the chill weather, and he shuddered.

A woman emerged from the doorway across from his, only a few feet ahead of him. Her hair was long and blond, and she was striking, willowy, athletic—and surprisingly busty, he wasn't too distracted to notice. His smile was easy, it didn't just pop up like some cheesy car salesman—it started slow, and spread across his entire face, a warming effect that he'd practiced long and hard to achieve. He didn't feel much use for it right now, *but for her...* "Hello," he said.

She returned the smile. She was stunning, her hair falling to her shoulders, the green in her eyes giving her a warmth that he couldn't recall seeing in any of the women he'd dated recently. "Hello," she said.

"Wow, hey," he said, as she walked on, turning slightly to watch him as he continued to speak, "looks like we're neighbors." He almost slapped himself in the forehead for the sheer ridiculousness of that statement. He held the smile on his face in spite of it, and saw the return from her.

"Well, I guess I'll..." He watched her receding back as he admired everything about the shapeliness of it, "...see you around." *Still got it, at least.* His smile turned genuine again, but she did not turn to respond, and arrived at the elevator as it opened again, revealing the big man who'd ridden up with him.

His smile vanished and he pivoted abruptly to walk back toward his door, as though a simple change of direction could make the big man disappear. He cast a look back and the two of them were standing there, at the elevator, waiting, watching him. He felt a pang of uneasiness and looked in the other direction, toward the end of the hallway where the stairs were. There, waiting, was the blond man from the street, staring down the hallway. With him was a shorter, muscular man with a blunter face and blond hair a shade sandier than his companion.

He drew a sharp breath and felt a tremor of recognition, seeing all four of them now. *They're here. Blocking the stairs and the elevator. No retreat.* He hesitated only a moment as he fingered his keys in his pocket and felt for the right one, knowing that movement would seal his fate, would spring them in motion against him.

He felt the key, the grooves, how it differed from the plastic top of his car key, how much larger in size it was from the key to his padlocked storage unit in the basement or the one that unlocked the safety deposit box at his bank. He looked again, and they had all begun the walk toward him, all four of them—*Katrina Forrest,* he thought, looking at the blond whose eye he had been trying to catch only a moment before. *Kurt Hannegan*, the big man, *Scott Byerly*, the blunt—faced man near the stairs. *And Zack Davis. Of course he looked familiar. He's* her *boyfriend...*

He brought up the key and lunged the last few feet to his door, fumbling, sliding it down the side of the lock, as he missed on his first attempt. He looked again, and Byerly was coming at him now, leading Davis, with Forrest coming fast from his left, walking, but faster than any human had any business doing. He felt the panic rising now, as the key plunged into the lock and he turned it as he worked the handle.

He threw himself through the door and slammed it behind him, throwing down the deadbolt and hitting the hand lock. He let his head fall against the door and his hand dipped into his pocket, retrieving the phone within. His fingers dialed the number by memory, and he thrust it against his ear, feeling it rub against the stubble on his cheek that he had thought was so sexy when he cultivated it. A deep breath, then another, and he heard it ring.

He felt a presence, and he felt the first THUMP! outside his door as footsteps stopped in front of it. He turned his head to the right and saw the figure in black, shorter than he, a mask covering all but the eyes. He saw the flash of blue in them as the figure started to move.

"What the—" The butt of a submachine gun came up and clipped him across the jaw, hard. He felt the phone slip from his fingers as he hit the ground. The phone skittered across the wood floor of his apartment, and he could hear a small, tinny voice from the speaker as it did so. He felt his palms pressed against the cool of the wood, felt his cheek land on it, tasted the blood in his mouth as he bit his tongue and spat it, the deep crimson getting lost in the dark cherrywood tones.

He rolled to his back and saw the figure standing over him, clad all in black, mask covering everything save for the eyes. "Overly dramatic, wouldn't you say?" he asked. "All black, in the middle of the day, in downtown Minneapolis?"

The black—clad figure's head cocked and he took his opening, hitting the figure with a fast kick that it had to dodge. A woman, he realized as he clambered to his feet, noticing the curve of the hips under the black clothing, the shape of breasts hidden under the tactical vest—*she's good, though,* he thought. She wheeled back, away from his kick, and he saw the submachine gun fall from her grasp, caught by the strap hung diagonally across her shoulder. He pressed forward as she fell back and he threw a punch that she dodged, as his fist carried through the drywall, making a hole that swallowed him up to the elbow. "I don't like to hit girls," he said in a low tone, pulling his hand free of the wall, "but you're not leaving me much choice."

"No, you don't hit them." Her hands came up in a defensive posture. She let loose a kick that hit him on the jaw and sent him to the ground. "You just kill them."

His face slammed into the floor, bouncing off the boards. A spinning sensation caused his inner ear to waver, and he let his hand remain under him, as it snaked its way back into his coat. He heard her move over him, and just as she got to him, he turned over and the pistol came with him, pointed into the face hidden by the black mask. Her submachine gun was pointed at him, his pistol at her. Her eyes got wide, and he started to squeeze the trigger.

A gust of tornado—force wind blew through the apartment and caught him, lifting him off the ground and hurling him against the wall. He landed on a table and heard the wood crack and splinter as he broke through it, then felt the shock of his nose colliding with the floor. He shook his head, feeling the blood run down his upper lip. Through cloudy vision, he saw another figure by the sliding glass door to the patio, this one a man. An expansive view of downtown Minneapolis was stretched behind the man, this one without a mask. He had a camera rig headset on and was silhouetted against the light shining behind him. *Reed Treston*, he thought,

head swimming. *Alpha. Son of a—*

The woman reappeared over him, the submachine gun barrel pointed right into his eyes. At this range, there was no dodging, only pain, and if the shot were true, certain death. "Looks like you got me," he conceded, "so what are you gonna do? Shoot me here?"

"Oh, I don't think so," came the voice, softer than he would have predicted. He blinked as her hand tugged at the mask and it came up to reveal soft, pale features, complexion slightly freckled, then came off the top of her head to allow long brown hair to flow down.

He let out a sigh, this time of annoyance. "Sienna Nealon."

"James Fries," she said with a smile, returning her hand to the forward grip of the gun. "It would be my very great pleasure if you would try and resist again." There was a gleam in her eyes that he saw as she reached over and unlocked the door. It cracked open to admit the others from the hallway—Davis, Hannegan, Forrest and Byerly. "Extraction on the roof in five," she said, and smiled down at him again, taking a pair of glistening handcuffs off her belt. "You can either put these on and walk or refuse and be carried." Her smile turned sweetly devastating. "Personally, I'm rooting for the refuse—and—be—carried option, because I get to be the one that beats you into submission."

The Black Hawk helicopter took off from the top of the building, unnoticed by nearly everyone downtown. A few heads swiveled as the sound of the chopper blades drew their attention, but they quickly went back to walking their paths, filing along the sidewalks. All but one.

A gray—haired man with a long face watched, his eyes tracing the flight path of the Black Hawk as it cut across the sky and out of sight behind the Wells Fargo tower. His face was wrinkled, his height merely average, and he wore a dark trench coat that looked only slightly out of place on a Minneapolis street in fall. His brown eyes were sunken into sockets that gave him a somewhat emaciated look, but there was intelligence in them, hiding behind the decrepit facade. When the helicopter disappeared from sight, his withered hand reached into the pocket of his trench coat and reappeared after a moment's search with a smart phone.

He stared at the brightly lit display that took up the whole front, so different from the first models he still remembered with fondness, the wall—mounted black behemoths that you cranked. He missed the operator, the voice on the other end that you could reach without even pressing a button. With a sigh, he touched the power button, causing the screen to flare to life. He pressed it twice more, and felt the wind pick up around him. "Call home," he said.

"I'm sorry, I didn't understand that," the phone replied, the soft, feminine computer voice almost lost in the roar of the wind.

"Call...HOME," he said again, his voice cracking, thickly accented.

"I'm sorry, I didn't—"

"Oh, to the dark world with you," the man replied, and thumbed the contacts button. Scrolling through the names on the list, he searched for the one he was looking for, then pushed it with his bony index finger and held it up to his ear. The digital ringing sound was loud. *Technology*, he thought, *equal parts triumph and terror—miracle when it works correctly, horror when it doesn't.*

A woman answered at the other end of the line, with an unmistakable British accent. "Federated Exchange."

"Ah, yes, this is—" He froze, dredging his memory for the code name given him before he had left headquarters. "Uh...just a moment, I'm trying to remember my—"

"Yes, may I help you?" the accented voice lilted.

"Yes, I need to speak with, uh...I forget his code name. Put me through to—"

"I'm sorry, sir," the voice came back over the line. "I have no idea what you're talking about."

"Oh, hell, this is—wait." He closed his eyes and tried to recall, then stomped his feet to try to stay warm as the chill wind funneled its way down the street between the buildings like a thousand icy needles hitting him in the face. "Oh, yes—this is Portal, calling for...uh...Alastor." He waited, listening for any sound on the other end of the phone, wondering if his hearing was failing him.

"I'll put you through straight away, sir. Thank you for calling."

"Alastor." The voice at the other end of the line was an ocean away, but he sounded as though he was right there, speaking into the old man's ear.

"This is Portal," the old man said. "I am in Minneapolis, and I just concluded a meeting with—" He hesitated, trying to remember Fries' codename, and felt the warm bloom of anger within. "Damn it all, I'm too old for this cloak and dagger business. I just met with Fries. He's been taken by the Directorate. I just saw their helicopter lift off from the top of his building."

"Has he now?" There was not even a pause on the other end of the line before the answer came. "Much sooner than anticipated, but unsurprising. Operation Stanchion will proceed as planned. You are prepared?"

The old man felt the tug of warmth within, the burning of a fire that had been with him all his life. "Ready enough. My pieces are moving into place."

A chuckle could be heard on the other end of the phone. "They thought we declared war on them months ago, these upstarts, this Directorate. They have no idea what war looks like, not most of them—none save for the *Jotun*."

"He is old," Portal said, feeling the shudder of the harsh Midwest autumn run through him. "Even compared to us, and he grows weaker since Peshtigo—"

"Yes," the voice came again. One of his oldest friends; the words came clearly, as though he were in the same room. *Miracle now, terror later, this technology*, he thought. "Do not forget, Operation Stanchion has but one purpose—and lest you forget, in the midst of all that must happen—"

"I will not forget," the older man replied, feeling the chill mingle with the excitement flowing through him. "The purpose of Omega is clear and has been since the days of old. I have not lost sight of it even if some of our own have. I will hold to Stanchion, to the plan I outlined for you—though," he said with a chuckle, "I may occasionally forget the code words for the operation. I am, after all, somewhat older than most of your current advisors, and have little taste for the intricacies of their so-called 'black' operations."

"I believe that is an outdated term," the voice came from the other end of the phone.

"So is the concept of gods who rule the world," the man who was codenamed Portal replied. "But that doesn't make it any less accurate."

"True enough. True enough. Take care, my friend. Take care of yourself-and our prize."

"Oh, I will." He let the smile tug at the corners of his lips, feeling the odd, drawn feeling from them as they began to chap from the wind. "I will ensure that Sienna Nealon will be ours."

"Good enough," the voice came again. "Until we meet again. Alastor out."

The old man heard the click through the speaker of the phone, and kept it up to his ear for a moment longer. "So long, old friend. I'll be home before you know it—with our prize."

"Let me do an internet search for chili cheese fries," a metallic, tinny voice blared from the speaker of his phone.

"What?" He held it up in front of him, staring blankly at the screen, which was lit up with a series of text bubbles. "No, I don't want you to do an internet search. And where did you come up with chili cheese fries?"

"Searching for a chili cheese fries app."

"What?" He stared at the screen, felt the confusion rise with embarrassment as a couple of teenagers brushed past him. He glanced up and saw one of them, a boy, looking at him, laughing. "Oh, shut up," he said, fumbling to push a button on the touchscreen with his fingers encased in a glove.

"Movie shopper—opening movie ticket app—"

He fumbled and pressed the power button, watching as the screen went dark. "Damnable thing."

"Let me do an internet search for a song to sing—"

He grumbled with irritation and pressed the button again, as the screen went black once more and the voice of the computer went quiet. His eyes came up again, back to Fries' building. "Stanchion. Oh, yes, Directorate, you will see. And Sienna Nealon, you'll be with us soon...whether you want to or not."

There was a moment's pause, then a muffled voice came from within his hand. "Let me do an internet search for bookstore oh yes director tools see you soon the new be us in—"

With a grunt of rage, he pitched the phone against the wall and watched it shatter into a cloud of plastic dust. He felt some of the debris sprinkle across his face, then shook his head at the momentary loss of temper and looked around. No one was paying attention to him. He sighed. "Now I'll have to buy another one. And doubtless it will work just as well as this one..." His eyes went back to the roof of Fries' building and the place that the helicopter's flight path had taken it only moments before. "No matter. Soon she'll be with us." He felt the smile return to his lips, revealing his teeth, exposing them to the cold .

"Soon."

2.

Sienna Nealon

The helicopter ride was smooth, surprisingly so for such a blustery day. It was my first autumn out in the world, out of my house, and I liked it better than summer and winter so far, but not as much as spring. The city of Minneapolis was fading behind us, the tall buildings and the skyline still a scene of mystery and excitement for me, even though I had been there more times than I could count now.

James Fries sat across from me, unspeaking. Of course, he had duct tape across his mouth and a black hood over his head, but I suspect even if he hadn't been so afflicted, he would have been smart enough to keep his mouth shut around me. It had been only about three months since he'd seduced me, using the fact that he was the only person I'd ever met whom I could safely touch to parlay himself into a romantic situation. It was not a shining moment in my memory. It left me with a few simmering resentments and a mess of regrets. Staring at him now, face hidden behind the hood, I liked to imagine that he might have felt a regret or two as well. You know, behind the duct tape.

The helicopter began its descent over the Directorate campus, the headquarters building with its white concrete and glass design visible below. The ground was covered with red and yellow leaves, drawing a slight smile and overriding my sense of cold satisfaction. Zack was diagonal from me, and I caught his gaze once, at least.

Around me, everyone was all smiles. Except Kurt Hannegan. He just looked stiff.

The campus was glorious, a miasma of autumn leaf colors standing out against the still—green grass that they lay upon. A few leaves still clung to their host trees stubbornly, apparently unaware that their eviction was imminent. That was okay by me, though, because I loved the colors, loved how they contrasted with the dull brown bark of their progenitors. I wasn't looking forward to the last of them leaving, because I knew winter was coming. I shivered; it was my least favorite time of the year.

The smell of gun oil in the cabin was strong, and I felt the weight of the chopper shifting as the wheels touched down. I reached across and grabbed James by the arm as Scott released his restraints. I tugged him to his feet as Reed opened the door for me and I pulled Fries out. He almost made a misstep but caught himself, and I pulled him along blindly toward the red-haired woman standing at the edge of the landing pad.

"Hello, Ariadne," I said with a smile. "We've got to stop meeting like this."

She raised an eyebrow. "You mean where you come back from a mission and I'm here waiting for you? You know how I worry."

"Hah. Yes, Mother."

She feigned a wounded look. "Coming from you, that hurts."

I pushed James around, front and center, and pulled his hood off. He seemed to flinch at the light. "Nothing we couldn't handle," I said.

"Good." She gave him a cold glare. "Nice to see you again, James. You probably didn't realize this, but we've been watching you for a while." I started to remove the duct tape over his mouth but she shook her head. "Leave it. I'm not interested in anything he has to say at this point."

"Okay. Say goodbye, James." I raised my gun and put the barrel to his temple. He struggled against my grip on his arm, but I had him held tight. I saw his eyes widen in surprise. So did Ariadne's a moment later when I brought the butt of my gun around and clubbed him in the side of the head, dropping him to the tarmac, unconscious, as the chopper's engine cut out and I heard the rotors begin to spin down behind me.

"I hope you didn't do any lasting damage," she said, looking to where Fries had crumpled at her feet. She stepped back, her high-heeled shoes clicking against the pavement, barely audible under the last noises of the rotors dying down. "He's here to be interrogated, after all."

"Hard to do brain damage when he didn't have a brain to damage," Reed said from next to me.

"Oh, he has a brain." I looked at my half-brother with a cocked eyebrow. "A horrific and sleazy one, but it's there. Cunning doesn't begin to describe this one."

"Yeah, well, let's get this cunning, sleazy bastard into lockdown," Scott said, Kat at his side. "Because some of us have plans for tonight."

"Carry him down," I said, giving the nod to Scott.

"Yes, ma'am," he said with a smartass salute, and reached down to pick up Fries's legs. "Reed, old boy," he said, affecting a British accent, "would you mind being a decent chap and help me carry him? There's a good lad..."

"What's with the British accent?" Reed asked, grabbing Fries by the arm and lifting him onto Scott's shoulder.

"Trying to make you feel at home," Scott said with a wide grin. "You know, because you haven't been home to talk to your bosses in a while."

"They're in Rome, not England."

"Oh, right," Scott said with a twinkle in his eyes, "then it must be cos' I want'd to sound a bit sophisticated, innit?" he said, changing his voice into a horrible Cockney accent. With a laugh, he sauntered off toward headquarters with Fries on his shoulder, Kat and Hannegan trailing behind him.

"Easy catch," I said, turning back to Ariadne as they left, leaving me with her, Zack and Reed.

Ariadne raised an eyebrow. "We were watching through the headset camera Reed was wearing."

I shrugged, and felt a slight trace of burn on my cheeks, not from the wind. "And?"

Ariadne kept her cool, I had to give her that . "The Director has...concerns."

"Concerns? Other than the fact that the frigid cold weather isn't getting here fast enough to suit him, what concerns does he have?"

There was a pause, then a flicker in her eyes. "Why don't we talk about it with him? We need to do a quick debrief with you as team lead, anyway." She looked from Zack to Reed. "Good work, gentlemen."

"It was a good takedown," Reed said. "We got him alive, and that's how it was supposed to be." I realized he was preemptively defending me, as though he was expecting me to get reamed for some reason.

"No doubt," Ariadne said with a tight expression meant to cut off any further discussion. "Gentlemen, we'll have a full after-action review with the two of you tomorrow morning. We'll email you a time and place."

Zack seemed to recede slightly. "We'll see you later, right? An hour?"

I managed a weak smile. "As soon as I'm free, I'll be along."

"Okay," he said, and took a quick step toward me, giving me a kiss on the cheek. "See you then."

Reed gave me a wave using only his fingers to waggle up and down. He followed Zack, and I watched the two of them make their way toward the dormitory. Ariadne was already on the move, high heels clicking as she walked the path toward headquarters. I followed a few steps behind, waiting for her to say something as we passed into the lobby and headed toward the elevators. She didn't speak again until we were in one of them and she had pressed the up button.

"How do you think you did?" She turned to look at me, but her arms were crossed in front of her. The doors shut behind us, quieting the buzz of activity in the lobby.

"I think we held to the mission parameters to bring him in, and that I got the job done." I watched her turn her head back to the front of the elevator car as it dinged and the doors opened. "Did I not get the job done right?"

"Sort of," Ariadne said, stepping out without waiting for me; she knew I'd follow. She walked stiffly, her tone terse but not unkind.

I followed in silence through the bustling cubicle farm that was ringed by offices on the top floor of HQ. Headquarters was only four stories high, but somehow the view it offered of the campus was still commanding. I walked into Old Man Winter's office a few steps behind Ariadne, and she took her usual position at his shoulder, like a parakeet. He remained behind his rough stone desk, the bright background of the autumn-tinged woods behind him through the window.

I stood at near-attention, my arms behind me in a military posture I'd picked up from Roberto Bastian, the leader of M-Squad. Old Man Winter was tall, commandingly so, almost seven feet in height, and that was evident even though he was seated. His skin was wrinkled and marked him as older than seventy. In reality, I knew he was at least a couple thousand years past that. He looked up as I entered, and his eyes began to bore into me.

"We watched the takedown," Ariadne said, drawing my attention to her. "We have our own opinions on how we think you did, and we want to discuss them with you."

Old Man Winter surprised me by speaking. "Fries broke loose of your ambush. He was a danger, he was mobile, he was clearly going for a weapon."

"Yes," I said, thinking he was done, "and I recovered from that as best I could—"

"You should have shot him," Old Man Winter said, stunning me. "You should have killed him rather than risk your own life. Fries is dangerous. You know he kills regularly, indiscriminately—for fun. You were in peril."

"Yes," I said, "but overall the situation was in control. My team was seconds away outside the door, Reed was waiting in the kitchen—"

"You put yourself at risk," Old Man Winter said, and I caught the edge to his voice, the first time I'd ever heard it. "Fries should have been put down like the pitiful rabid dog that he is at the first hint that he was going for a weapon. You are too valuable to put yourself at risk when it can be avoided."

I blinked. "The order I got was to apprehend him because we'd gone as far as we could by having him followed and tracked. I got the sense that he was valuable, that the intelligence he carried was worth us picking him up now—"

"Not the point," Old Man Winter cut me off, and his tone was flat, but blunt. "His life is nothing compared to yours. When you were entrusted with your team, it was understood that you would protect them. I expect you to protect yourself as well, and value yourself more than some Omega sop whose value is limited, at best. If you cannot do that, we need to re-evaluate your role and place you somewhere less..." His eyebrows arched, displaying the most emotion I'd ever seen him show, "...dangerous."

"No, sir," I said, and swallowed heavily. "I won't put myself in a position like that again."

"Do not be afraid to kill," he said, "not to save your team, not to save yourself. And certainly not for so low a form of life as James Fries."

"Yes, sir." I felt a slight contraction in my throat at their concern, a burning that I had failed them in some way.

Ariadne's eyes were soft, and she wore an almost sympathetic smile of understanding. "We just want you to understand your worth to the organization—and to us. Killing in your own defense is always preferable to placing your life at risk, and we want you to know that you'll always have our backing in that type of situation." She leaned forward. "No matter what. If your life is at risk, you are our priority. Not a stranger, not a random person, and certainly not an Omega operative. Pull the trigger next time, and we'll sort it out later."

"Understood," I said, and felt a slight tug in the back of my mind. "Is there anything else I can improve on?"

Old Man Winter said nothing, and Ariadne answered. "Nothing beyond the major concern we already voiced. We're going to let Fries stew for a night and then start the interrogation tomorrow." She smiled. "Should soften him up before we start asking questions."

"What do you think he'll say?" I looked at both of them, waiting for reaction, but found none.

Ariadne seemed to stare, cocking her head to look out the window. "I'm not sure, exactly. He'll probably be a tough one to crack. Hopefully he'll give us some pulse on what Omega's up to since they've gone quiet for the last few months after their assault on our agents."

"Assault is putting it mildly," I said. "They drew out and killed ninety percent of our human agents. They engaged M-Squad in a battle in Kansas that the news called an apocalyptic firestorm coupled with tornadoes."

Old Man Winter snorted. "The press is very easily led, in most cases. Especially when telepaths become involved."

I felt my jaw tense at the mention of the term telepath. I'd had my own encounter with a telepath only a few months earlier, and the memory was still with me. "Fries," I said, trying to bring the discussion back to center. "How do you want to handle this?"

"If you're up for it," Ariadne said, "I'd like you in there with Parks when he conducts the interrogation. You can play bad cop to his good cop. Just try not to go over the top with your performance."

"Fries is slick," I said. "He may see this coming."

"If it gets ugly," she said, "excuse yourself from the room. We'll figure out where to take it from there."

"All right," I said. "How far are we going to take this?"

I saw Ariadne's gaze flit to Old Man Winter, and his stone-faced response. He waited before answering, as though he were milking the moment of all the august pause he could put into it. "As far as it needs to go," he said. "Omega has you as their target, and they have intended to lay their hands upon you since day one. I will not let them have you." He let out a slow breath that fogged the air with frigid mist in front of his blue lips. "And I mean to know *why* they want you."

3.

I walked back across the campus after my meeting with Ariadne and Old Man Winter, his words echoing in my ears. Why did Omega want me? I wondered, too, and had since they'd first sent Wolfe after me almost a year ago. The leaves blew around my ankles as an eddy of wind formed, causing them to drift up in a whirlwind around me. I blinked and took my hands out of my pockets as two of them, maple leaves, ran across my face and tickled my nose. I saw Reed, his fingers extended to the glass from the lobby, a smile on his face. When he saw he'd caught my attention, he dropped his hand and the wind around me faded, the leaves drifting away.

He held the door for me as I walked up, my hands again snugged in the pockets of my coat. "Heya, brother," I said in as casual a tone as I could as I walked past.

"Heya, sis," he said, and let the door swing shut after I passed then opened the next for me. "How was your meeting? Or should I call it an ass-chewing?"

"Hardly." I walked into the lobby of the dormitory. It was a wide area, oblong and directed down two hallways to the left and right, the two respective wings of the dormitory. Directly in front of us was the entrance to the cafeteria. People were already lined up out the door for dinner; it was close to time. I was hungry, but I wouldn't be eating there tonight. "They just wanted to be sure I didn't hesitate to kill next time rather than let myself go into danger."

"I was wondering about that myself," Reed said, and I stopped, feeling my brow crumple as I gave him a look. The aromas of food came from within the cafeteria—meatloaf, I thought with a cringe. I could hear the chatter, some hushed whispers of a few newer metas talking about me in quiet undertones from near where the line formed for the cafeteria.

"Oh?" I let my head swivel; in a normal situation I'd have been looking for a threat. In this case, I was withering a nearby teenage boy with a glare for staring at me. He had brown hair and glasses, and he didn't look away from me, didn't turn red, didn't break eye contact. Annoying. "Why's that?"

"Because," Reed said, lowering his head from the top of his lanky frame as though he were trying to bring it into view for me because I was much shorter than him, "Fries had a bead on you. He would have killed you, no hesitation. But you? You didn't fire, even though you could have."

"I was told to get him alive, so I got him alive," I said with only a little hostility. Defensive much?

"And if they'd told you to bring him dead?" Reed's right eyebrow was higher than the other. He held eye contact with me just a second too long for my taste. When I didn't answer, he spoke again. "Why are you trying to scare off the newbs with your frightening glare?"

"I don't like the way they look at me," I said, turning back to the teenager who I'd caught staring. "Like I'm some kind of freak."

"Umm, no," he said. "They're not looking at you like you're some kind of freak."

I frowned at him. "What are you talking about? They stare, they whisper—it's a full-blown epidemic of gossip, just like it has been since the beginning—"

"Wrong," Reed said with a little more energy and a slight smile. "Some of that, yeah. But they're staring at you because they're teenage boys, and because you're—"

"What?" I let my voice rise and drew looks. "You're way off."

"Not so. You may be my sister—"

"Half-sister," I corrected.

"—but yeah, I still know. And they're not looking because they're gossiping."

"Awkward," I said with raised eyebrows. "But thanks for that."

He shrugged, but wore a smile. "I'm here to help." His face shifted a little, expression almost pensive. "I never asked you this, but you really didn't know I was your...?"

I let my face scrunch up to show my incredulity. "How would I have known that? Do you think my mother gave me a lesson in family history?"

"Just curious." His eyes went back to the teenaged boys in line behind me, and I followed his gaze. All but the one with glasses averted their eyes before we caught them looking. The one with glasses, he didn't seem to care, staring back at me, absolutely cool. "So you didn't ever feel like..." Reed let his words trail off.

"Like what?" I tore my eyes away from the teenager in line and looked back to Reed. "Like you were an awkward teenage boy?"

"Hah! No." He nodded toward the kid again. "You know...like he is towards you, but...towards me? Because you didn't know?"

A slow dawning came over me. "What? You mean like..." my voice turned hushed, "romantic? Ugh. Awkward much? No. No, never." I watched his olive skin darken and his brow furrowed. "I mean, nothing personal, you're a good guy, but—"

"Yeah." He held up a hand in a dismissive wave. "Friend zone. I got it."

"You're my brother, for crying out loud!" I kept my exclamation to a low whisper, but I still drew some swiveled heads.

"Yeah, but you didn't know that," he said, and nudged me in the ribs with his elbow. After a minute he grinned, and I shook my head, a smile of my own on my face. "Just needling you. You know, you should probably smile more often, Ms. Squad Leader. Maybe be more approachable. You might end up expanding your circle of friends."

"I'm good for now, I think. See you in a little bit?"

"I'll be there," he promised, and gave me a wave as he turned and walked out of the dormitory.

I watched him go, then turned and caught that teenager and his friends looking at me again. I shook my head and walked to the elevator bank just down the hall and pressed the button, causing a loud ding to sound immediately as one of the elevators opened for me. I stepped inside and pressed the button for the third floor, and waited for the doors to close as I pondered Reed's words. I had imagined myself to be rumored about in unkind ways, just as I had been a few months ago. It had always been that way for as long as I'd been at the Directorate, since I stood by and let Ariadne and Old Man Winter protect me while Wolfe was slaughtering his way through innocent people to get me to surrender to him.

The thought of people talking badly about me was nothing new, and easily enough dealt with; I had friends to help me cope, after all. The thought of people talking about me in more pleasant terms—for some reason, that bothered me. I had seen people steer away from me in the halls, and I preferred the idea of being feared to the idea of being lusted after. It creeped me out and brought back associations with Wolfe in unfavorable ways.

I felt a stir in the back of my head as the doors dinged open, and I realized it had been almost twenty-four hours since my last dose of chloridamide, the medication that kept my demons in check. Wolfe and Gavrikov were with me, always, and I could feel them through the medication sometimes, moving in the back of my head, like faint voices in an empty room. The chloridamide made it possible to (mostly) ignore them, to shut them away where I didn't have to deal with them on a constant basis. A couple months ago I had gone a day with a diminished dose to see if I could control them naturally; the increased chatter from the two of them was exhausting. They fought over the most inane things, bickering enough that after three hours I had no desire to listen anymore and took a shot of chloridamide just to shut them up.

I stepped out of the elevator onto the third floor, and walked down an open hall. To my left was a series of windows that looked down on the cubed structure of the cafeteria and to my right were doors, spaced every hundred feet or so down the hallway. The paint was fresh white, and the pungent smell of the primer and lacquer was still in the air. I took a deep breath of it, trying to ignore the fact that the chemical was probably not healthy for me. It made the place smell new, fancy, as if it had been built just for us—which it sort of had. I walked past four doors before I came to one marked with a gold plate that saidss "S. Nealon" on it. I heard the scanner next to the door beep as it reacted to the proximity of the key card I had in my pocket, and I reached for the handle and opened the door.

I had lived on the first floor of the dorms for most of the time I had been at the Directorate, but a few months ago, when I left training, Ariadne handed me a key card and pointed me to the third floor. I'd never explored up here, and I found to my surprise that this was where M-Squad lived. It required a key card on your person to even access the floor, and there were only the eight of us up here—the four members of M-Squad, Kat, Scott, Reed and myself. There was a fourth floor, of course, and I knew Ariadne and Old Man Winter both had quarters up there. I'd seen it only once myself, though.

My suite was light, open and spacious—lots of sunlight pouring down from the three paneled windows that opened into the living room, which was two steps down from the entryway where I came in. There was a kitchenette to my left and a subtle dividing half-wall that ran between the kitchenette and the living room. A set of French doors opened onto a balcony just beyond my living room, and the ceilings were high enough that even as a meta, I'd have had to put some effort into jumping to touch them.

The sun had finally come out from behind the clouds and

was lighting the room beautifully; it wasn't long until sundown, however, and I had a few things to accomplish before then. I went to the fridge, a new, beautiful stainless-steel model, and opened it. A few party trays were sitting on the shelves, with twelve-packs of cola. Along with my new quarters, I had access to a pool of assistants who could run my errands for me, paid for by the Directorate. I had sent one of the gophers to a local catering company to pick up some hors d'oeuvres earlier—finger sandwiches, miniature pastries, and a few other things for what I had planned for this evening. I pulled the trays out and set them on the table in the dining area.

I opened one of the cartons of cocktail wieners, smelled the rich, sweet barbecue and smiled. I pulled the toothpicks out of the cabinet and speared one through the middle, taking a bite. The fat had settled into the sauce, and it was delicious, a sweet tangy flavor almost melting on my tongue. I poured them into a porcelain bowl and stuck them into the microwave per the directions taped to the top of the dish. While they were warming, I pulled an ice bucket from below the sink and filled it from the freezer. When I was done, I grabbed the soft drinks and started burying them in the ice.

I heard a knock at the door and froze, my eyes turning toward the clock on the microwave. Fifteen minutes early; I smiled and walked to the door.

When I opened it, Zack was standing outside, a bottle of wine in his hands. I looked at it and gave him a smile. "It's illegal for anyone under the age of twenty-one to partake in that, you know."

"I'm here to make sure you kids don't get out of control," he said. "This is for later, for the two of us." He glanced at the label. "Maybe not tonight, but sometime soon."

"Ah," I said with a nod, letting my smile thin my lips. "I'll pass, but you can have as much as you want."

"None?" He asked with mocking grace, holding the bottle up by the neck. "You can't think of anything we should celebrate? Like, for example, your first successful mission as team leader of the new second rank of M-Squad?"

"Ah, yes, my role as the venerated leader of the B-team," I said with a forced smile. "I'm glad the mission went well, but we should probably save the celebrating for something big, not the forced abduction of a third-rate jackass."

"You really don't want to celebrate?" His face fell a degree, and I watched the bottle lower a little.

"I do," I said, and beckoned him in, giving him a very brief kiss on the lips. "But you know I'm not that keen on alcohol at this point...for obvious reasons," I watched his face contort slightly as I said this; it soured and he forced a smile, "so as long as you're all right with me toasting with a cola, I'm okay with it."

"I'm all right with you toasting without alcohol," he said as he brushed past me. I felt his hand run along the line of my belly, a soft caress as I leaned against the wall to let him enter my quarters. "Looks like you're really taking movie night seriously," he said as he cleared the wall and turned his attention to the food already on the table.

"I just want everyone to have fun," I said as I closed the door. "Help me get the last of the stuff out?"

"Sure."

With Zack's help everything was ready long before the next knock at the door—Reed, at a minute to five, and then Scott and Kat at five after.

"Reed, we need to get you a girl," Kat said with a frown as we all stood around the living room.

"You don't like me hanging around like a fifth wheel?" He asked as he scooped ice into a red plastic cup and poured cola over it—or pop, as they called it in Minnesota. Having learned everything in my life from television, I was still adjusting to that one.

"I just figure you'd be more comfortable with a girl of your own," she said, prompting Scott to nod his head in agreement. "You know, maybe help you feel less awkward when we hang out."

"Awkward? I'm just trying to be respectful of my sister's feelings," he said. "I figure having one more couple hanging around being overly handsy would probably just be salt on the wound." He turned his back on Kat and Scott, hiding a grin from the blond girl as she froze, Scott's hand planted on her hip, her back pressed to his chest. They looked like they were glued together most of the time. I couldn't deny that, but I never resented them for their ability to demonstrate affection.

Kat broke from Scott self-consciously, causing Scott's brow to pucker in a frown. He held himself awkwardly without her pressed against him, as though someone had yanked a blanket off him. She stood a foot away, shuffling back and forth on her feet with a forced smile planted on her lips. "What's that all about?" Scott asked. "Just because Sienna and Zack can't touch doesn't mean we can't."

"It's fine," I said with stifled amusement. "Really. We're okay, honest. It doesn't bother me if you guys are all lovey-dovey around us; I doubt I'd be that way even without my..." I let my eyes drift to Zack, who looked away, "...condition."

"See?" Scott leaned forward and his hand landed back on Kat's hip. She reddened, but made no move to displace it. "Sienna's a good sport about it." He pulled her tight to him again. Kat, for her part, held her body at an angle from his, as though she were trying to touch as little of him as she could get away with.

"If you two do get too frisky, though," I said, stirring the cocktail wieners in their bowl, "I will turn loose the firehose on you."

"Try it," Scott said. "I bet the water ends up going somewhere unexpected—like the front of your boyfriend's pants."

"I wouldn't bet on it," Reed said. "I have a feeling the wind might catch it and turn your girlfriend into a wet t-shirt contest winner." I heard a snicker from Zack and saw Scott's shoulders shake with quiet laughter as Kat remained posed awkwardly.

"Have you guys ever combined your powers to make, like, a water twister?" Zack looked from Scott to Reed, and I watched the silent conversation between the two of them as they both gave it a moment of thought.

"That's kind of a cool idea," Scott said, and separated himself from Kat with all the effort of turning loose a feline held against its will . "Should we?"

"Not in here," I said, replacing the lid on the dish and putting the spoon in its rest, splattering barbecue sauce on my tablecloth. "I need a metahuman power experiment in my quarters like I need Ariadne to dock my pay for a major remodel."

"Outside?" Scott suggested.

"Let's do it."

The two of them went through the French doors to the balcony, Zack a few steps behind them. Kat remained behind on the sofa, her face pressed into her hands. There was a light chill as the doors opened and shut, a gust of wind as they went out and Reed held the door for Zack. When Zack shut it behind him he gave me a little wave through the glass. Even though I knew he couldn't see me through the tinted pane, I waved back.

"Things seem to be going smoothly again between you two," Kat said. I noted a wet handprint on the side of her white jeans and my hand came up to indicate it with a point. "Hm?" She looked down. "Oh, yeah. When Scott gets excited, sometimes he gets a little, uh...out of control with his power, doesn't realize he's using it." She flushed and looked out the French doors to the balcony, where Reed and Scott stood side by side, Zack a few feet away at the edge of the terrace.

"Yeah, Zack and I are doing better," I said. "It's easier now, somehow, since we broke up and got back together, I guess." I grabbed a mini sub sandwich that had been sliced into one-inch segments, and took a bite. Roast beef, turkey, ham, lettuce, tomato, mayo and mustard combined in my mouth with oil and vinegar.

"Seems like that cut some of the tension out of the relationship, the inflated expectation because we'll never be able to, uh...well," I hemmed, "you know."

Kat's eyebrows rose. "Have sex?"

"Yeah. That."

"So you don't know how your mom did it with your dad?"

"Kind of, I think," I said, pinching the sandwich between my fingers with enough force that it pulped and I mashed it into my mouth before it came apart. "But I mean...I don't know. It doesn't seem very romantic, what I've figured out. There's not a lot of contact, you have to wear protection, it just seems..." I shrugged. "Cold. Calculating. Like Mom, I guess. Not warm and affectionate at all, everything at a distance except...well. Pretty sure I was an accident based on what she told me. I don't know, we've been doing..." I felt myself redden, "other stuff that seems to make him happy, so I haven't really wanted to venture into dangerous territory by trying something potentially fatal."

Her eyes widened. "'Potentially fatal' does seem to be on the far side of exciting."

"Not quite the kind of excitement I'm looking for, no..."

There was a noise out on the balcony, and I looked up to see Scott throw his hands in the air in exultation. "YES!" I heard him call through the glass.

"Oh, good, they've created an elemental disaster that they're super excited about," Kat said without any enthusiasm. "Do you suppose he'll notice if I'm not as thrilled about it as he is?"

I watched Scott turn around as the three of them came back toward the door, heading inside. "Nope," I said, "He's gonna be happy about this whether you are or not."

"That. Was. Amazing!" Scott said as they opened the door again, letting the chill wind follow them inside. Reed and Zack trailed behind him. "We totally did it, created a waterspout right in the middle of the lawn, out of nothing—"

"Yes," Zack said, unimpressed, "and promptly ran it over a line of meta teens that were leaving the building."

"Pfeh," Scott said with a wave of the hand. "Nobody got hurt."

"No," Reed said, "but that one kid looked scared as hell when he flew about ten feet into the air." I watched my brother's expression; he did not seem pleased.

Scott snickered. "Yeah, but...it was funny. You could have just dropped him the minute he walked into the path of it, you know."

"First of all," Reed said, "he didn't walk into the path of it so much as he veered like a moron into it and got sucked into the air, second, I didn't want to drop him because he was at least ten feet off the ground, third," he reddened, "I bet he never stares at Sienna in the cafeteria line again."

"Aww, you were taking up for my honor?" I gave him a fake smile. "The little one with glasses?" Reed shook his head. "Oh, well, still, how sweet. Next time, though, run your water tornado into Clary's room and wash the place out. Of course, that'd be a labor on par with cleaning out the Augean stables, though I bet it'd take more than a day, even if you used the entire Mississippi..."

"Can we get the movie going?" Scott asked, wiping his hands on his pants and leaving behind dark water marks where he touched. "I don't want to be out too late tonight."

"Why?" Zack asked, peering at him with snarky amusement. "You afraid of the dark or are you gonna start going to bed early like an old man?"

"Yep," Scott said with a nod as he slid back onto the couch in front of my widescreen TV, "I am going to bed early tonight. I want to be in bed by nine so I can be back out again before ten."

"Why would you go to bed just so you can get back up again?" Kat asked with a frown. "That doesn't make any sense— oh." The rest of us remained silent as her hand came up to her face, covering it from sight.

"Movie?" Scott asked again, a Cheshire smile twisting his lips into a grin as he turned his head around to look at me, still at the table.

After starting the movie, I settled down and let myself begin to relax, my preparations done. The couches were set up in a right angle in the little pit that was my living room. Scott and Kat sat on one couch, Kat's head resting on Scott's shoulder, her blond hair entangled in his brown, fuzzy mohair-looking sweater. I pondered that fashion statement until I realized she was wearing a similar one and that she had picked the ensemble out for both of them.

Reed sat next to me, slouching against the big, overstuffed armrest. He turned his head to give me a casual look. I didn't blame him for keeping his distance; after all, a brush of skin contact with me for more than a few seconds was painful. I returned his smile and watched him lean his head against the back of the couch, his focus back on the TV screen where Keanu Reeves was running into a flip off a pillar as bullets tore the lobby of the building apart around him, gray stone turning to dust and flashing through the air as he moved in slow motion.

"I could do that," I said under my breath. The bullets fly around Keanu and his billowing black trench coat as he kicked a black-clad guard so hard the man flew through the air.

"That looks so fake," Scott said. "How old is this movie, anyway?"

"1999," Zack said. "I was in middle school at the time, and it was the coolest thing I'd ever seen when my dad rented it for us to watch."

"You're kinda like that creepy thirty-year old guy that waits for his teenage girlfriend outside the local high school," Scott said, shaking his head.

"Excuse me?" I said with a raised eyebrow. "He's twenty-five and I'm eighteen. Your girlfriend had a centennial."

"What?" Kat's ears perked up. "Yeah, but I don't remember any of it. I'm just as mature as you guys."

"Setting the bar kinda low there, Princess," Reed said under his breath.

I saw Scott laugh, his face split into a wide grin. "She may not remember any of it, but I'm telling you she's got muscle memory from—"

Kat slapped him on the shoulder, her mouth open in faux outrage. "Shush!"

"I rest my case," Reed said with an upturned eyebrow.

It got quiet again after that and the noise of the onscreen action took over. I leaned my head against Zack's arm, and felt his heavy sweater against the back of my neck. I lolled my head to look at him as he watched the movie, focused intently on the screen. He was handsome, still as much so as the first time I had seen him. His spiked sandy blond hair and brown eyes were winning combination to me. My eyes followed his smooth jawline, and I found myself wanting to reach out and run my fingers over his face, no glove, but I resisted. I settled against his arm and watched the movie, feeling warm. The smell of the food and the light dab of my boyfriend's cologne combined into a single, hearty, familiar aroma that put me at ease.

The last light was dying outside the windows, the sun sinking below the horizon. The flickering of the TV from the movie was reassuring, and kept me looking back even as my eyelids started to get heavy. I took a slow breath, and a moment later I jerked back to wakefulness. The sun was gone, the TV was off, and Zack was looking at me with a faint smile.

"Did I fall asleep?" I asked, blinking at him.

"Yep," he said, still sweetly endearing. He had a glove on his hand, and it brushed against my cheek, coming to rest next to my eye as he kissed me on the temple.

I looked around; the couches were empty. "Everyone else...did they leave?"

"Yeah," he said softly. "They left a while ago, when the movie was over. We didn't want to wake you."

"Did they at least have fun?"

"Yes," he said and brushed his hand against my hair, stirring my bangs.

"Oh, good." I ran a gloved hand over my face, as though I could brush the sleepiness out of my eye. I felt wetness at the corner of my mouth and wiped at it. "Was I drooling?"

He laughed under his breath. "Just a little."

I felt sleep bear down on me again, teasing my eyes to close. "Okay. If they're all gone, I'm gonna go back to sleep."

"Okay," he said in a whisper. "I'll carry you to your room." I didn't protest as I felt him take up my weight and lift me from the couch. I heard him strain as he did it, but every step was smooth, and he was warm; I was pressed against his chest, the soft cotton of his shirt, with his smell filling my nose.

He lay me down on the bed and I felt his lips again, this time on mine. "See you tomorrow, sweetheart."

"Stay," I said, and my hand went to his face, and I traced the line of his jaw as I watched him through half-closed eyes.

"You want me to?"

"Mmmhmm."

I rolled to the far side of the bed and felt it shift as he got in, but he kept a foot of space between us. It was the only way to be sure I wouldn't accidentally roll over in the middle of the night and press my face against his. I could hear his breathing in the darkened room. The lamps outside radiated a faint glow that spread along the ceiling and the corners of the room. After a moment I heard him murmur something. "I love you," he said.

"I love you, too, Zack." My hand made its way across the bed and found his in the usual place, and I felt our fingers interlace through the leather both of us wore. It should have been so cold, so distant, but I felt the warm reassurance of his touch, even through the cowhide. I threaded my fingers through his and gave a gentle squeeze before I drifted off again.

"Hey," Zack said, his face clear in front of mine. We lay on the bed, and the light was more intense now, sparkling against the walls, almost surreal. Zack's skin carried a darker tone, as though the shadows around the room infused it, casting him in stark black and white contrast.

"Hey," I said, and reached out. My gloves were gone, and so were my sleeves, and everything else. Naked, my fingers brushed against his jaw, he drew a sharp breath and his eyes closed. "Hurts?"

"Just the opposite," he said, suddenly close to me, his skin pressed against mine. "I could stand some more of it." He smiled without showing his teeth. "So, does this make you the girl of my dreams?"

"You always use that cheesy line, you know."

His kisses were like fire, like a sweet hot shade of touch. I knew they weren't real, yet they felt fuller than the real thing. I looked into his eyes and felt the stir of something else there, like I could look deeper into him, and I resisted the call from within to do it. I focused on the sense of his skin against mine in the dream, and held onto that moment, that feeling.

"How do you do this?" he moaned as I ran a hand over his chest, causing him to tingle.

I could feel what he felt as I did it. "Dreamwalking is part of my metahuman abilities," I said, kissing him on the neck and sending him into ecstasy. "You know that."

"Yeah, but I get the feeling that the other people you've talked to in your dreams didn't get this..." He shuddered, his mouth opened slightly and he let out short, gasping breaths, "...sensation from being in a dream with you."

"True," I said, and kissed him on the bicep, causing him to sigh loudly. "But that's because with them, I was insubstantial; a ghost without touch." I felt myself fade into a shadow, as though I had become blurry, and I passed through him, reappearing at his back, where I planted a series of slow kisses and a caress along his shoulder, causing him to shudder. "I'm only real in your dreams."

"I'm...not complaining. But you seem pretty real when I'm awake, too."

"Yeah, but you can't touch me there. Not like this. Not like here. I wish we could..." I ran a hand over his shoulder.

"This is working plenty well enough for me," he said and moaned again as I traced my fingers along his spine. "This is unlike anything I've ever...it's just...so good."

I smiled and kissed him again, back in front of him now. I looked into his eyes through the haze of the dreamwalk, and I paused. His eyes were normally perfect, creamy brown, like the color of sugared and creamed coffee. "What?" he moaned as I hesitated, and he pushed himself against me again, brushing against my skin, and he sighed, a little noise of ecstasy. I held fast, though, unmoving, as he moaned in pleasure from the feel of my skin against his in this dream world, and he dissolved into the sounds of a man deeply, totally satisfied.

I held back though, frozen, unable to move, locked into the dream and the horror of thoughts I couldn't—wouldn't—share with him.

His brown eyes were gone, replaced with blue—bright, crystalline, cerulean—exactly like the ones I saw when I looked in the mirror every morning.

4.

I walked into Ariadne's office at the crack of nine the next morning to find her already behind her desk, a file in her hands, her reading glasses on. She wore them infrequently, only when she was actually reading, and as soon as I appeared at the door she hurried to put them back in her desk drawer, laying the file down in front of her.

"Why do you do that?" I asked as I flopped down in the chair across from her.

"Do what?" she asked, almost looking innocent.

"Put away your glasses when someone comes into the room?" I nodded at the drawer to her side where she had stowed them. "Everyone knows you wear glasses when you read."

"I..." She paused, as though thinking about it. "I don't know, actually. Just one of those things I've never given any thought to. Vanity, I suppose."

"But you don't wear make-up and you don't worry about how you dress...?"

I watched her face sag a little, before she formed a tight smile. "What can I do for you, Sienna?"

"I'm here for the interrogation. I thought I was gonna play bad cop, worse cop, with Fries this morning."

"Not 'til eleven," she said, picking up the file and opening her desk drawer again. She slid her glasses on and looked at me over the half-lenses. "I do have something you can do until then, though."

"Oh?" I perked up. "I hope it involves beating someone up. Because I like to play to my strengths, you know. Also, physics.

I'm good at math."

"Not physics, nor beating people up. You're behind on your quarterly physical exams," she said, running a finger over the file as she read along with it. "You need to see Dr. Sessions."

"I'll get around to that one of these days," I said.

"You'll go today, right now, if you want to continue to be cleared for duty." She looked up and found me with her gaze, more severe than usual. "This isn't negotiable, and it isn't just for you; we expand our knowledge base about metas from these exams, so help us out, will you?"

"O-kaaay," I said, dragging out the last syllable. "But only because you asked me nicely."

"Thank you," she said as I made my way to the door. "And Sienna?" She looked up at me as I turned around at the door. "Try not to kill Fries. Now that he's here, we want him alive."

"You sure? Because you told me if I felt in peril, I could kill, so it might be that he gets a little smart-mouthed with me and I feel threatened—"

"No."

"What if I didn't kill him, maybe just took a spleen or something?"

"No."

"But it'd grow back!"

She shook her head. "Take it easy on him. It's an interrogation. You're there to extract information, not his gallbladder."

"The gallbladder would be easier. Maybe less messy, too."

"Parks is an expert interrogator," she said. "Follow his lead. You're only there as a counterpoint, watch him work. This isn't a one-time interrogation so don't be surprised if you don't get much in the way of results. We have him now, there's no reason to get impatient when he's not going anywhere."

"Yeah, yeah."

I made my way across the campus. I was successful at

suppressing the thought in the back of my mind about Zack's eyes turning into my own during our dream rendezvous last night. After all, it was just a dream. I toyed with the idea of bringing it up to Dr. Sessions, but he knew so little about succubi I doubted it would be of any use to me, though he was certain to fawn over it like he did any other piece of irrelevant but interesting data.

The cool air was comfortable against my skin; I preferred the chill of autumn now that it was here, because I didn't look so out of place walking the campus in long sleeves, long pants, gloves and a coat as I did in the summertime. Talk about stares, especially when I went to the mall. Just as well, the skin on my legs and arms was beyond pale; I might as well have been a vampire. Well, not exactly like one. At least not the ones I'd seen.

A pile of leaves had blown into the small entry alcove to the rebuilt science building. It was different than it had been before Aleksandr Gavrikov had blown it up; the old building was brick, a 1970s facade and an interior not much more updated. Now it was all new and modern concrete, a more rounded profile instead of the square, blocky facility it had been before. I wondered how much of the Directorate had been destroyed and rebuilt since I had arrived. The proportion was not in my favor, whatever it was.

I knocked at the door to Dr. Sessions' office. The doctor looked up from his desk at my arrival, his bald head shining by the light of a lamp that was lit on his desk. He looked at me through his overlarge glasses, taking a moment to readjust them. "Oh, Sienna. Good." He blinked a few times, and then stood up, hitting his knee on the underside of his desk. I watched him cringe. "Ouch. If you'll come with me." He gestured toward the hall as he limped his way past me.

I followed him past the new drywall panels, and the glass windows that looked into the various labs. There were a few men and women in white coats working within them, messing around with who-knows-what as I walked by. We stopped at a room with a wooden door and he opened it for me. I shrugged and walked in. "Gown on the back of the door," he said. "I'll be back in a few minutes."

"Doc, is this really necessary?" I looked at him with constrained irritation. "Dr. Perugini has told you I'm healthy after conducting a physical, I feel fine—"

"Research, Sienna," he said with a suppressed smile that tightened the lines around his eyes. "We understand so very little about how metahuman abilities work, frankly, so it's important to take every opportunity to further our understanding. I promise I'll make it as quick as possible."

"Fine," I said with a sigh, and he closed the door. I took off my clothes in silence as I put on the gown, felt the cold touch of the tile floor on my feet, the nip of the air as I removed my shirt and jeans. The heat exchange above me was faintly letting out some warm air, which helped. I sat on the examination table, a padded monstrosity that sat in the corner. The faint smell of alcohol from the disinfectant station above the sink permeated the room, and the soft groan of the table felt like it could be audible three buildings away. "I'm ready!" I called out, hoping Dr. Sessions was still standing outside the door and hadn't wandered back to his office and forgotten about me.

The door creaked open and he stepped inside, wearing a buttoned-up lab coat. "This won't take long," he said, as he closed the door behind him. A blue latex glove rested on the handle as he closed it, catching my attention.

"That won't protect you," I said, pointing to the glove. "Keep that in mind."

"I'm well aware of the spectrum of your powers," he said as he circled around behind me. I kept a wary eye on him as he walked to the sink and started pulling things out of the cabinets above the counter. "I am, after all, the one who did the experiments to test those powers."

Shortly after I had arrived, Sessions and a few of his lab assistants (I never caught their names) took turns touching my exposed skin. It never lasted more than a few seconds, but they determined the threshold at which most people begin to experience effects from my touch (three seconds) and how long it takes the average human to pass out (about six seconds). For obvious reasons, we never definitively answered how long it would take me to kill a person. I was pretty sure it was something like twenty seconds. I'd never seen them pass out from it, though. I'd just seen them scream all the way to the end.

"I'll need to draw some blood," Sessions said. "I'd also like to get saliva samples—"

"You want me to spit in a petri dish?" I looked at him with a combination of loathing and skepticism. "Are you a real doctor or did you get your degree in the Caribbean?"

"Harvard   Medical   School,"   he   said   with   aplomb. "Highest Honors."

"Your mother must be so proud."

"Oh, she is," he said, as though what he were saying were of no more import than giving me a weather update. "Very proud indeed."

"I wonder what that's like," I said, muttering under my breath.

"Shall we begin?" He lifted his head up and smiled brightly, causing me to stir. I felt his touch as he pushed up my sleeve, and I watched him as he started to draw blood. His blue latex glove was on my bicep, and I resisted the urge to flex hard and knock it away just to show off. My muscles didn't look all that big. Actually, they were roughly the size of any of the other non-meta women at the Directorate. I had the strength where it counted, though—performance.

After a moment, a thought broke through and I reached to swipe at his hand. "Doc, the glove won't protect you for more than—" I stopped, and looked up at him, his face broken wide into a grin. He squeezed my arm for emphasis, and I realized he'd been holding onto me for well over ten seconds, and he was still sitting there, unaffected. "How?"

"New material," he said, and kept his hand on me. "I won't bore you with the technical details, but it's the same approximate thickness of a latex glove, but slightly more flesh-suitable, shall we say?" I felt his hand resting on me, and he was right. The glove wasn't rubbery, it didn't tear at my arm hairs as he ran it down to my forearm. It felt smooth, soft, almost like skin but not quite. He gave me a squeeze and brought the needle out with his other hand. "Might as well get this done while we're at it, but my plan is to keep a hand on you throughout the exam to test how long this material holds up." He gave a little shrug. "If it works, we could look at getting you some gloves made from it."

I stared at his fingers, draped in the blue material, snugged tight to his skin. "How about more than that?"

"More than what?" He blinked and readjusted his glasses. "More than gloves?"

"Yeah," I said, as I licked my lips. "What about...like...a bodysuit?"

His eyes seemed to stare off into space and his face scrunched up in thought. "Why would you need one of those? Your hands are the weapons, keep them contained and you should be fine—"

"Because," I said, cutting him off, "maybe I don't want to always be a weapon."

"Then wear gloves," he said, clearly not getting it. "It's simple, puts the safety on, if you were to continue the weapon analogy— you stick with long sleeves, long pants, shoes, and as long as you don't touch anyone with your face, you should be fine."

"You've never known the touch of a woman, have you Doc?"

He stared at me, inscrutable, for another few seconds and then the intense look of study dissolved. "Oh! Oh, for intimacy! You want a bodysuit so you can..." He blinked again, and his look of revelation cascaded into discomfort as his voice lowered in pitch and his face fell. "Oh. Yes, I mean...it is theoretically possible to make an entire body encasement of the material, and it's not that difficult for us to synthesize here in the lab." He gave my arm another squeeze and gently stuck another needle in my arm. "That is certainly something we could look into for you."

I stared straight ahead, considering the possibilities. "How... resistant is the material to breakage?"

He didn't even raise an eyebrow. "It's tougher than latex, can take more pounds per square inch of pressure before suffering a rupture. For something of that nature, it would need to be measured and specially fitted in order to give the level of...ah...protection... you'd require for uh...such activity."

"So it is possible?" I tried to look him in the eyes, but he didn't bother to look up from drawing his fifth vial of blood. "You can do that? Make a suit for me?"

"Yes. Although," he said, placing the last vial into the little row in the container he had for them and withdrawing the needle from my arm, "I might suggest that for your purposes, it would be easier for your paramour to be the one to be fitted for the suit." He flushed. "Assuming that your...ah...partner...would be male rather than female."

"Fair assumption in this case." I cocked an eyebrow at him. "Zack Davis. You know him?"

"An agent, I believe?" Sessions seemed to give this some thought. "I'm certain I've met him, but I can't place a face offhand. Regardless, if you intend to engage in...activities of the sort you'd indicated, it would be easier on a purely mechanical level for the male to wear the suit."

"Sure," I said with a vague sense that I was agreeing to something, but not really caring what it was. "Whatever you say."

"If you wish for...Mr. Davis to have a suit of this material, send him over to me at his earliest convenience. Taking measurements is simple enough, and it'll take a few days to fabricate. It's hardly a panacea that will solve all your ills, but we could probably synthesize another every few weeks if need be."

"That would be marvelous," I said with a hunger. I felt a buzz in my stomach, a nervous energy that stemmed from excitement coupled with nerves. "Thank you, Doctor," I said, and genuinely meant it.

"I haven't done anything yet," he said, once again blank. "Except draw your blood, I suppose, though I don't know why you'd be thanking me for that."

"I'm thanking you for telling me about this," I said, trying to stay calm. Sessions was a dolt, complete and utter, clueless about basic human need or desire. "It's a chance for me to live a normal life."

"Oh, I see," he said, but I could tell by his voice he didn't. "Well, that's good. Now, if you can just open your mouth," he brandished a swab, "I need to get a sample of cheek cells..."

I sighed, and opened my mouth. The swab was long, white and had cotton on the end. It was not pleasant, not fun, but it didn't matter because my head was already elsewhere. This suit was something that could change my life, could make me able to touch my boyfriend, to feel him against me without two layers of clothing to separate us. We could sleep in the same bed, could stop fooling around in our dreams...and start doing it in the real world.

And I wouldn't have to worry about his eyes turning colors anymore.

5.

The exam lasted longer than I wanted, and was far more invasive than I really cared for. I sighed with relief when I was done. That I'd learned about the new material was worth the inconvenience of dealing with Sessions and his complete lack of humanity . When finished, I dressed and worked my way back to headquarters, where I found Parks in the watch room next to the basement interrogation chamber where Fries was being held. I watched Fries, who sat with a black hood over his head, handcuffed to the metal table in the center of the room. There was no cot in the cell, and I wondered if he'd slept sitting up in the chair. Actually, I wondered if he'd slept at all.

"Would you have, in his place?" Parks asked when I voiced that thought to him, "We'll be able to get an idea of his state of mind when we pull that hood off." His gray hair flowed over his shoulders, somewhat more controlled today than it normally was. Its usual state was to be bushy, but it looked like he had washed and perhaps combed it. "Let's take a look, shall we?" His expression was almost wolfish, his teeth bared as though he were a feral creature ready to strike. He strode out of the observation room and into the hallway, unlocking the door using a key card. The door opened with a gentle *whoosh*, and I walked in first when Parks gestured for me to.

Fries wore the same clothes he had when I had encountered him yesterday in his apartment—suit coat, black pinstriped pants, leather shoes, no tie. I could see the top of his chest in the space between the hood and his unbuttoned shirt; I had seen him with it off, and he was muscular, in very good shape. I suspected he spent some time on that, probably more as a vanity thing than any sincere desire for the added strength his definition would bring him. I circled him and came to a stop just to his left. His head moved under the hood, swiveling to follow the sound of my footsteps.

Parks took up position at the shoulder opposite me, and looked at me over Fries' covered head. Parks reached down and took hold of the hood and gave me a questioning look. I nodded. He gave me a wink and then yanked the hood off, causing Fries to blink at the brightness of the light. He shut them harder when I yanked off the duct tape.

Fries blanched, then slowly opened his eyes, keeping them squinted as he stole a look first at Parks, then at me. "Oh, good, it's you," he said upon seeing me. "I was hoping it'd be you."

I stared at him, forcing my face to carry an expression that I hoped conveyed bleak humor. "Because I didn't hit you hard enough yesterday to satiate your masochistic desires?"

"No," he said, and formed a smile that caused me to feel another desire to pound his face into tenderloin. "I just like seeing you, that's all."

"I assure you, the feeling is not mutual."

"Enough of this crap," Parks said. "Fries, we've got questions for you."

"I'm sure you do," Fries said, turning to face Parks. His expression went from a grin to something more concealed, calm. "I doubt I have any answers for you, though. At least none that would satisfy."

"You, unable to satisfy?" I arched an eyebrow. "Common occurrence."

"I don't hear any complaints," he said with a light shrug and a smile.

Something primal and brutal welled up inside me, and I

couldn't contain myself. I hit him before I even realized I was going to, leveling him with a punch that sent his chair over backwards and snapped his head against the floor with a crack that I felt reverberate off the walls. "That's because the women you seduce are dead before you finish," I said, leaning over him. I reached down and forced my gloved hand against his throat and lifted him back up, setting his chair upright against the wall. "If you didn't kill them, they might tell a different story."

I heard him take a deep breath around my hand, his wrists still attached to the chair courtesy of the handcuffs. "I do know how to make the girls scream." He coughed. "I didn't hear you complain."

I restrained myself from hitting him. "Oh, I didn't? Sorry. I was very unsatisfied with the look I got at your equipment. It seemed pitifully inadequate to the task before you."

I caught a flash of rage in his eyes that disappeared behind another smile, this one faker than any of the others he'd used on me. "Heh. Very good. But you wouldn't know what satisfaction is, would you, Sienna?"

"Enough," Parks said, and I felt his hand on my shoulder, gently. I looked back and saw that there was no mistaking the look in his eyes—*Back off*, it said. I walked back to the table, seating myself on its edge. "We're here to talk to you about your employers."

"I've got nothing to say about my employers," Fries said, leaving the smile plastered on. I heard the click of his handcuffs against the chair as he rattled them.

"You sure about that?" Parks gave him a dead stare, cold and unmoving, without a trace of warmth.

Fries smiled tightly. "Yep. If you're planning to torture me, though, I suggest you get started. It might take a while to get to the good stuff."

A sound came from the door, unlocking and opening, cutting short Parks' reply. We turned to see a flash of red hair as Ariadne stuck her head in. She flushed at the sight of Fries, who smiled back at her. "I need to speak with the two of you for a moment."

"Nice to see you again, Ariadne," Fries said with a little shrug . His hands clinked the cuffs as the chain reached maximum extension. "I'd wave at you, but I think you can see I'm a bit tied down here."

"Just the way I prefer you," Ariadne said. "Parks, Nealon...a word, please."

I cast a look at Parks, who shook his head in a warning that took me a moment to decipher. I realized he meant I shouldn't show hesitation in front of Fries, but when I looked at Fries he was already grinning at me. Too late. I followed Parks into the hall where the door slid shut behind us and Ariadne activated the lock.

"This one's gonna be tough without getting physical or using chemicals," Parks said the moment the door clicked shut. "He's got a serious reserve of self-confidence that ain't bluster. Probably been trained to resist interrogation."

"Doubtless," Ariadne said, "but that's not why I called you out here—"

"He said it was nice to see you again," I looked at her pointedly. "You know this scum on a personal basis?"

She shook her head. "In passing. I didn't realize it at the time, but he tried to flip me a few months ago."

"Flip?" I looked from her to Parks. "Like...physically?" I lowered my voice. "Like..."

Ariadne let out a hiss. "No. As in flip me from the Directorate to Omega. I didn't know who he was at the time, and it was a clumsy attempt, but it had..." I saw some of the life drain out of her, "...repercussions. I'm not going to go into detail, but suffice it to say the Director is fully aware of what happened, and you needn't concern yourself with it. We have something else brewing."

"What's that?" I asked.

"Just a moment," she said, and I caught movement at the far end of the hall, by the door to the stairwell that led out of the basement. "Here he is."

A thin man in skinny jeans, with thick, square-rimmed black glasses came bouncing down the hall in a worn olive green jacket that looked like he had been paid by the Salvation Army to get it the hell out of their store. His black, wavy hair was spiked into an angled fauxhawk.

"J.J.," I said as he walked up, tablet computer in his hand. "It's always so nice to see you leave your cubicle for a little while."

"Because the air here in the dungeons is so much fresher than what we get on the fourth floor?" He looked at me with a querying eyebrow. "Ariadne asked me to tell you what we found."

"Found from what?" I asked.

"Fries' cell phone," Ariadne replied, smug. "Reed bagged it during your raid. Go on, J.J."

"Recent history was kind of a boon ," J.J. said, holding up the tablet so I could see. "The man's not what you'd call real communicative, so it's not like there was a ton to sift through in his thirty-day history."

"I've heard that incubi and succubi can be a little unsociable," I said without a trace of irony.

"That might be underselling it for him," J.J. said. "Two numbers, that's it. One's a cell phone that I backtraced. Area code says it's from Manhattan, but it was last used in downtown Minneapolis yesterday afternoon at about three-thirty p.m." He held up the tablet and a city grid showed up on the screen. "It wasn't logging the GPS, but just based on the cell tower data it looks like the user was pretty close to Fries' apartment when the call was made. After that, it went dark, completely offline, no record that it's been on the network since."

"Whoever's using it is either odd or cautious," Parks suggested. "They might have seen your team bag Fries and figured you could track them down if they left the phone on for the networks to follow."

"Or they might just be on planes or not wanting to be disturbed," J.J. said with a shrug. "It's not usual behavior for most users to go dark for that long, though, so I think we can assume that the phone is probably disposed of."

I stared at the map on the tablet computer. "So that's a dead end unless the phone goes active again. What about the other number?"

J.J. broke into a little smile. "That one is a landline for a house in Des Moines, Iowa."

"Iowa," Parks said as though it were some sort of curse. "I hate Iowa."

"Why?" I asked, and caught a flash of the wolf on Parks' face when he came around to answer.

"Because between it and the damned Dakotas, there ain't a more boring place to drive in the entire United States." He bared his teeth again in a scowl. "I'll get M-Squad together, though, and we'll—"

"No," Ariadne said. "I want you to remain here with Bastian and Eve." She let her eyes flick to me. "This seems like another good opportunity to test our new team in the field."

"What do you think this is?" I asked. "An Omega safe house?"

"Based on anomalies in the property records, yeah," J.J. replied. "It's registered to a Peter and Sophia Larson, but the names and social security numbers in the property tax rolls don't match any employment records, birth records, et cetera, that are legitimately alive anywhere. No employment history? No social security work or payment history for either?" The geek raised a hand as though he were offering an open palm. "Not likely to be a real person. No bank records, either, so who knows how they're paying the property taxes and gas bill."

"So I take my team, we reconnoiter the house, and if it seems suspicious, we break and enter?" I gave Ariadne the eye, waiting for her approval.

"Yes," she replied. "But take Clary with you."

I felt the enthusiasm for what I was about to do wither and die in a half a heartbeat. "Please, no. Can I have Bastian instead?"

"Bastian is M-Squad's leader," she said, as though patiently explaining why I was wrong. I looked at Parks and cocked my head to indicate him. "Parks has been your instructor, so you're more likely to defer to him and his judgment rather than cleanly lead like I want you to."

"There may be some virtue in drawing from superior experience," Parks said to her with an edge of reproach.

"No doubt," Ariadne said, "but this is a time of trial."

"What about Eve?" I said hopefully.

Ariadne's face flickered with a moment's hesitation before she answered. "She won't take orders from you, she's too stubborn."

I let that hang in the air for a moment, not letting her escape my gaze. "Know that from experience, do you?"

Ariadne stared coolly back. "Clary will listen, and he's strong enough to be of use if you run into trouble, powerful enough to overcome almost any meta you run into."

"He'll listen?" I asked, dubious. "First time for everything, I suppose."

Ariadne ignored me. "Go to Des Moines. Find this house, and get to the bottom of what Omega's up to."

"Don't you have anything ominous to say about this?" I asked. "Something like, 'Our very existence hangs in the balance' or 'the fate of the meta world depends on you'?"

"No offense, but if I thought the stakes were that high, I'd send M-Squad. Experience trumps youth and enthusiasm. Besides, Omega is headquartered in Europe. Whatever you find won't be more than the five of you can handle."

I let my jaw hang slack, and favored her with my best disbelieving stare. "So...what I'm hearing you say is that there will probably be a whole army of Omega's thugs and minions there, as well as some of the old gods. Got it."

She blinked and drew back in disbelief. "I just said...how did you get that out of what I said?"

"You jinxed me." I started toward the stairwell. "I can't believe you just jinxed me like that!"

"It's a safe house!" she said, trailing along behind me. "A house, in the city of Des Moines. Two-thousand square feet, tops. It can't possibly house more than a few metas—no army, no minions. And I think gods would travel in a bit higher style."

"You don't know." I pushed through the exit door. Parks and J.J. had been left behind, but Ariadne trailed in my wake. "They could have one of the old gods in this place." I paused and held the door for her. "They could have Thor. And when he smacks me upside the head with Mjolnir—or possibly mesmerizes me with Chris Hemsworth-like abs—I'm going to say, 'I told you so, Ariadne'." I frowned. "Assuming I survive."

She squinted at me with one eye crinkled, slightly appalled. "'Chris Hemsworth-like abs'?"

"You wouldn't understand," I said, and started up the stairs. "The point is, I'm not the biggest believer in luck, but Omega has this tendency to whack us every time we underestimate them. It's like turning the crank on a jack-in-the-box, and when the damned song is over, the jack pops out with a mallet and beats the hell out of you."

"Wait...what?" She shook her head. "You're talking about abs and jack-in-the-boxes. This is a straightforward mission. Go to Des Moines, do recon, if it looks bad, call for backup. Don't endanger your team unnecessarily. There's no shame in admitting you might be in over your head if you see something suspicious. We can dispatch the rest of M-Squad if needed."

I paused at the top of the stairs. "Yeah, all right."

"Are you sure you're okay with this?" She halted next to me, her eyes looking into mine with the barest hint of concern. "You don't normally get worked up about these things—you're cool, calm, efficient—not predisposed to rattling on about jinxes or some faux God of Thunder's abs. If you don't want the assignment, it's fine. I'll send M-Squad."

"It's not that," I said, feeling my fingers wrap around the thick metal safety rail. "It's just..." I halted. "These guys sent Wolfe after me and Henderschott. They tried to get Fries in my pants, then flipped Mormont—or whatever you called it—and turned loose a couple of bloodthirsty vampires to try and catch me." I shook my head. "It feels like every time we've got a grasp on what we're dealing with, something else comes popping out that's more horrific than the last thing they set loose."

"You think Henderschott, Mormont and the vampires were worse than Wolfe?"

I felt myself freeze and stiffen, all motion stopping around my body. "No. Nothing is worse than Wolfe. And nothing has stayed with me like him, either."

"Yes, well, having a monster stuck in your head isn't the sort of thing that goes away, I suppose," she said. "This is our best chance to get to what Omega's doing now, and if you don't feel comfortable with it—"

"I'm going," I said, firm, feeling it all the way down. "I'm just...cautious, okay? They're not world-renowned for coming at us open-handed. You've got their slimy mouthpiece in there, and he's just grinning up a storm, like he's just having a conversation with us sitting on his couch. It worries me that Fries is so cool. They must have known we'd come for him—that I would, after what he did."

"He hid," Ariadne said. "He changed identities, he changed apartments, he probably thought we couldn't find him after Eagle River. He was wrong. Just because he's been trained to play it cool when most of us would be showing some concern doesn't mean anything. Omega is not some invincible organization with limitless resources and the ability to know our every move before we make it. The fact that your mother hit them so hard, in places they didn't expect, proves that they can make mistakes." She lowered her voice. "The fact that they lost Andromeda, someone so important an entire facility was dedicated to her, proves they're not invincible."

I felt a sliver of fear mingled with sadness at the mention of Andromeda's name. "And I might feel better about that if we had turned that win into something, anything that worked to our advantage. But even the autopsy left us with no clue what she was, or why they wanted her, or anything really, beyond the fact that we pulled two traitors out of the Directorate's inner circle that we wouldn't have had a clue about if she hadn't told us before she died. Let's face it Ariadne—these guys have been kicking our asses since day one, and we know almost nothing more about them beyond the fact that they used to be gods, than we did when we started. I don't know about you, but when someone's pounding my skull in, I like to think that after nine months of it, I'd have at least some handle on who they are and what they want."

"We know what they want," she said. "The same thing they've always wanted. You."

I hissed, expelling all the air from my body. "But 'why?' is the more valid question. And, by the way, just as an aside, sending me to their secret safe house when we have no idea what's contained within? Not the best idea ever for keeping what they want out of their hands."

She twitched and looked away, her gaze swiveling to the white concrete block that surrounded us in the stairwell, looking out over the banister. "The Director thinks you're one of our best resources against them because whatever they throw at you, you seem to be able to turn around relatively easily."

"Relatively easily?" I stared at her openmouthed. "Wolfe nearly killed me. Fries nearly—" I stopped. "Mormont would have taken me to them if Zollers hadn't saved my life."

"You're not going after them alone, nor do you have to go at all if you don't want to," she said. "Your choice."

"You're damned right I'm going after them," I said. "I just... ugh. I hate everything they've done to me so far. I hate them."

"I'd feel the same if I were you."

"Whatever." I shook my head. "When does the chopper leave?"

She looked at me in surprise. "Chopper? I'm not having you take the chopper to Des Moines. Not for this. The uncertainty of the mission coupled with the recon element means you'll need to approach quietly, with some subtlety, and a chopper hovering over a suburban neighborhood with people deploying out of it on zip-lines doesn't exactly fit the bill. You'll take a van; it fits the mission profile better."

I grimaced. "How long of a drive is it to Des Moines?"

"Four, maybe four and a half hours?"

"Dammit," I said, and my hand came up to massage my eyebrows. "This is bad."

"What now?" Ariadne said, her voice rising with alarm. "What is it?"

"I'm going to be stuck in a confined space with Clary for the whole drive."

6.

"...and that's why I left Nebraska," came the droning, cornpone voice of Clyde Clary. Scott was driving and Kat was riding next to him, her face suffused with boredom. Reed and I were seated in captain's chairs directly behind them and Clary was in the back in a massive rotating chair that was anchored to the floor in front of a computer console. It was all kind of sci-fi, or FBI, but I didn't really care. I was so annoyed and bored by Clary's stupid stories that I was ready to reach forward and yank the wheel out of Scott's hands so I could put us into the ditch and end all of our suffering. I had mentally checked out of Clary's stories throughout the whole ride, until they all blended together. The parts I remembered involved a grain silo, three heifers and an old Cadillac. For all I knew, they were all from the same story.

"We're almost there," Scott said with a note of hope. "GPS says it's off the next exit."

"Thank God," said Kat and Reed in perfect harmony. I was thinking it.

"You know, this reminds me of this one time when—"

"Hey, Clary," Scott said, raising his voice to talk over Clyde. "Can you do me a favor and start booting up the computer?"

"Yeah, sure," Clary said, and after a moment, he spoke again. "Say, you weren't telling me to boot up the computer because you're sick of hearing me tell stories, are you? Because I figured none of you were talking because you thought they were interesting."

"If you could just go ahead and start it up—" Scott began.

"You really didn't think that, didn't you?" Clary said, and I could hear the rising disbelief. "Y'all are assholes. At least when Bastian and Parks want me to shut up, they come out and say it."

"Shut up, Clary," Reed said, his arms folded in front of him.

"Hey, you can't talk to me like that, Alpha dog."

"Sure I can, Beta dog," Reed said. "Pretty sure I just did, in fact. What are you so pissed about? You told me to come out and say it, so I did."

"Yeah, like an hour late."

"More like four hours," Scott said from the driver's seat.

I felt Clary seething behind me as Scott took us off the exit ramp and into a neighborhood that didn't look that different from the one I had lived in back in Minneapolis; tall oaks jutting skyward around us, red leaves falling and clogging the gutters, filling the channels on both sides of the street. The houses were older but not in bad shape, for the most part. Some were stucco, some siding, with the occasional brick facade just to break up the monotony. The lawns were all beginning to turn brown, the cool weather leeching the lively green from them as a signal that vitality and warmth were retreating for the season.

Older cars were parallel parked at the sides of the streets. The houses were built high off the road on either side of us. They had no front yards to speak of; instead a concrete terrace came four feet above the sidewalk, with a staircase in front of each house that led up to front porches. The whole place had the feel of a valley, with the houses overlooking the street.

"Omega put a safe house here?" Kat idly mused from the front seat. "Why?"

"If they're recruiting metas like the Directorate," Reed said, "it helps to have operations all over the map. That way, say a meta in Sioux Falls manifests and you get wind of it, you can dispatch someone to get to them before anyone else does." He shrugged. "It makes a difference when you're building an army."

"An army?" I paused and turned my head to favor him. "Alpha doesn't have safe houses all over the U.S., do they?"

"Nope," Reed said with a casual shrug. "They have intermediaries like me to keep an eye on things, to try and get to any really powerful metas that come to our attention; our main focus is Europe. We're really more of a token presence here, though, trying to watch Omega's North American operations rather than offer any serious interdiction efforts."

"Well," Clary said, leaning forward over my shoulder, causing me to almost gag from the stink of his breath, which smelled like rotten fish, "you better watch and learn, Alpha dog, because we are about to do some serious interdicting." He giggled, a low-pitched sort of thing that reminded me of the time I'd heard Scott choke on a hotdog in the cafeteria.

"Interdiction means interfering or stopping," Reed said, looking at Clary with undisguised disgust.

"Well, we're gonna do that too," Clary said with a nod.

Scott slowed the vehicle as he looked across Kat and out the front window as the GPS dinged. In the back, we had no windows to speak of; there were none on the sides, and the rear windows were covered with a Velcro foam that kept anyone from looking in at us while we were running surveillance.

"I'm gonna turn us around," Scott said, as the van accelerated again. "I'll park us with a clear view and we can get the cameras going."

"Or we could just go up and ring the doorbell, see who's home," Clary said.

"Clary, our mission is to recon first," I said. "Ringing the doorbell isn't exactly a subtle way to find out who's inside."

"What, you wanna sneak around the back and peer in the windows or something? Screw that." I heard his seatbelt unsnap and he was already moving toward the back doors, even though we were still moving. "Let's get this party started!" The back door swung open and he was out.

"What the hell is he doing?" Scott said, and he slammed the brakes. "Is he seriously going to go knock on the door? What is he thinking?"

"Clary doesn't think, does he?" Reed asked.

"Dear God, I hope he gets the right house," I said, already unfastening my seatbelt. I ran the ten feet to the back door and jumped down to the pavement, racing to catch up with Clary, who was already up on the sidewalk. The air held a dampness, and the sky was hazy, a light fog still lingering thanks to the cloud cover.

"Clary!" I said, trying to keep my voice down, knowing he could hear me. "Clary!" I said again, now only a few feet behind him. He had reached the steps at the bottom of the house and was starting to ascend the first when I caught him. "Clyde," I said with a hiss as I laid a hand on his shoulder. He brushed it off.

"Girl, ain't no one calls me Clyde," he said as he continued up the steps.

"What are you doing? I am in command of this mission— Ariadne is going to have your ass if you don't get back in the damn van."

"I'm gonna get this show on the road," he said as he reached the front porch. A squeak of an old floorboard caused me to cringe, as though it were attached to a wire that would report directly to Omega HQ that we were, in fact, here. I felt as though they were watching us through a pinhole camera and could see stupid Clary in his Ugg boots and me trying to get him to listen to reason. "Why tiptoe around these clowns when we can just push 'em right out into view and start kicking ass?"

"That is the dumbest thing I've ever heard," I said, "and not the mission." The paint on the siding was peeling, leaving cracks of dark, old wood peeking out from behind the dirtied white paint, the chips still laying scattered with leaves all around the porch. "We're supposed to investigate first—"

"Well, we gonna investigate right now." He smiled at me with that gap-toothed idiot look of his and slapped his hand against the screen door, hard, rattling it on its flimsy hinges. He swung it open, then smacked his palm against the interior door five times, loud enough that I was sure that they could hear it at Omega HQ, wherever it was, even if they didn't have any microphones anywhere in the state. "Hey!" Clary shouted. "Open up, Omega! It's the Directorate. We've come to kick y'all's asses, so get on out here."

I closed my eyes and placed a gloved hand over them, as though I could blot out the horror of what was happening as easily as I could cut out the light around me. "Did you really just tell them we're from the Directorate?"

"What's wrong?" his voice came around my hand, though I wished it didn't. I wished I had an invisible wall or a happy place I could flee to that was as far from Clyde Clary as Pluto was from the sun. "Fine, I'll be subtle. Girl Scout cookies! No, wait, I got it. Avon calling!" He raised the pitch of his voice on the last one, turning his normally deep timbre into something horrific.

"Oh, dear God, kill me now," I whispered. "Please let Chris Hemsworth answer the door, and then let him smite me with lightning and abs."

"I think it's working," he said as I took my hand away from my eyes. "Someone's moving around in there, I think they're coming to the door."

Before I could brace myself (or call him an idiot, because I was going to do both) the front door blasted off its hinges and Clary vanished behind it. They flew through the air, off the steps, and down the ten or so feet to the street below, where he came to land on an old-model Ford that flipped when he hit it. He fell behind it and was obscured from my view.

I turned back to the doorframe, which had become a cloud of dust and fragments, and looked within. A man stood at the aperture, taller than me by a head, hair brown and short, flecked with white from the demolition he had just perpetrated. He was big, big enough to make Clary look small by comparison. I took an involuntary step back, placing myself into a more moveable stance. The man looked at me with eyes that were so light blue that they almost seemed white. A few scars dotted his face as he emerged from the gaping hole in the front of the house.

"Umm, hi," I said. "Sorry about my associate. He's an idiot." I glanced back to where Clary had landed, and saw not even a sign of movement. I wanted to curse and scream, but since I had darted out of the van so quickly I hadn't put in my earpiece, no one but Omega would hear it. "Umm...we were just wondering if you'd like..." He stared at me, angling his head as though he were pondering me, "... some Girl Scout cookies?" I heard the lameness of my words and wished I could just flip a switch that would shut me up.

I heard him let out a breath all at once, deep and throaty. "I'm about to pulverize you, Thin Mint."

I blinked at him. "Thin Mint? You really think so?" I felt myself perk up a little. "You know, I have been working out—" He charged at me, shoulder first, and I threw myself through the porch rail backwards as he stormed through the space where I had been standing only a moment earlier as though he were a rhinoceros coming across the African plains. I hit the terraced step below and caught myself as I saw him burst through the support beam for the porch and fly over me to land on his feet on the sidewalk. The earth itself shook, I swear it, as I rolled to my feet. The narrow strip on which I stood allowed me to look at the back of his head as he came to a landing, and I knew if we were going to fight, which we were, there was no better opening than the one I had right now.

I jumped, leading with a front kick, my leg extending as I caught him perfectly in the back of the skull. He staggered and caught himself on a rusty Honda, knocking the car out of its parking place at a ninety-degree angle. I landed on the sidewalk and felt the impact run through my legs; I had hit him at a height of nearly seven feet off the ground and the drop was not small after that. I landed and regained my balance, wobbling only slightly.

The gargantuan beast in front of me turned, placing his hand on the car that he had knocked out of the way. I grimaced. "Hi. Still thinking over which cookies you'd like?" I kicked him in the knee as hard as I could, causing him to grunt and me to bounce back a step. "May I recommend some Samoas?" It wasn't exactly like kicking a rock as I could see I was causing him pain, but there was no doubt he was tough. I followed up with another hard kick to the thigh, hoping I could at least give him a dead leg to stagger him.

"How about a Thanks-A-Lot?" he grunted and swung at me in a backhanded slap that connected and caused a ringing in my ears as it lifted me off the ground and hurled me into the concrete terrace. I heard the retaining wall crack, possibly along with my skull, as I tried to blink the dots and colors out of my eyes.

When my eyes refocused, I saw him take a limping step forward, dragging the other leg behind him. He was still in the street, at a perfect right angle to the Honda he had hit. "I know you," he said in a gruff, scratchy voice. "Sienna Nealon. I'll make you my prize, take you back to the boss; Operation Stanchion will be over even before it starts—"

He stopped speaking when a squeal of tires came from his left. The van slammed into the parked Honda next to him, spinning its front end around. The front of the car hit him from behind, catapulting him into the air. He flew to my right and struck the terrace wall about ten feet from where I lay, shattering the block and causing the first level to collapse on him. His legs stuck out onto the sidewalk, his dark gray trousers and beat-up tennis shoes the only thing remaining that weren't covered by concrete and dirt. The broken blocks had buried him to the waist.

"Are you okay?" Reed jumped out of the van and was making his way toward me. I shook my head, feeling as though my brain were rattling inside it.

"I think so," I said. "Took a little bump to the noggin on that one. Glad you guys came back to join the fight."

"Hold still," Kat said, appearing out of my peripheral vision. I felt her touch against my skin, short contact that only lasted a few seconds, and I felt better. "I can't do any more than that," she said with a low gasp as she pulled her hands away. "Not without...you know. Losing my soul, or whatever, and I don't think I'd want to spend my life in your head. I have a feeling it's a creepy place."

"What are you trying to say about me?" I stood with Reed's assistance, his hand on my arm, helping me up.

Kat's face went agape, and I saw her jaw move up and down as she started to stammer. "Nothing. No, nothing at all."

"You could at least try and lie better," I said, and pulled my arm from Reed. "Did anyone check on that Omega operative to make sure he's good and down? That man hits like a frigging asteroid—"

As if to punctuate my point, a concrete block hit Reed in the face. I saw the whole thing as if it were in slow motion, the impact, the concrete shattering, blood geysering from my brother's nose and his bone structure deforming from the impact. His body dropped to the sidewalk, his eyes invisible beneath puddles of blood already forming in the sockets. His jaw was hanging at an odd angle; he was almost unrecognizable.

"Kat!" I screamed. "Fix him!" I positioned myself between her and the next concrete block that came winging at us. I hit it with my fist, knocking it to the side, shattering the window of a nearby car. Another one came from the Omega monster as he wound up and pitched it, and I slapped it out of the way. I felt the pain in my hand and hoped I could keep up. My meta reflexes allowed me some leeway, but not much; it was all I could do to keep the bricks from hitting Kat.

The next I caught too late and it exhausted most of its force against my forearm. The face of the man from Omega was a wreck from his trip through the wall, off-axis from the impact and swollen. I knew it would heal, but for now his lips had shifted several inches to the right and blood was flowing down his shirt, which had a rip halfway down his abdomen, revealing a muscular stomach that I might have found appealing on a less violently disagreeable man.

He winged another block at me and I knocked it aside with my good hand as I closed on him. He paused and his hands went to his face, feeling it, fingers tracing the lines around his jaw and nose. I couldn't see much reaction because I presumed his facial nerves had suffered some damage, but there was a pronounced twitch and more eye motion as he touched himself. "You..." he said, and his words were slurred by the movement of his jaw, which bounced up and down as though it were a garage door off its track. "You...did...this..."

"I didn't," I said, as he grabbed another block and came at me with it like a club. "But I must say, it's quite the improvement. Before you were just an ugly son of a bitch; now, you're ugly *and* you can't speak worth a damn." I caught his forearm with my good hand as he brought the weapon down hard enough to cleave my skull from my body with it. I slammed a heel onto the instep of his foot, and he did more than grunt this time, he let out a little yell. I dodged the retaliatory backhand and let go of him as he pulled the concrete block above his head again. I ducked out of the way as he brought it down and shattered it onto the sidewalk, sending fragments in all directions. I kicked him in the knee as I sidestepped and it buckled with the force of my attack.

I hit him behind the ear with a punch that caused him to falter, his eyes crossing slightly. He whipped another fist around but I stepped out of the way, keeping light on my feet and using my speed to outmaneuver him. "Come on, Shortbread," I said lightly, glad that Kat had healed me, "you're getting your ass kicked by a Thin Mint." I hit him in the face with a roundhouse kick as he turned; I heard snapping sounds from his jaw after the impact and his face realigned. He stared at me through a droopy eye and I didn't hesitate before kicking him squarely in the groin. He doubled over, his knees finally hitting the ground and I kicked him in the head, which ricocheted off the concrete, sending a spiderweb of cracks down the terrace wall as he fell over. "You might have to call your boss and tell him Operation Stanchion is still on, since you failed—"

He scissored out with a kick that took my legs from under me before I even realized what had happened. My back hit the sidewalk and my head bounced against the grass. I lay there for about half a second while my brain assessed what he had done. "Or not." I rolled my weight to my shoulders and bucked, vaulting back to my feet in a martial arts move that Mother had taught me to master when I was eight. I raised my fists as the hulk got back to his feet, menace in his eyes. "Busting through the door when someone knocks? That's taking the get-off-my-lawn attitude a step too far, old man."

"Do you...ever...shut up?" His accent dragged the words, even through his broken jaw. I had caught a hint of it before, on the porch—Eastern Europe, I would have guessed, though I couldn't be certain now.

I didn't answer, instead doing a backflip onto the higher terrace as he came at me in a shoulder-down charge. I kicked him in the side of the head and backflipped again to the topmost level, landing on his two-foot stretch of "lawn." "You should criticize; you're pretty chatty for a guy whose face is hanging off. Maybe you want to explain this Operation Stanchion to me now, so we can get on with our lives—me to mine, you to a cell in the Directorate prison in Arizona for the rest of yours?"

He stared up at me from the sidewalk, his jaw clacking together as though he were trying to speak; I didn't even want to think about how much pain it was causing him to talk. I wanted to inflict more of it.

From my elevated position I saw Scott on the street below next to Clary, who was sitting up. The car next to Clary was destroyed, oil leaking all over the pavement, coating him in black liquid that it took me a moment to realize wasn't blood. Reed was bleeding next to Kat, though he was looking better than he had when last I saw him. Kat was paler than I could ever remember, her wool coat looking like black granite next to her complexion, which was drained of all color.

"You sure you don't want to come with me?" I asked him. "We could give you all the things your heart desires—three square meals a day, reconstructive surgery for that face—you know, for after it heals, and you go back to looking the way you did before?" He took a leap up the terrace in one bounding jump and I veered sideways and up, clearing the porch steps and landing back at the open hole where his front door had been. "We could give you a nice, quiet place where you'd never have to worry about some annoying strangers knocking on your front door again—you know, because that sort of thing seems to stress you out..."

With a bellow of fury he jumped up to the porch and charged again, tearing through the rail as he raged ahead. I turned and sprinted into the house and up the staircase inside the door as he crashed through the wall behind me. The foyer was sparse, old dark wood faded to a light brown, aging plaster and wallpaper that wouldn't have looked out of place fifty years ago.

I paused at the landing as I heard his feet hit the first steps behind me. "You seem to have some anger management problems, too," I said from above him, and launched off the stairs in another kick that hit him in the face. "Unless you think it's healthy to act like a bull in a china shop all the time." I heard more bones break, he let out a howl of pain, and I flipped myself by pushing off his head with my foot. I came to a landing on my feet in the middle of the square foyer. "Like a cat," I whispered to myself. "Always landing on my feet."

My foe let out a roar of rage and I watched him double at the midsection; he brought both hands down and hit the floorboards, causing the whole room to shake. There was a calm, a quiet, and then a cracking noise as my enemy disappeared through a hole in the floor. Just a second later, the splitting of wood reached my ears and I jumped, a moment too late, as the floor crashed down around me and I fell to the basement.

The shock of the landing snapped my head back, my head hitting the boards that I had fallen with. A dazed sensation overwhelmed me, as though everything in my vision had taken a mighty sway, like it was all jerking around me. "Apparently, I don't always land on my feet," I said, and felt a sharp pain in my back. "And more's the pity for it..."

The dust was thick in the air, choking me with the smell of the wreckage. Particles of wood, plaster and concrete, oppressive and thick, coated my tongue and nasal passages. I coughed, trying to expel it, even as I tried to sit up. The floorboards of the house were all around me, at odd angles from the landing, and the dust was so thick I couldn't see much of anything, even if I'd had my eyes open for more than a few seconds at a stretch without them filling with tears. I could taste the foul stuff that hung in the air, a dry, awful flavor like the oldest bread on the face of the earth coupled with paint.

I stood and finally got my head above the dust in time to see the beast of a man roar at me again and charge. I threw myself to the side, smashing into an old piece of wooden furniture as he went by. "If I ever get out of here," I said over the noise of my enemy hitting the far wall with shattering force, "I will personally beat Clyde Clary to death with nothing but an old shoe."

There was a sharp increase of moisture in the air, I could feel it, as though it were about to rain, the cool, clammy sense that I was sweating and chilled. "Why a shoe?" I heard from above me as the sound of someone dropping to the floor of the basement and hitting the broken lumberyard that lay across it reached my ears. "Why not something really good, like a hammer or a mallet?"

"Because I won't be emotionally satisfied by the sound of a hammer hitting him over and over," I said, keeping my eyes trained on the dust in front of me, even as the moisture began to pull it from the air, clearing my vision. "I think it might take a while to work out my rage on him, and I'd like to have the enjoyment of the sole of it slapping him in the face over and over again."

"Yeah, well," Scott said, and I saw a thin aura of moisture around his hands as he pulled it from the air and then dispersed it in front of us, "tell him yourself in a second; Kat's getting him ready to fight again right now. Hopefully he'll be down here in a minute."

"Reed?" I asked, and caught a twinge of pain in Scott's expression. "That bad, eh? I should have known."

"He'll be fine," Scott said. "But Kat can't fix him *and* Clary without draining herself dry, so…"

"So you'd rather have an idiot at our backs than a guy with a brain? How very thoughtful of you. It's almost like you want the enemy to kill me."

"Hey," he said, looking vaguely offended. "I'm down here with you, aren't I? Besides, in this fight, brawn seemed to be the needed thing, more than brains, at least."

"Oh, that's well thought out," I said, watching the last of the mist clear to reveal a shattered, dark hole where my enemy had charged into the foundation wall of the house, now empty, "I'd be more upset with you, but I'm too busy wondering where this Omega jackass went—"

"GERONIMO!" I heard from above, then the sound of something impacting on the stairs, followed by the breaking of all manner of wood as the stairs collapsed.

"Wow," Scott said. "Maybe you were right about that idiot bit."

I rolled my eyes at him in the barest control of my fury. "Ya think?!" I adjusted my footing and stared into the black, gaping hole in the foundation; it was so dark in the basement I couldn't see into the depths of it. It could be a foot deep or twelve, and I wouldn't be able to tell. "Clary, you just destroyed our escape route, you moron."

"What do you need to escape for?" Clary's voice came along with the shifting of boards as he prised himself free of the wreckage of the stairs, which had dissolved about six steps down. "We got him right where we want him, now!"

"Oh, do you?" A voice came from the darkness next to the staircase, and I heard something massive shift, stone moving against skin, and then something flew through the air. I was slow in my reflexes and I felt Scott slam into me, knocking me to the floor as Clary's rock-skinned body passed over me and hit the support beam behind us, causing the ceiling to cave in again. Panic threatened to overwhelm me as the remains of the upstairs collapsed on us. Scott took the brunt of the impact, shielding me with his body. He lay across me, trapping me in place, confined, unable to move more than a few inches.

After a moment of pause for everything to settle, I coughed and tried to move. The pressure of Scott's body lying across me made it difficult, and I felt warm liquid run down onto my clothing, seeping through against my skin. I pushed against him, but he was limp and silent, offering no suggestion that he might be conscious. I thought about crying out for help, but I didn't know if Clary was even in a fit state to assist me. If he was down, then Kat was the last one standing, and she wouldn't be much use in this fight, assuming she could even hear me outside. I tested moving Scott and felt the wreckage shift a little as I pushed up on him. I paused and tried to listen for movement, but my ears were still ringing. I pushed again and worked my left hand free.

I batted a few stray pieces of floorboard off Scott, then pushed three medium sized slabs of the subfloor off him before rolling him to the side and off me. He was still breathing, but it was shallow, slow, and there was blood soaking his clothing, a piece of rebar jutting out of his back. "Dammit," I breathed, still unable to hear myself talk. The only light in the basement came from above us, and most of that from the hole where the front door had been, the gray soft light of the overcast day visiting what it had upon us. Scott's eyelids fluttered as I slapped him lightly, and he coughed blood that ran down his cheek and chin. "Dammit all to hell."

The crunch of a foot behind me signaled the presence of someone else and I launched myself back, the only direction I was conveniently poised to spring—and right into a pair of tree-trunk like legs. I knocked my enemy off balance as I saw a shattered face, split with rage. I caught the flash of a crow in my mind's eye as he fell upon me, his upper body landing on my lower, and I brought a knee up to "cushion" his landing, and it caught him full in the face. He tried to return the favor, jerking his legs as though to kick me with them but I knocked one of them aside and punched him in the groin. Twice. For luck. And possibly spite.

I kicked him in the face and rolled him off me as I pulled a glove off my left hand with my teeth, spinning around and lunging to land on top of him, bringing a knee into his groin again. There weren't going to be any points awarded for the cleanliness of this fight, and I didn't care. I just wanted to survive it. I got astride his abdomen even as I wrestled to get the glove off my fingers; the moment they were free I jammed my bare hand against the skin of his neck, choking him as hard as I could. With the other, I slammed him with punch after punch, driving his already broken nose into his face. "What..." I said, forcing my words out even as I evaded his hands, which were reaching for me, "...is...Operation...Stanchion...?"

I counted the seconds as he writhed after every hammer blow I landed. "What...is...Operation...Stanchion?" I felt my knuckles crack but I hit again, ignoring the pain, smashing him down with one hand while draining his life with the other. "Answer me!" I felt him go limp in my grasp, his body slack underneath me, and I held on for just a few seconds longer before I let my ungloved hand release him. I hit him in the face a few more times, just to be safe. Maybe more than a few.

I let out a long breath, a sigh, and slid from him, laying my head against the ground. All my strength was gone, completely and utterly, as though it had disappeared with nothing more than a dozen pains to mark its passage. "You son of a bitch," I said, and kicked at him, hitting him in the arm. I took another breath and forced myself to my feet. "What the hell is Operation Stanchion?"

7.

There was a sound behind me of rubble shifting, and I prepared myself to deliver another attack to my downed foe if necessary when I heard a familiar voice. "Damn, that sucked," came Clary's stupid baritone. "What the hell was that?"

"Our enemy, you brain-dead jackass," I said. "You've successfully almost gotten us killed, you unbelievable moron. I just have one question for you—are you working for us? Because I honestly don't think Mormont or Zollers could have made worse choices for us than you just did."

Clary's husky figure emerged from the shadows and rubble in the corner of the basement. "Well, yeah, I'm working for the Directorate," he said as he stepped over Scott's body to stand next to me. "I mean what do you think—"

I grabbed him with my bare hand around his neck and heard a GURK! "You. Idiot. You almost got Reed and Scott killed—not to mention me—and you're so damned oblivious you don't even realize it." I watched his piggy little eyes move back and forth and I saw the pain emerge on his face as he felt the first stirrings of my power working on him. He didn't resist, even as he began to grunt. I threw him loose and let him fall in a pile of broken boards. "If you...ever...come on a mission with me again and fail to follow my orders when I'm in charge, do you know what I'm going to do?"

His double chins obscured his neck, but I saw the bob of his Adam's apple. "You'll...uh...kill me?"

I leaned down, and wondered for a beat why he didn't turn to rock before I realized that he was afraid of me. "I won't kill you, Clyde. I'll drain so much of your mind that what's left will have all the cognitive ability of a pumpkin." I narrowed my eyes to glare at him. "Which, in your case, will be nothing but the sharpest of improvements." I brought my hand around and patted him gently on the cheek, which he flinched from. "Clear?"

"You..." his voice wavered as he regained his capacity for speech, "you can't talk to me like that!"

I grabbed him again around the neck and lifted him up. He was taller than me by a full head, so I tilted my back at an angle so that he was above me and his feet couldn't touch the ground. I felt the swirling start in my head, and he shrieked, so I let him go, and he fell back into the refuse pile he had landed on a moment earlier. "I can. I will. You will listen to me while you're alive or I'll make you my slave after you're dead."

There was a moment of glare between us, and then I raised my voice. "Kat! KAT!" I kept watch on the space where the door had been when we had first come to the house, and I saw a blond head peek in from the porch, her face waxy pale, as though the life had been drained out of it. "Get Reed in the van," I said. "We're moving in five, just as soon as Clary and I can get our prisoner and Scott up there." I looked down at Scott, who was still bleeding on the floor. "And I hope you saved some of your strength for your boyfriend."

It was an operation, and I cursed Clary a dozen times over the next few minutes for cutting off our easy exit by destroying the stairs. The clouds of dust had cleared, and Clary gave me a boost up to the front of the house after I asked him only once. He was strangely silent, cowed into submission at last, no trace of guile or anger on his face; he reminded me of a shamed child, someone bullied into submission and broken in their will. I didn't have time to feel bad about it, though, because Scott was still bleeding profusely. With Kat's help I got him up and into the van as the sirens became audible in the far distance.

"Dammit," I said under my breath. I looked back to the house to see a body ejected out of the basement, hitting the second of the four supporting pillars that held the roof off the porch before taking a slow arc and landing on the same Honda that the van had rammed into my opponent during the fight.

"Oh, God," Kat said, wavering, as though she might fall at any moment. Against the backdrop of the gray skies and leaf-strewn wet street, she looked like a leaf herself, ready to wilt and fade. "Do you think anyone noticed that?"

"I think we're pretty much out of time and luck if we want to get clear of this ridiculous turkey of a mission," I said grimly. "And I hope like hell that the body that just flew out of there wasn't Clary, because we have no time to subdue that other jackass again before the cops get here."

"You don't have your FBI ID?" Kat asked me in slight surprise.

"I don't think an FBI ID is going to explain us out of this disaster."

She looked for a moment like she was going to answer, then paled and promptly got sick on the road, hitting her knees.

"Are you gonna be okay?" I asked as I trotted over to the wrecked Honda. I cast a look at the house, where I saw Clary climbing out of the wreckage, then to the road, where Kat was on one knee still retching, and the Honda, where the Omega stooge was laying limp. In the distance, the sirens drew closer.

"I'll be fine," she said. "I just...need to get to Scott." She crawled into the back of the van.

I dragged my Omega enemy off the wreckage of the car and tossed him in the van next to Kat, who was already ministering to Scott as Clary trotted up. "Clary..." I said, favoring him with narrowed eyes.

"What?" he said, perturbed. "I was just trying to make sure we got out of here! If you had a better, faster suggestion to wrap this up other than tossing him like a lawn dart, I would have loved to hear it."

There was a creaking noise from behind us and I turned my head. The porch roof began to cave in where Clary had taken out the support pillar with his throw, which prompted an additional collapse of some side rooms as the second floor came down on the first. A cloud of dust blew out in a billowing, bellowing mess that swept over us, obscuring my vision.

I held my breath, closed my eyes, and let myself stand there immovable as the white cloud swept over me. I counted a slow count to ten, and when it was done, I opened my eyes and saw Clary standing in front of me, still, his lip quivering, his face caked in white. I looked at my hands and surmised I was likely covered in the dust of the collapse. It was in my nose, my hair, and I felt it cake my face like the worst, driest facemask I could ever have imagined. I glanced briefly at the house; it was as near as it could be to gone, fallen in on itself, with little to show but wreckage, a crater of boards, beams and roofing tiles with almost no structure left on display. Clary stared back at me and I almost thought he was going to cry.

"Let's go," I said, controlling my instinct to toss Clary back in the cellar and let whoever found him deal with him. I made my way to the driver's seat. "Clary, cuff that Omega stooge. Hands behind his back. Then cuff his ankles together, and then handcuff the cuffs together like—"

"You want me hogtie him?" The cornpone was a little too evident in the way he said this.

"Whatever you call it, just make it happen," I said as I stepped on the accelerator and heard the sputter of the van's engine. "Kat, get on the phone and call HQ, we need a new vehicle, this one's been seen leaving the scene of a..." I thought about it for a moment, "...a housing crisis."

"She's passed out," Clary said.

"What?" I looked back, at the pile of bodies on the floor. Kat was indeed passed out, her skin pressed against Scott. "Get her off of him!"

"What?" Clary frowned at me, one eyebrow knitted. "I thought you told me to cuff—"

"GET HER OFF OF SCOTT!" I swerved to avoid oncoming traffic, and I heard flesh hit metal in the back and prayed that Clary could carry out my command.

"Okay, okay," I heard Clary after a moment. "She's moved, but, you know, there ain't much space back here with all the damned bodies—"

"Shut up, Clary," I said, reaching into my coat pocket. I fumbled, pulling out a cell phone that was shattered into three distinct pieces. I dropped all three of them onto the floor and started rummaging; Kat's coat was on the seat next to me. I searched the pocket while keeping one eye on the road and pulled out a phone in a pink plastic case. "For real, Kat?" I thumbed it on and was presented with a screen prompting me to enter the eight—digit lock code. "Dammit!" I shouted and swerved again, trying to drive the heavy, overladen van with one hand. I tossed the phone onto the seat. "Clary, do you still have your phone?"

"Yeah, hold on a second." I waited, almost holding my breath, the cars streaking by as I got us onto the interstate. "Here you go," he said, handing it to me, a small, thin lump of plastic about half the size of the phone I carried.

"Thanks." I started to hold it up to my head but stopped, looking at it, confused.

"Hey, you want the rest of it?" I glanced back; he still held the other half of it.

"DAMMIT!" I started to hit the steering wheel out of sheer frustration and thought the better of it at the last minute, realizing my meta strength would enable me to break it into pieces and leave us stranded. I hit the gas instead as we made the turn onto the on-ramp, and I throttled up the gas as we raced up the interstate.

"Status report," I said after a few minutes of silence.

There was a hesitation, then Clary spoke. "You talking to me?"

"No, I'm talking to the four unconscious people. Use your head, Clary! Of course I'm talking to you."

"Umm," he withered under my glare. "Scott's still bleeding, but not as bad. Reed's out and his face looks like someone took a brick to it." He frowned. "What happened to him, anyway?"

"Someone took a brick to his face," I said, clenching my jaw. "What about our friend from Omega?"

"Oh, yeah, he ain't movin'." Clary's voice revealed a hint of self-satisfaction. "I got him trussed up real good, three sets of our heavy handcuffs on his wrists, two on his ankles, and one holding it all together like that plastic thingy they use on six-packs."

"How's Kat?"

"She looks like she ain't been out in the sun for about a hundred years," Clary said, no trace of irony. "But she's breathing and all, seems all right. I pinched her on the tit and she didn't move, though, so I think she might be out pretty hard."

I let that settle for a second. "You did...what?"

"Well, I—"

"Never mind. Keep your damned hands off her, Clary, and see if you can find a way to call the Directorate."

He was silent for a moment. "Maybe a pay phone?"

I thought about that. "Do you know the number?"

"No. It's in my cell phone—"

I sighed, but not really at him. The sad truth was, I knew the number, but I was still working through things in my head. "Is Kat all right? Still breathing?"

"Yep." I heard a silence for a beat. "She's definitely still breathing and all. Feels nice and warm."

I turned my head at a snap to look at what he was doing and found him with a hand on her chest. "Clary, you pervert! Hands off!"

"I was checking her pulse!"

"Her pulse is way north of where you were checking for it!"

"I was trying to see if I could feel her heartbeat, you know, close to the heart itself, because it would be stronger there, right?"

"Never mind," I said. "No one's in critical condition. They'll all survive...so let's just drive. Really fast. We'll stop in a few minutes and change the license plates and then we'll just haul ass to get home." I bit my lower lip. "And hopefully everything will work out."

8.

We pulled through the gates of the Directorate a few hours later. The ride had been quiet, the opposite of the trip down, Clary keeping himself silent. Our prisoner did not awaken, nor did any of our other passengers. When we stopped, I did a quick check of Reed and Scott. My brother's face was a mess, but had already started to heal because of his meta abilities and what Kat had done with her powers. Scott, on the other hand, was pale from what I assumed to be extreme blood loss. He'd started to regain his color by the time we were pulling up to the gates, but I wasn't terribly eager to hear Dr. Perugini's assessment of what had happened (or Old Man Winter's, come to think of it, or Ariadne's).

We pulled up to the front of headquarters and I found Ariadne waiting for us. As I stepped out, her jaw dropped and she rushed forward. "What happened to you?"

"Clary," I said through gritted teeth. I wasn't over it yet. "We've got wounded—Kat, Scott and Reed—but we also have a prisoner." I opened the back doors of the van. "Can you get Dr. Perugini out here?"

She nodded sharply, her phone already in her hand. "Isabella," she said. "Get to the front of HQ, we've got wounded." I heard the soft beep as she cut the connection. A cool wind picked up as I opened the back doors to the van and Ariadne let out a gasp as she looked inside. "What the hell happened? Why didn't you call?"

"No phones," I said. "And I didn't want to slow down. We had to leave Iowa in a hurry."

I heard doors opening behind me as Perugini came rushing out of the building, rolling a gurney covered in white sheets. Her lab coat matched the sheets perfectly, as though she were a part of the gurney herself. "What the hell...happened here?"

"I led a mission," I said tightly, "and Clary came along."

Clary stepped down from the back of the van, pulling Reed out and setting him on the gurney. "It was an accident, I swear."

"It was a..." I held my tongue. "...Charlie Foxtrot. I'll carry Scott, you get Kat."

"Done and done," he said with a little too much enthusiasm.

"Cancel that," I said. "I'll get Kat." I lifted her up in my arms, trying to cradle her so that her thin neck didn't bob. "What do we do about the prisoner?"

"I'll get him," Clary said with muffled disappointment. "You want him in the cell block, Ariadne?"

"Yes," Ariadne said, a little pale. "That'll be fine. What a catastrophe."

"They'll be okay," I said.

"Oh, are you a doctor now?" Perugini said from where she stood over Reed. Her dark skin was flushed red in the lamplight. "No? Then shut up and carry them in while I do my work. Come back for the other one."

I nodded and started toward the entrance when the door opened again and Zack emerged with Kurt Hannegan. Zack saw me and his face pinched in concern. "What happened to you?" he asked as he approached, his suit flapping in the wind. "You look like you got rolled in dough."

"Here," I said and handed Kat to him. He took up her weight, cradling her in his arms like a baby. "I'm going to carry Scott." I turned back to the van, where Clary was lifting our prisoner over his head, carrying him on his shoulders in a bowed shape. I picked up Scott in my arms and tossed him over a shoulder with as much care as I could. "Clary, get that man to the cell block and don't let him out of the restraints once you're there. Let him sleep like that; he's too strong to let loose."

Clary nodded as we entered the marbled lobby, the black stone flecked with white that didn't even show in the dim light. All the recessed lighting had dimmed for the night and Clary made his way toward the stairs, evading the beams shining down from overhead as though he were trying to stay to the shadows.

"I want a full debriefing when you're done seeing to them," Ariadne said. "The Director will want to be informed."

"I'll be there once I finish dropping them off," I told her. "Give me about ten minutes?"

She nodded and disappeared toward the elevator banks while we filed down a long, narrow hallway.

"Good to see you," I said to Zack, and got a tight smile in return. "How was your day?"

"Not as exciting as yours, I'm guessing," he said with aplomb, repositioning Kat in his arms. "What happened on your mission?" There was a clatter as Perugini rolled the gurney down the hall ahead of us, hitting the small grooves where the tile separated from the carpeted areas.

"We destroyed the Omega safe house."

"Uh...weren't you supposed to surveil it?" Zack asked, his face contorting as though he were trying to find a diplomatic way to ask the question that was on his mind.

"Clary," I said simply as we walked through the doors of the medical unit. I set Scott on a bed, being as careful with him as possible. "He decided to walk up and knock on the door."

"And then what happened?" Zack asked, laying Kat on the next bed over from Scott.

"Then Clary go boom," I said, brushing Scott's curly locks off his forehead. There were some scabbed-over cuts still there. "Our prisoner answered the door by blasting it off its hinges. He's quite strong, that one."

"What is he?" Zack asked, lifting the rail on the edge of Kat's bed into the locked position to keep her from rolling out.

"Clary? An idiot." I lifted the rail on Scott's bed and started to adjust it to sit him up at a forty-five degree angle. "As for the meta we picked up at the Omega safe house, I have no idea what type. He didn't really show any other abilities that I noticed other than an uncanny knack for destroying everything around him." I frowned. "Is there a nuclear bomb type?"

"Yeah. Aleksandr Gavrikov," Zack said with amusement. "No fire, though, right?"

"No fire," I said, as he made his way around the bed and over to me. "Just a lot of property damage that resulted in a house caving in."

Zack brushed his fingers over my forehead. "Did you get hurt?"

"Not bad," I said, and ran my fingers through my hair. They came back coated in white dust, and I coughed involuntarily. "I did inhale a few rooms worth of plaster, though, so if I spit out a whole wall later tonight, you'll know why."

"I can't believe Ariadne sent Clary with you," Zack said, stroking my hair, brushing the dust out of it. "Everyone knows that guy is an idiot."

"A useful idiot at times, though," I said.

"You're not mad at him?" Zack looked inquiring.

"Oh, I'm super pissed," I said. "I'm thinking about killing him, actually, and I don't tend to think about that, ever." Zack raised an eyebrow. "Not seriously," I added. "But it would be satisfying to smack him around for a while." I nodded. "And I did, actually. I think we understand each other now."

Zack looked at me, wide eyed. "You...smacked Clary around? Like, really did?"

"Yeah. Like, I really did. And we're good now."

"And he didn't...splatter you all over a wall?"

I slapped his shoulder lightly. "He's scared of me. We're good."

Zack thought about it for a moment and gave a slight shrug. "I don't blame him."

"Would you two please take your pitiful necking activities out of my medical unit?" Dr. Perugini bustled over. "There are sick people here, and if I have to listen to any more of your banter, I will be one of them."

"You've got a great bedside manner, Doc," I said with a smile. "Did you learn that when you worked for La Cosa Nostra?"

"Oh, you are thinking you are funny!" She jabbed a finger at me as she prodded at Scott with her stethoscope. "But let me tell you something, the disasters you bring me are not funny, they are sad."

"Will everyone be all right?" I asked.

"Does it look like I have examined everyone yet?" She wagged her finger at me again. "Your brother is fine. Cosmetic damage will heal in the next day or so, but he doesn't look so pretty until then." She looked down at Scott. "What happened to this one?"

"Internal and external bleeding," I said. "Will he be all right?"

"Away from me," she said, waving me off. "Go to the corner, neck for a few minutes, then come back when I am done."

"How about your office?" I asked. "We could—"

"Away!" She flailed an arm at me.

"She seems more uptight than usual," Zack said as we made our way over to Reed's bed. "Seriously, though, physical stuff aside, how are you holding up?"

"I'll be all right once I get a shower and..." I let my voice trail off as I pulled my jacket off. It was ruined, the black leather torn in several places. "Bleh. I should have known better than to wear something I actually liked on a mission."

"Your gun," Zack said and pointed.

I looked down to where he had pointed, to the holster under my arm, and I pulled out my pistol. The barrel was bent at a ten-degree angle, either from one of the times I was hit or one of my landings.

"Damn. I liked this one, too."

"You didn't use it?" Zack asked.

I looked at the black finish. "No. I didn't even draw it. Guess I was too focused on subduing the prisoner."

Zack raised an eyebrow. "People tend to get pretty subdued when you put a few bullets in them, especially if they're a meta and can heal from that sort of thing."

I slid the wrecked gun back in the holster. "They also tend to die sometimes, in case you don't remember that certain girl—"

"Andromeda?" Zack's mood shifted. "Kinda hard to forget."

"Yeah." I tried to think of something happier. "Oh. I saw Dr. Sessions earlier today. He's discovered something...interesting."

"Oh?" Zack's face locked into a grimace. "What's that? A new way for you to kill people?"

"Ah, no. The opposite, actually." I smiled at him. "He can manufacture a suit for you that will allow you to touch my skin."

"A suit?" A raised eyebrow again. "Like with a tie?" He tugged at the bottom edge of his coat.

"No, like..." I eased closer to him, and stopped when I realized I was covered in dust. "Like a plastic one that adheres to your body. Like...skintight."

He frowned, his brow crumpling. "Like spandex? So I can dress like a superhero?"

"No," I said. "Like...skintight thin latex. So you can...touch me."

There was a moment's quite pause, the only sound coming from the beeping of Reed's pulse-oxygen monitor. "I can already do that," Zack said, breaking into a smile. "In dreams."

"Yeah," I said, "but this way you could touch me in real life. And in *every way*." I raised my eyebrows at him, trying to be suggestive.

"You mean like..." He froze, as if it was almost computing, then his eyes got wide. "Oh. Skin tight, totally skin tight, and form fitting." He looked pensive. "How do I get into something like that?"

I thought about it for a beat. "I don't know, maybe it comes in pieces? Or maybe it's like a jumpsuit with a zipper on the back. I don't really know and I don't care that much, either, as long as it works. It means we could actually..." I awkwardly started to place a dirty glove on his shoulder and then stopped myself. "Sleep together."

"We've slept together before," he said, keeping his voice low and looking over toward Dr. Perugini, who was still working on Kat. "And I kinda like what we're doing now, with the dreams. It's a pretty amazing feeling. I think it may be better than the real thing and I never thought I'd say that about...uh...that."

"Well, I'm glad it's good for you," I said, trying to stay on the side of the line of sheer irritation I was feeling, "but it's not really all that...for me, if you know what I mean. And I'm a little worried about that power of mine. We don't know how it's supposed to work. I doubt the main application is getting my boyfriend off without touching him."

"Why not?" he asked. "Maybe it's an adaptation to allow a succubus to keep a mate without being able to touch them."

"I kinda doubt that," I said. "In my experience, my powers are seldom that innocuous."

"If you're done with your little make out session," Dr. Perugini said from beside Kat's bed, "I can talk to you now."

"Just tell me what you want me to do and I'll do it." Zack placed both his hands on my arms and kissed my forehead. "If you tell me to get the suit, I'll get it and we can—"

"Well, since you're so excited about it," I said, almost snapping. "Forget it, we'll talk about it later."

"I'm sorry," Zack said, and I saw the genuine contrition in his eyes. "I guess I just thought we had a good thing going on with the dreams—"

"*You* had a good thing going with the dreams," I said, and

my voice rose higher than I intended it to before I lowered it. "Personally, I'd still like to be able to touch my boyfriend, to feel him against me, really against me, without having to dream it."

He nodded and I saw a little retreat from him. "Okay. I'll talk to Sessions."

"Try and muster some enthusiasm about it or let's not even bother."

"No, really," he said. "I just felt...intimate with you already. I'm sorry."

"Let's talk about it later." I started toward Dr. Perugini.

"Oh, good," Dr. Perugini said, looking up at us, her olive skin flushed as I arrived at Kat's bedside, a snarl posed on her lips. "I didn't mean to interrupt your personal conversation with my tedious medical report about the people who were injured on your mission." She smiled, her every word a dagger. "Scott will be fine. Katrina appears to be fine, physically. They'll both awaken in the next few hours, I expect. Katrina did some preliminary healing at the scene, yes?"

"Yes," I answered, looking down at Kat's face, which was drawn, almost as platinum as her hair.

"That saved us from serious problems, especially with Scott," Perugini said, a clipboard positioned in front of her. "I can tell from the damage that his injuries were much more severe, that they have been healed considerably. Without that, he would likely have died."

"He saved my life," I said, looking back to where Scott lay on the bed. "Saved me from getting hit, pushed me down and blocked me with his body." I shook my head. "That was a complete cluster—"

"And you were in charge?" Perugini eyed me accusingly.

"In charge, yes," I said. "In control of the situation—sadly, not."

"And whose fault is that?" she asked with more than a little accusation.

"What happened?" I heard a faint, groggy voice. I looked down to see Kat staring up at us, her curled blond hair lank and hanging loose around her face. Her eyes were open but only barely, the green of her irises peeking out at us from behind heavy lids. "Sienna?" She said my name as if trying to drag it out of herself.

"I'm here," I said, and started to reach for her hand, but hesitated when I remembered how dirty my glove was. I only froze for a second and then I took hold of her hand and picked it up. "You're gonna be fine, Kat. We're back at the Directorate. What do you remember?"

"Directorate?" Kat asked, blinking at me. "What happened?"

"We were on a mission," I said. "In Des Moines. We were supposed to keep an eye on an Omega safe house, and things went wrong. You saved us, Kat—you healed Scott and the others, kept them from dying."

"Scott?" She scrunched her eyes at me. "I saved him?"

"You did," I said. "He's going to be just fine."

"Oh." She seemed to nod, but her eyes were distant, far away, glazed over. They came sharply back into focus, and found mine, and she squinted as she concentrated, trying to speak again. "Who is Scott?"

9.

Interlude
Des Moines, Iowa

Red and blue lights flashed in the Iowa night, casting their colors over the street. The streetlamps were out, and he was left to wonder if they had functioned in the first place. The house in front of him was blocked off by a line of police cars and officers, all of them out of their vehicles—*and buzzing around like little bees*, he thought. The news vans were out as well, and they were worse than bees—they were like flies that gathered around manure in a pasture, always gravitating toward the largest pile.

Residents were out, the damp street showing the reflected red and blue, the same refracting off the faces of the men, women and children who were on the scene with him, the crowd that had gathered in their heavy coats, trying to put anything between them and the cold autumn night. The wind picked up but didn't blow the leaves the way it had in Minnesota only a few days earlier; here, everything was damp, weighed down by the wetness of a rain that must have passed in the morning but failed to dry under the cold grey sky. The smell of it was still in the air.

He pulled his own coat tight against the chill, not quite to the point of having to stamp his feet to keep warm, but only because of the crowd gathered around. He watched one of the news anchors, a pretty blond woman, delivering her palaver to the camera, after which she pulled some poor resident of the neighborhood over to answer her questions. "What did you see?" the reporter asked the woman.

"It was like there was a bulldozer coming through here or something, like I think maybe the gas line exploded?" The woman shook her head at the reporter. "I saw a car hit another car at one point, and there were people moving around, and lots of dust because the house came down...it was crazy. I think some of them were fighting."

"The police are calling this a building collapse," the reporter said, turning to face the camera, "that came in the wake of a gang battle. At least one vehicle fled the scene shortly after the collapse, and vandalism by the rival gang is strongly suspected as the motive for this bizarre activity. Whatever the case, this Des Moines neighborhood is still reeling from the destruction." She stopped and seemed to relax. "That was good, right?" The producer next to her nodded. "Perfect."

"Fools," the old man whispered under his breath, but it was lost to the wind. He backed through the crowd, then turned from the scene of the chaos, and began a slow stride back down the street to where he had parked his car. His grey hair was cropped short, and he bore not even a limp from his seemingly advanced age. *Eat, sleep, drink, and know nothing about your world. Deny all you see, and don't bother to try to explain it outside the framework of your silly beliefs,* he thought. His car was ahead, the old Cadillac he had picked up at a used car lot only a few days earlier—steel gray, this one, perfectly suited to his needs. He'd driven it down in the morning, when he'd heard the report that the safe house had gone offline. The drive was terrible, as all drives were, but it was necessary. *As I knew it would be when I originated Operation Stanchion.*

He felt for the key in his pocket, felt the loose jangle of the change, and suddenly he knew he was not alone. There were presences all around him, familiar in their intent. The police were just around the corner—*but far enough away that it won't matter*. He felt himself tense slightly, and smiled. *What a fine opportunity*, he thought. He let his fingers go slack around the keys and turned, leaning his back against the car. "Hello," he said, his voice sounding normal to himself, but probably drawing the same confusion from the youths that surrounded him as his accent seemed to with everyone else that he encountered on his trip. "It's a fine night for a walk, isn't it?"

"I was just thinking that," said the young man in front of him who wore a chain from his nose to his ear. His head was shaven clean, his skin a pale sort of cream, along with the two boys who flanked him on either side. "I was thinking that if you gave me your car keys and your wallet, you could just keep walking." Tattoos on their necks caught the old man's interest and he cocked his head at an angle to look closer.

"You are bold," the old man said, keeping his hands folded one over the other in front of him, "with the police in force just around the corner."

"They'll never get here in time." There was almost a sneer in the young man's face. "Even if they heard you." Behind the bravado, the sneer, the old man could sense the faintest hesitation. *A broken nose, then.*

The young fellow at the front turned to say something to his comrades. The old man smiled, and was already moving as the head began to swivel back at the sight of motion. The impact sent the young tough to the ground, hands slapping the pavement, catching him. His mouth was open, a thick stream of blood already coating his upper lip, dribbling down his face as he looked up at his attacker. "As you said," the old man repeated, "they'll never get here in time."

The two youths that were still standing began to move, but they were too slow; the older man's methodical motions were gone now, replaced with a fluid grace as he spun into a low kick that swept the legs of the thug on the right, sending his head cracking against the asphalt and followed that with a punch that fractured the skull of the one on the left. The older man returned to his position, leaning against the car, taking a deep breath of the night air, feeling the vigor return to his joints in a way that the walk hadn't been able to restore.

"Let me tell you something," the old man said to the young leader, the only one of the three still conscious, "because I like to aid people in their transitions. Your life, short and pitiful as it is, will be even shorter and more pitiful should you keep walking the route you are. It's a path fraught with peril, not to be trod lightly upon, and even less so by one as mortal as you." The old man looked down, and saw a quivering lip, the young man watching him frozen, as though the cold had claimed him. "If I were you—which I am not, and never would wish to be—I would go a different way, because a short life is much less preferable to a long one, wouldn't you agree?"

"Y-yes." The reply was mumbled and stuttered, some rare combination of nerves and pain.

"Good, I'm glad we sorted that out." The old man leaned down. "I look at you and I see someone who could still live long, at least for your people, should you cease this pointless, circuitous route of jail and robberies and beatings and eventually murder. That would be a shame, even for one with as little potential as you." The old man stood, and felt for his keys again, his hand sliding against the fleece of his old coat, the skin feeling thin as paper against the wind. "Good luck in your transition, should you choose to make it. I can show you the door, but you must walk through it yourself."

With that, the older man unlocked the car and eased in, shutting the door behind him. He looked out the window, saw the little cloud of fog gather on the glass from his breath, and saw the face beyond it, a scared young man, his nose broken, humiliated by a man who looked at least four times his age. *An easy mark.* The old man smiled. *Not so easy. Not such a mark. Never have been.* He started the car, fumbling the key slightly in the ignition, and reached into the old, faux leather armrest. He pulled out a new cell phone, a disposable one that he'd bought in a chain store only a few days earlier, then pulled a small 3 x 5 index card out along with it, and dialed a number. *This time, I remember.*

The female voice answered at the other end of the line, peppy for it being so early in the morning there. "This is Portal, extension 4736, please." He waited a moment before the connection was made, and the voice on the other end of the line sounded groggy. "Bjorn has been taken. Stanchion moves to phase two." He paused, waiting for a response. "No, I was supposed to get extension 4763... well, just forget what I said, will you? Connect me to the operator."

He sighed as he heard the familiar ring again, of the call being connected. "Let's try this again," he said as the female voice picked up. "Message for extension 4763...Stanchion proceeds to phase two. Will advise. Janus out."

He pressed the end key and replayed his words again. "Dammit! I meant Portal. Portal out." He shook his head, teeth clenched. "Shit."

10.

Sienna

"Her memory seems to be...selectively gone," I told Old Man Winter and Ariadne, standing in his office before the massive stone desk. The smell of the plaster and dust that coated me was still there, now evident to my nose because of the thoughts my brain was fixed on, of what had happened in Iowa, of how we had failed. Of how I had failed. "You told me once before that when she heals someone too much, she loses memory..."

"Yes," Old Man Winter said in his rumbling tone. He stirred against the black background of the windows behind him; the lights that lit the Directorate campus were dimmed at this time of night, and stars were visible on the horizon behind him, a thousand points of light over the trees in the distance. "So far as I know, her memories, once gone...remain gone forever. This has, of course, happened to her before, which is why she remembers her name as Katrina Forrest rather than Klementina Gavrikov a."

"I get that," I said, and ran a hand over my forehead, stirring a small cloud in front of my face. "But there must be something that we can do. He's her boyfriend, and she doesn't even remember who he is. We had her look at him and it was a blank stare, nothing, no recognition, as if they'd never met before in their lives. But she remembers me," I shook my head, "hell, she even remembers Reed. It's like her memory about him just...vanished."

Old Man Winter templed his hands in front of his face. "For a Persephone-type, the first memories to go are those most crucial—

the core memories, if you will. The best of times, the most intimate of companions, these are bundled together in some sort of way that makes them closest to the edge. What remains, even after a fully draining event, is ancillary things, the trivial and unimportant. The rest is just fragments."

"There must be..." I sighed. "There has to be something we can do."

"She'll receive our full attention," Ariadne said from her place next to Old Man Winter. "We'll have Perugini and Sessions working every angle they can to try and restore her memory, but this is...not something we've ever dealt with before, nor is it something where there's an overabundance of information waiting out there to steer us in the right direction. It's doubtful we'll be able to do anything for her, because as with everything else, our experimentation with meta abilities tends to leave us with more questions than answers, more knowledge of the results than what causes them."

"She saved him, his life," I said, quiet. "She must have known she was close to the edge of losing memories, because she'd already healed me, Reed, Clary—she knew, and I think she did it anyway, and she ended up passing out on him." I felt my jaw tighten before I loosened it to speak. "She saved his life, and she can't even remember his name because of it."

"Perhaps we should discuss this another time," Ariadne said gently, looking to Old Man Winter. "This has obviously been an emotional day—"

"I'm fine," I said, cutting her off. "I'm the only one who is, but I'm fine."

"Clary appears uninjured," Ariadne said. "Perhaps you can explain what happened—"

"It all went to hell," I said. "This meta, he greeted us at the door, blasted through the wall with his strength and sent Clary into a parked car—"

"Why were you at the front door?" Ariadne said, and for once the ice extended from her words, not Old Man Winter's. "Your mission was reconnaissance first—"

I didn't answer, and tried to look past them, out the dark window, but the lights inside the office reflected me, only me, me and them.

"Did you go to the door?" Old Man Winter asked, "Or were you following Clary while trying to dissuade him from knocking?"

I felt a moment of tension. "It's my responsibility either way."

Old Man Winter did not back off. "And how did it happen? Did Clary disobey your orders and leave the van or did you tell him to do so?"

I felt my innards twist. To admit that Clary had disobeyed me felt like admitting I was a weak leader, unready to be doing what I was doing. But the alternative was lying. "I'm responsible either way—"

"The truth," Old Man Winter said, "if you please."

"Clary left the van against orders," I said. "He did not listen to my repeated requests to return to it, and knocked on the door before getting himself taken out of the fight by the Omega meta." I straightened up, bringing myself to attention. "I apologize for the failure of my leadership—"

"You have no need to apologize for having a teammate who disregarded your orders," Old Man Winter said, impassive. "But the Omega meta—I have seen the footage of him in holding. I am familiar with him, his name is Bjorn. He is deadly. You did not draw your weapon?"

I pulled the pistol from beneath my tattered coat. "It was damaged."

Old Man Winter stared deeply into my eyes. "You have a backup weapon, yes?"

I hesitated. "Yes."

"Did you attempt to use either of them, at any point, during the mission?" Old Man Winter's icy gaze was on me now, a winter's storm of a glare that was absent any malice, but intense in its power.

"No," I admitted. "I...don't know what happened. Perhaps I was trying too hard to subdue the meta so we could find out about this 'Operation Stanchion' he mentioned."

"'Operation Stanchion'?" Ariadne leaned over the desk. "He just...spilled that out?"

"Something about calling it off if he was able to capture me," I said, hoping that maybe the information would cause Old Man Winter to take his gaze away from me. The thought was making me uncomfortable, the idea that I hadn't used my weapon...perhaps if I had, things would have been different, the others might not have been hurt. I felt the sting inside and shoved it down, ignoring that heartsinking feeling.

Ariadne and Old Man Winter exchanged a look, a much more obvious gesture from him than most. "We will...discuss it...when we interrogate him tomorrow," he said, breaking away from Ariadne to look back at me.

It took a moment for it to register with me. "I'm sorry...did you say 'we'? You mean me and Parks, right?"

There was a moment's pause as the air shifted in the office, and I would have sworn the air conditioning had switched on if I hadn't known better. "Things have come to a point where I can no longer allow them to proceed as they have been," Old Man Winter said, drawing himself up in the chair, but making very little expression. "I will be handling the interrogation of Bjorn myself.

"And you will assist me."

11.

I left Old Man Winter's office in awe. The entire time I had been at the Directorate, I hadn't really seen Old Man Winter do much of anything. Once, he threatened Wolfe and scared him away from me through sheer, intimidating reputation—or so he professed, since he claimed that he lacked the power to actually stop Wolfe. Other than that, he had been nothing but a mystery, an enigma, a quiet voice that delivered the occasional surprise, revelation or something else.

I certainly didn't think of him as an interrogator.

I returned to the medical unit but was run off by Dr. Perugini, who shooed me away the same way an old lady might shoo birds out of her yard with a broom. I didn't want to fight, even though it was my teammates and my brother under her care. It's not like I could do anything for them, and I was tired anyway, so I went back to my room.

I lay down on my bed after taking my injection of chloridamide. I felt the pinch of the needle as it left my arm, and I put a little piece of cotton over the hole, letting it rest for the minute or so it would take to stop the bleeding. I looked around my room: bare walls, plain carpet. I'd been in Kat's suite before—the one she barely used because she was so busy sleeping with Scott most nights—and it was totally different. I lay back on the bed and pictured it from the time I'd been in there with her while I waited for her to change.

There were posters on her walls. Justin Bieber. One Direction. I snorted at the memory, and hadn't bothered to avoid laughing at the time. She just smiled in that infuriating, uber-confident way she had—not really like a cheerleader at all, just more comfortable in her own skin. She said she liked them. Her decor was like something out of bad set design for a fourteen-year old's room. She didn't even have a TV. Her wardrobe was super cute, at least everything she wasn't wearing when she was working. Great taste in fashion. Mine was abysmal compared to hers. She had like...a thousand pairs of shoes. I had ten. I'm still a girl, after all.

I thought about her room, and how empty mine had felt compared to hers, and I wondered if she'd be staying in there for the foreseeable future.

I lay my head on the pillow and stared at the whirls of texture on the knockdown ceilings in the sparse light of the single bulb of my nightlight. I thought about Kat, about what she remembered of her life before the Directorate, and I realized that I hadn't really asked her about it. All she had told me was that she couldn't remember anything before the scientists at the facility in the Andes. I wondered how she'd gotten there, if she'd loved someone like Scott before in her century-plus of life, and if she'd love someone like that again and end up forgetting it.

I thought about Zack for a few minutes, then consciously made the effort to put him out of my mind before I fell asleep. Nothing could be worse for him right now than me coming to him in his dreams, and I needed that worry like I needed another mission with Clary at my side.

I woke to the screeching of my alarm, fading into consciousness with sunrise still somewhere over the horizon. I yawned and wondered why I had bothered awakening before seven. Then I remembered—food, get dressed, interrogation—all of which were important things.

My morning routine was half-speed, for some reason. I didn't ache as if I had been in a fight, but I definitely knew I'd been in one, because a few little pains remained. I remembered the times before my powers manifested, when my mother and I would spar in the basement. I was left with bruises that took a week to heal, with pains that stayed with me for days. Yesterday I'd been thrown into a concrete retaining wall and had a house dropped on me. My back hurt a little, like I'd slept on it at the wrong angle. I kneaded at the knots in my shoulders with my hands; even with the weak muscle control I sometimes felt in the mornings it was more than enough to cause me pain. If I squeezed full strength, I had the ability to break the skin and draw blood. Well, that was as hard as I had ever squeezed myself, at any rate.

The cafeteria was already filled with activity when I got there, from the crowds of people going about the start of their daily routine. I thought about texting Zack to see if he would be in for breakfast, but I didn't want to be a clingy girlfriend, especially after last night. I suppose it was a compliment that he enjoyed our nighttime activities so much, but it worried me, and the pleasure was all his. To me it still felt fake, like trying to touch a shadow. I wanted to feel the real thing.

I waited in line, lost in thought. The crowd and conversation went on around me, hundreds of voices rising and falling in a chorus that reminded me of white noise as I tuned it out. The smell of eggs and bacon were prominent, as were the onions for the Denver-style eggs. All the cafeteria workers were dressed in brown aprons, their hairnets making them into a line of mushrooms blooming against the white, sunlit walls.

My fingers, still covered by gloves, ran along the glass window between me and the food, as though I could somehow impart the tactile sense of taste along with the touch, something small to calm my raging stomach, which was reminding me I had skipped both lunch and dinner yesterday. It had a bad habit of holding me accountable for missed meals (which happened increasingly often due to work lately) with a bad case of the rumblies. I could almost taste the food as I slid my tray down the three steel rails that ran the length of the counter.

"Excuse me," I heard from my left. I turned and saw that teenaged boy who had been staring at me only a couple days earlier, the one that had been in the cafeteria line. He had hair that seemed to droop around his head in a bowl, falling to just above his neck. It was a careless sort of haircut, and his brown eyes were hidden behind a thick pair of glasses. "Can you pass me an apple?" he asked, pointing just past me to where the apples and oranges waited in bowls at the end of the line, in an area reserved for self-service foods like crackers and condiments, cereal and such.

I thought briefly about why he was bothering to ask me when in two seconds I would be clear of it and he could get whatever he wanted, but I put it out of my mind in the name of civility. "Sure," I said, and tossed him an apple. He caught it, cradling it against his red t-shirt like it was some treasure. He looked familiar, I thought as I gave him a moment's more look before turning away and finding a table of my own. And not just from the cafeteria line yesterday, but from somewhere else. He didn't look much different in age than me, but...I shrugged. Not my worry.

I scarfed my eggs and ham without much delay, sitting by myself. It was a little unusual; I'd fallen into a pattern of eating my meals with Reed, Kat and Scott, or at least Zack. Failing that, sometimes I would eat on the run or skip a meal. I looked around the cafeteria and found myself unsettled at being alone. Which was strange for a girl who used to eat almost all her meals by herself, with only Mother occasionally around for company.

I finished and walked back to headquarters, ignoring the fall chill in the air. I hit the lobby of HQ and the heaters kicked in the moment I walked through the doors, spreading slowly over my skin as the cool air faded. I felt the heavy dryness of it in my sinuses as the soles of my shoes clipped along on the tile floor keeping pace with all the other civilian employees of the Directorate who were making their way in to go about their daily jobs. Suits and ties abounded, women wore darker-toned dress pants and jackets, and almost everyone was already wearing full-length winter coats.

I veered behind the sweeping double staircase on either side of the lobby and made my way to the emergency stairwell at the back of the building, the one that also led down. The concrete walls around me established a pattern that ran all the way to the emergency floodlights at each landing. The sounds of the people milling about the lobby on their way to their serious, professional day disappeared as I heard the heavy metal door to the stairwell shut behind me, an echo bouncing around in the four-story room like a thunderclap after lightning.

I pushed through the door at the basement entrance and found myself in a long, narrow hallway. The walls were beige, a kind of wallpaper on them made up of tiny lines that intersected like fine wire mesh, a texture so small that I wondered if the non-metahuman eye could even perceive it. Black doors lined the walls, and I realized for the first time I had no idea how many of them were actually cells, and if any of them were occupied besides the two filled with our Omega friends. Just outside the staircase entrance were the more luxurious cells, the ones that were almost like standard living quarters but more secured; the further one got from the stairs, the more they became like a square without any sort of differentiation; an arrangement designed to keep the prisoners contained within off-balance, and Spartan enough to give them almost nothing to work with in planning any sort of escape.

Old Man Winter stood in the middle of the hallway like an imposing pillar holding up the whole building. He wore a winter coat like so many of the other men, but I blinked in surprise—it had to be close to eighty degrees in the hallway. He always tended toward heavy clothing, but I wondered if perhaps it was to hold the cold in, toward him, rather than keeping the warmth in as it was for most people. I watched him as I walked, and he seemed to take no notice of me until I was within a few feet, at which point he swiveled on a heel and looked down at me. Almost seven feet tall, that was no challenge for him, since I was not even five and a half feet tall myself.

"You are early," he observed, arms folded over his coat.

"It doesn't pay to be late when you're working with the boss," I said. "Are we going to be interrogating James Fries as well, while we're here?"

"Pointless, I think," he said, his rumbling voice given resonance by the acoustics of the hall. "Fries is a messenger boy, a strong meta, but not one of the privileged of Omega. Bjorn, on the other hand, was the son Odin, before he passed."

"Odin's son?" My face scrunched up and I pondered the oversized man who had wrecked my whole team in Des Moines. "He looks nothing like Chris Hemsworth."

Old Man Winter ignored me. "He will, I think, be a better choice to speak with. More...knowledgeable, having been brought to America specifically for whatever this Operation Stanchion is."

"How do you know that?" I asked, feeling a flash of confusion coupled with the fear that I had failed to read something that had been prepared. Unprepared was not a good feeling, especially in front of the boss.

"This morning, J.J. ran a...tracking program, I believe he called it...searching through U.S. customs for certain patterns. One emerged, detailing passport irregularities." Old Man Winter peered down at me, cold blue eyes seeming to glow in the fluorescent light of the hall. "After comparing them to photographic records, he found Bjorn." Old Man Winter let out a deep breath, fogging the air in front of him, something that reminded me of the smell of a December wind. "Unless Omega is planning something else, that means that Bjorn is here for Stanchion."

I thought about that for a moment. Stanchion had something to do with me, plainly, because Bjorn had inferred as much when I was fighting him. If Omega was sending in more operatives to capture me, this was nothing new. They'd been sending them at me for almost a year, to the point it was now almost comical in result. Or it would have been, except for what happened to Kat. Their last two operatives had ended up decapitated (and I didn't even feel bad about it, because they showed no human characteristics at all), the one before that was locked up in a cell even now, the one before that had been thrown off a building by the one predating him (by Wolfe, who was locked in my head).

"You seem unworried," Old Man Winter said, jarring me back to the here and now.

"I don't know. It's hard to keep getting charged up about this. If I did, I'd spend all my time worrying. Whatever comes, I can deal with it."

"You should not be so cavalier," Old Man Winter said, somehow more serious than the way he said everything else. "Omega is a very serious threat, one which you have defeated through a combination of luck, skill, power and the assistance of others. Bjorn is not to be underestimated, though he is no great thinker. Whatever they are planning now seems to indicate a deeper consideration for long-term strategy rather than just throwing whatever they have on hand at you. Using Wolfe as their opening gambit should not be overlooked; he was the best they had to offer. They do not hesitate. Their means are brutal, and they will do whatever it takes to achieve their aims." He looked at me, steadily. "What are you willing to do?"

"What am I willing to do...to what?"

"To find out the truth about Operation Stanchion and what it means for you." Old Man Winter was unflinching. "To discover Omega's aims. These are all questions which could be of great use to us if we were to find answers."

"I'm willing to question Bjorn as long as necessary to get some answers," I said.

Old Man Winter reached out to the door, finally looking away from me. He placed his hand in his pocket and withdrew a key card that looked no bigger than a scrap of paper in his massive palm, and ran it over the reader in front of the door. The glowing red light on the reader turned green with a subtle beep. "Follow," he said and opened the door to the cell.

The room was small, ten by ten by ten, like the rest. The squares that made it up seemed to blur together for me, and I put aside my thoughts about all else to focus on Bjorn. He didn't look quite as he had yesterday when I'd been fighting him. His short brown hair was still powdered with the dust of our battle. He had blood on his face and chest that had gone uncleaned, though his wounds were gone. His shirt was missing, along with boots and any other sort of clothing save for his pants, which were a dirty corduroy and speckled with all the evidence of our fight. He was shackled to a chair that was metal, bolted to the floor in the middle of the room, and he was still cuffed about the wrists and ankles.

"Bjorn," Old Man Winter said in some form of greeting. "It has not been nearly long enough."

"So it is you, Jotun," Bjorn said, his brow arced in a forty-five degree slant on either eyebrow. "I had heard you were the head of the Directorate, giving shelter to this one. Do not expect me to remember the old times fondly and cooperate with you."

"I do not expect you to remember anything fondly," Old Man Winter replied, his breath still frosting the air. "But you will cooperate with me, or your memories will go from less-than-fond to a much darker place."

Bjorn's back straightened at this, his shoulders squared, even with his arms trapped behind his back. "You will get nothing out of me, Jotun. Do your worst."

Old Man Winter stopped in the middle of the room, towering over the seated Bjorn, who was not exactly a small guy. "Do you remember that time in...what did they call it, the Huns who lived there? I find myself forgetting the names the Germanic tribes gave to the old places. I have heard that in old age, humans default to their childhood remembrances. I find the opposite is true for me, that I cannot remember the names of the places from my youth, though I can recall the sight of them in vivid detail. For example, I recall that maiden that you bedded, that local girl from a tribe, how you called her a virgin sacrifice, and how when her brothers came after you in the morning, you caved their heads in with your fists as the girl cried behind you and begged you to stop. Do you remember what happened after that?"

Bjorn showed little reaction, only the slightest of a smile. "I remember her voice, but not her name. Is that strange? I don't remember any of their names."

"That does not surprise me at all," Old Man Winter said, surprisingly gregarious, even as I was trying to keep down my breakfast in the midst of these discussions. "I wanted to kill you for that, did you know?" He bent at the waist, as Bjorn's head jerked in surprise. "My respect for your father kept me from it, though. You lived as a god, and all you wanted was there for the polite taking; there was never a need for the sort of violence and thuggery that you and your kind visited upon the humans. But for you it was never about receiving the gifts of those who worshipped us for our power; it was about taking that which they did not wish to give freely." Old Man Winter rumbled with every word, and the temperature seemed to drop in the room. "Strength over kindness, as it were. Force over grace. Did you thrill to the thoughts of what you did there?" Old Man Winter leaned in closer to Bjorn's ear. "Did it keep you warm on the cold nights when we returned to our homeland? Did the memory excite you long after you killed the girl, her father, her brothers and all the others who did not stand idly by while you murdered their kin and fellows?" Old Man Winter's hand landed on his shoulder, resting there. "Is that the way you like it?"

I cleared my throat, and both of them looked up, seeing me as though for the first time since I entered the cell with Old Man

Winter. "Perhaps we could...return to the main subject?" I asked, wondering if I was overstepping my bounds and figured I was about to get a warning to shut up from Old Man Winter. Or at least a gaze that would freeze me in place.

"Quite right, Sienna," Old Man Winter said, returning to his full height. "Bjorn, you will tell us every detail of this Operation Stanchion—its purposes, its players, its timeline, and you will do so now."

Bjorn did not laugh this time, nor smile, nor react almost at all. He kept his head facing forward, and I saw the slightest shudder from him. He opened his mouth as if to speak but faltered, taking a moment to recover before speaking again. "No. I will not."

"Very well, then," Old Man Winter said, now beginning to orbit Bjorn slowly, one small step at a time. "Then we seem to have reached an impasse."

I blinked in surprise at Old Man Winter's change in attitude. Was this as far as he was willing to go? I didn't exactly want to be party to torture, but I assumed that perhaps there would at least be a face punch or two for Bjorn, who, as Old Man Winter had just established, richly deserved it and probably quite a bit more.

Old Man Winter remained quiet for only a moment. "You realize, of course, that Sienna is a succubus?" He took a step around to the front of Bjorn and waited there, indicating me with a long, extended finger pointed at my chest. "That she drained the very life and memory out of Wolfe? That she can take your memories and leave you as thoughtless as a legume, break you to her will and make you no more?"

Bjorn's eyes flicked toward me, then went straight ahead again. "I had heard she was a succubus. I didn't know you allowed meta-draining on your campus, Jotun. How low you've sunk, to allow a soul eater to go to work on your own kind." He spat in Old Man Winter's face and I flinched. "Let her do her worst. I won't cooperate with scum, with her kind, or with you if you're the sort who does that."

"I have not yet begun to sink," Old Man Winter said, using his sleeve to wipe slowly across his face but not bothering to stand up and remove himself from spitting distance, "but perhaps, very soon, you will see that I will do whatever it takes to defend those under my protection." He stood and glowered down. "Sienna." He looked back at me. "Find out what he knows."

I froze for a moment, as surely as if he had just used his frigid breath to ice me into place. I felt my legs come back to me, and I took halting steps to get behind Bjorn, who watched me, his blank affect showing the first signs of strain. I began to take off my glove, wondering which would come first—Bjorn breaking or Old Man Winter telling me to stop. I walked a slow arc around Bjorn, trying to keep my calm, trying to portray winter's cold, like the Director, to look like this was nothing, no big deal, something that happened all the time. I kept my lips a narrow line, ignored the stuffiness of the room, the lack of movement, the air currents that my body made as I swept along. It was as though all particle motion had stopped, neither Winter nor Bjorn were speaking, and I felt every step I took.

The clammy feeling of a sweat crawled across my skin as I took up position behind Bjorn. I could tell by the twitch of his muscles that he was trying not to look at me as I stood behind him. I lay my discarded glove across his shoulder, and he blanched at the feel of it. It fell to the floor and made a soft plop as it landed. I looked up at Old Man Winter, but he was still on Bjorn, unyielding. I put my gloved hand on Bjorn's other shoulder, and he looked at it as though a spider had crawled on him. His shoulders were tense, his muscles at full flex, hands still locked behind him.

"Last chance," Old Man Winter said. "Before she extracts your soul like a walnut, leaving only a broken shell behind."

Bjorn held his quiet for almost a minute, and finally, Old Man Winter nodded to me. I lay my bare hand on Bjorn's shoulder, and he tensed once more, as though he could shuffle off the chair and away from me. I felt the stir in my fingers first, as though the blood were running to them. I was warm now, my breathing slow but deep, each exhalation a sweet release. I felt the rush as my skin tingled all over, the sweet, warm sense that Charlie had talked about, desire and pleasure filling my mind as I heard the first scream leave Bjorn's lips. It was a small howl, not only loud in the physical space, but in my head, through the tie between us created by my touch, the drag of his soul against the bond with his body as my power tore at him, ripping a little bit of him from it moment by moment. Thoughts began to cascade through my mind, flashes of images, faces, emotions, and I held my hand on him for only another second before I tore it away, my breathing turned ragged, painful. My hand shook, and craved what it had held only a moment before, and the rest of me did, too.

I hunched over, hands on my knees, drawing slow breaths and unable to pull myself back up. I turned my head sideways to Old Man Winter, who looked over Bjorn and down at me, the closest thing to concern rimming his eyes. "Are you all right?"

"Fine," I said. "But if I touch him any longer, he's going to be a permanent spectator in my life like the others, and frankly, I could use fewer sickos in my head, not more."

Old Man Winter held his position, towering above Bjorn, far, far above me. "Sienna...you must extract this information from him. He will not tell us. Sifting it out yourself is the only way...and is necessary to begin to gain hold over your powers."

"I can't..." I said. "I can't keep them at bay without chemical assistance. And I don't want another one in there. Not like this. Not ever."

Old Man Winter took two steps around Bjorn and knelt to one knee, still almost able to look me in the eye if I had been standing up, which I wasn't. "You know the dire predictions of what is to come, not only from Omega now, this Stanchion, but of the other warnings, the storms that come for us and all our kind—indeed, all humanity as well. You will be one of their protectors, but to do so, you will need the strength to do what is necessary."

"I can't," I said. "I can't even control them without chloridamide. I can't do it."

"You must," Old Man Winter said, his voice an urgent hiss that dragged out the word must. "You are vital to our success."

I stared at him. "What do you know that you're not telling me?" The cold inside me was almost indescribable, my body crying out for the warmth of Bjorn's soul, mine for the taking if I only reached out—but from Old Man Winter, for once...it wasn't cold at all.

"That you are key." He stared at me, and the iridescent eyes of blue warmed. "But it is all at risk. If you are unwilling to do what it will take to protect even yourself, how can you protect anyone else?" His hand came to my shoulder. "You must learn to control your power. To not fear it." He looked to Bjorn. "And you must be willing to kill when it is necessary."

"He's a prisoner," I said, and looked past Old Man Winter to Bjorn, whose eyes were open wide but rolled back in his head. His mouth hung open and spittle was rolling down his chin. The smell of fear and sweat filled the cold air in the room. "He's helpless. Give it time, we'll break him."

There was something I saw, a flash in Old Man Winter's eyes, and he stood abruptly. "Time is not a luxury, and nor is it something we possess in abundance. This Operation Stanchion rumbles closer to fruition, and we remain like children running about in the woods after dark, unaware of the danger about to unfold around us." He placed a hand on Bjorn's shoulder. "You will not use your power to unearth his plans?"

I stared at the back of Bjorn's head. The man's head was turned, looking back at Old Man Winter, and just far enough that I could see the edge of his eye under his heavy, Cro-Magnon brow. "No," I breathed, "not like that. Not him, not anyone. I just...I can't."

He didn't even flinch. "Your mother would."

I, however, did flinch. "I'm not her." There was a pause. "We can find out another way. He'll talk." I drew a deep breath and stood, coming up to my full height. "We'll break him."

Old Man Winter closed his eyes, as though pondering something, and then opened them again, now impassive. "You are correct. We will break him." I felt the temperature in the room plunge, this time no product of my imagination. My skin, once clammy, felt ice form along the wet dampness of it, the freeze crawling up around me as a winter frost manifested before my eyes.

Old Man Winter's hand glowed where it lay on Bjorn's shoulder, and a thin sheet of ice was forming around it. It grew thicker, denser, as I watched astonished, the frost crept down Bjorn's arm to mid-humerus and beyond. Bjorn let out a cry, followed by a sustained scream. "Oh, yes," Old Man Winter said, removing his fingers from Bjorn's arm as the air in front of his mouth formed a cloud that was visible against his thick, black wool coat. "He will break."

With a subtle move, Old Man Winter brought his fingers back down in an open-handed slap that sent a cracking noise echoing through the room. Bjorn's entire hand dissolved into shards of ice and cascaded to the floor in a pile, no more substantial than a mound of discarded snow. "If it takes losing every limb he has... he will break. And if that fails..." Old Man Winter placed his hand on Bjorn's chin and held it up, looking into his eyes. "Then we will wait until tomorrow, when he has regrown his limbs...and begin again."

12.

I was out the door before I realized I was walking, my key card granting me exit. I put my back against the wall in the hallway and listened, but heard nothing from inside, nor in the hall save for the vent fans and my own heavy breathing, sharp, punctuated with a gasp every few minutes as I tried to hold in strong emotion.

The door opened quietly a few minutes later and I averted my eyes to keep from looking inside, and whatever was left of Bjorn. When I glanced, unable to control the instinct to look, Old Man Winter obstructed my view until the door was closed. "You don't approve of my methods," he said, stating the bloody obvious.

"You tortured him."

"He would kill anyone who got in the way of capturing you, harm you in any way it took to get what he wanted." Old Man Winter made no apologies as he stood there before me. He stood just as tall as he had in the room, just as imposing. "Why would I do any less to protect you from them?"

"They're a joke," I said, almost expelling the words as a breath. "Everything they've sent, we've beaten. To cave to their tactics, to drop to their level—"

"They will beat us, regardless of level, if we refuse to do what it takes to get to the truth of what they are planning," he said, and I caught heat in his words for the first time. "You wish to believe foolishly that no matter what comes, you can simply overcome through some sense of unlimited potential or magical destiny, but that is folly. Your life hangs in the balance." I could hear an urgency from him I'd never heard before, a stirring in his words that hinted at something darker, something deeper. "Omega and all hell that follows is inching closer by the day, and we have little time to prepare you for the role you will take when it comes." He drew up again and hesitated, and I saw a hint of sadness. "I won't always be around to protect you—to do what you will not. Soon you will have to do these things for yourself, to be ready to take your place—"

"Are you leaving?" I asked, not sure how to respond, and not even sure why I was cutting him off. He stared coolly back at me. "Checking out? Bailing in the middle of the fight?"

"I am one of the oldest metahumans on the planet," Old Man Winter said, and the tiredness in his voice made it fact more than any of the words did. "I have seen much, done much, endured much. My power fades, even now, from a battle I fought over a hundred years ago that scarred me and left me weaker than anyone knows." The glisten in the blue of his irises was unmistakable. "Even still, Omega fears me." The frosty sensation grew in the room, as though his skin were growing cold and infecting the air around him. "When the day comes that they find me—and find me they shall, sooner or later—I will be the first to fall." His eyes glistened ever brighter. "But not the last, unless you are prepared to do whatever is necessary to fight the battle that they will not expect you to fight. Unless you are ready to do whatever it takes to win, to protect the metas and humans of the Directorate."

He moved his hand to my shoulder, a heavy, leaden weight, but the way he did it was unlike how he had touched Bjorn. "It is much responsibility I place on your shoulders, I know. The weight of the world, perhaps, it feels to you. But I do this because you...are the only one who can bear it. There is no other." His shoulders were slumped now, his black coat billowing around them as though there were extra space, and the shadows from the fluorescent lights on his face made it seem like he was gaunter, bonier, more shadowed and skeletal than he had ever looked before. Like death, frozen and forbidding, as though he were already dead, as though it had settled on him down to the bones, and he simply had yet to stop moving.

"Do you think they'll be coming soon? For you, I mean?" When I asked, I sounded like a scared little girl.

"I have no idea." I heard him breathe again, back to life. "This Operation Stanchion is concerning...to see them moving resources toward us and not know their specific aim." He grew quiet for a moment. "You must prepare. You must ready yourself for what is to come. To turn blindly away from this or to trust fate to be kind is a fool's lot, and yields a fool's results." His voice grew hard like iron as he stood again. "And you are no fool." He turned and walked toward the end of the hall, leaving me behind.

I felt pitiful, scared, feeling the true dread of Omega, of what was coming, in a way that I hadn't since the arrival of Wolfe had forced me to hide in a cell here in the basement, hoping he would eventually leave town, leave me alone. Henderschott hadn't scared me, not really. He had hurt me once or twice, but not enough to drive the fear into me the way Wolfe had. Same with the vampires they sent, and Mormont, whom they turned from the Directorate's service. None of them scared me like Wolfe did, none of them hurt me like Wolfe did.

Except Fries. That little rodent. Exempting Wolfe, they couldn't beat me in a fight, not even with Bjorn, who was a bruiser. But Fries came at me sideways, touching on all my insecurities at a time when I was vulnerable. Then he betrayed me and twisted the knife, the snake. The hallway seemed narrower now, the air thicker, and the chill had left with Old Man Winter. I started toward the stairs, the beige walls blurring together. Now they were after me again, maybe after Old Man Winter, too. If they wanted to topple the Directorate, knocking over Old Man Winter seemed like it would be the way to go about it. Who'd step up after him? I liked Ariadne, but I got the sense that she relied on him to do more than was obvious on the surface.

My legs carried me up the stairs, through the lobby and out the door. I hit the crisp air and took a breath. All the feelings of confinement began to fade, that tightness in my chest as if I couldn't breathe for what I had to contemplate. Breaking a man's arm off out of fear for what was to come, for what he knew but wasn't telling...I don't know that I would have had it in me to harm even Bjorn in such a way.

But I didn't know that it was totally wrong, either. Not when we were dealing with the same people who sent Wolfe, the man who tried his best to rape and torture me. It sounded as though Bjorn was cut from the same cloth.

I cut across the campus on the way back to the dormitory; heading to the training room was my first instinct, but I couldn't bring myself to do it. I needed quiet. Operation Stanchion bothered me. Who named their little plans in such a grandiose and evil way? A stanchion was just a pillar, after all, a post, and what did that have to do with me? Or did it refer to Old Man Winter, the pillar of the Directorate?

The leaves were packed to the ground, and a frost had come with morning, turning everything a silvery, shimmering white when the sun hit it. The blades of grass crunched under my boots in a way that was almost alien to me, so different from their sweet give in summer. The frost was in the air, too, crowding into my sinuses and nose, freezing the little hairs inside. It was bitter—too bitter by far for October.

The entry to the dormitory was quiet; the younger students were in their classes. It wasn't close to lunchtime with the bustle of all the administrative employees coming to the cafeteria in droves. I wondered how much they knew about what we did here. There were hundreds of employees, after all, and most of them lived off-campus. I doubted most of them even worked with the metas, which left me curious. There was a divide between the admin and school business, I knew that, and I supposed a person could even work in the administration building without ever knowing that the kids at the school had anything different about them; it wasn't as if any of them had scales, or had snakes growing out of their shoulders, or anything like that. The most bizarre thing on campus was Clary, and that had more to do with his personality than his power, except when he shifted his skin.

On the other hand, seeing Eve Kappler flying past a window might be a hint that something was not quite what it seemed on campus.

I inserted my key card in the elevator and rode up to the third floor. When I arrived, I stepped off and walked down the white hall, noticing a few potted trees that hadn't been there before. Decoration to brighten up the dull landscape with winter coming, I supposed.

I paused as I reached my door. The one next to mine, the one that belonged to Kat, was open, the card reader's bar an angry red, and a buzzing noise coming from it, the quiet sound of low-voltage electricity arcing. I walked toward it tentatively, the thought that I might be walking into trouble only a faint idea in my mind. I lay my hand on the door, which was half open, and I could see the light flooding in from the windows. It was a sunny day and the room was lit like mine, bright and pleasant. I took a quiet step inside, then another. The living room and kitchen were silent, nothing moving as I came around the wall and got a full look.

Kat's furniture was roughly the same as mine and in the same layout. All her appliances were Directorate standard, though again, she had taken some effort to spruce up the walls with the posters I didn't care for. I heard a faint scratching from the bedroom, and I walked through the middle of the apartment on my way to the bedroom door, which was drawn at a forty-five degree angle.

With a touch I sent it open, the oiled hinges allowing it to move without making a sound. The bed was against the far wall, and someone was sitting on it, a man in jeans and a black t-shirt that went perfectly with his darker, more tanned complexion—something I had always thought bizarrely out of place in Minnesota, especially going into winter. "Scott," I said quietly, and he looked up, his blond curls bobbing, his eyes only slightly puffy. I would honestly have expected more emotion, but it was possible he had been here for a long while.

"Sienna," he said, and his voice was scratchy, like a needle run over a record. He cleared his throat and tried again. "How are you?"

"How am I?" I looked at him with incredulity. "I'm fine. I'm a little worried about you, though."

"Dr. Perugini said I'm okay." He held something in his hand, and I realized after a moment it was a CD, and he lay it on the bed, the clear plastic case catching the light.

"I kinda doubt she examined you in the way I'm talking about," I said. "I realize you're fine, physically—"

"Well, we don't have a psychiatrist anymore to make sure I'm gonna be all right mentally, so..." He shrugged fatalistically. "I guess I'm just gonna have to limp on in my own way, kinda like every other teenager who just lost a girlfriend."

"That's one way to look at it." I edged a little closer to him. "Kind of a healthy way, too, I suspect."

"Well, I'm all about my health here," he said, waving vaguely to his body, which I admit, was well sculpted. In spite of being unserious about almost everything, working out and eating right was something Scott did almost to distraction. And it showed. Not that I noticed, of course, but because others had told me. And I saw him with a shirt off, once, at the beach. Maybe more than once. And not always at the beach. Anyway.

"I don't think too many people have had their girlfriend completely forget them," I said. "That might be new territory. Something you could stake your claim to."

"Why does that matter?" he asked with a shrug. "Lots of people wish they could forget their breakups."

"But Kat wasn't breaking up with you," I said. "She sacrificed her memory of you to save your life."

"Yeah, I get that," he said, and I saw a flush hit his cheeks. "She's brave and self-sacrificing, and now she can't remember me, or any of our little inside jokes, or that we slept together every night, or anything...at all...from the last nine months. I might as well not have existed in her life."

I swallowed heavily. "I'm sorry, Scott."

"Why are you sorry?" he asked, and his eyes were narrowed in genuine confusion. "You didn't make her lose her memory."

"It was my mission." I sat down on the bed, leaving a few feet of distance between us. "I was in charge. It's my fault that—"

"Listen to me," Scott said, and all the brittle was gone from his voice. His eyes were lidded, puffy, but they burned with inner fire. "I want you to hear this, and maybe it'll make me feel better, too. What happened at the safe house wasn't your fault. You took a beating to keep us from dying, and without you, we'd all have croaked, I'm sure, after tangling with that big bastard. What happened in Iowa was Clary's fault, because he's an idiot. And we knew he was an idiot, that there was nothing but rocks in his damned skull. We would have been better off without him." The last part was spat out like a curse. "No one on that mission could have controlled Clary. No one."

"I appreciate what you're saying—"

"But you're gonna blame yourself anyway?" He looked away, and his hands came behind him so he could lean back, legs still draped over the edge of the bed. "Might as well. Plenty of that going around."

"It wasn't your fault either, Scott."

"Nope," he said, staring into the window on the far edge of the room, to the blue sky beyond the tinting that made looking out bearable. "Doesn't stop me from blaming myself, though." He shifted position a little. "Would you mind leaving me be? I kinda just want to be alone right now."

"Sure," I said with a perfunctory nod. "If you want to talk, later, I'll—"

"*If* I want to talk, no offense but I'll look for a more sympathetic ear," he said, looking at me almost pityingly. "You're a lot of things, Sienna—leader, badass, friend—but camp counselor you're not."

"Pretty sure friends listen to each other when they have problems." I felt that curious clench in my jaw. "I want you to know...I'm here for you if you need—"

"Please don't get sappy for the first time in your life, ever," he said, and he looked at me with a hint of pity. Then after a pause, "Thank you."

"You're welcome," I said, easing my way back to the door, which I drew closed behind me as I made my way out of the apartment.

13.

Technical services called me on my new cell phone an hour later, a secretary with a perfunctory message asking me to come to Ariadne's office immediately. It was a bit of a puzzler, honestly, because usually she either called herself or a messenger slid a paper note under my door if it was considered to be an unholy enough hour to give someone a phone call that wasn't urgent. I made my way into the Directorate lobby and rode the elevator to the fourth floor, the lift filled with administrative employees coming back from lunch. I'd skipped mine (again), not really in the mood for conversation after running through everything in my mind for an hour straight.

Ariadne's door was ajar when I arrived, and already filled to near capacity. Clary was sitting in one of the chairs, his bulk slumped over, not as jovial as usual. His head was down, as though he couldn't bear to look at me. It didn't seem to be a reaction solely to my entry to the room, either; he was quiet long before I walked in. Eve Kappler was in her usual position, leaning against the hutch behind Ariadne. I had a feeling Ariadne's skin was ready to crawl from her casual lingering there. Ariadne was not the sort given to public displays of affection, or even association, and her relationship with Eve was an open secret, much gossiped about in the halls of the Directorate. While she tried to keep it quiet, Eve did everything in her power to subtly remind every one of us that she was sleeping with the second-in-command. I wouldn't have wanted that sort of political game played around me, but I wasn't Ariadne, so I didn't have to worry about it.

Roberto Bastian was looking dark as ever, leaned against the wall just past the door. "Ma'am," he said with a nod to me. I liked Bastian; he was a pro, always respectful, and he never disregarded anything I said just because I ran the junior league version of his team. Parks was next to him, and the grey-haired older man gave me a nod as well when I came in. Reed was hanging in the corner behind Clary. Every one of them had been in these exact positions in this office before when I'd come in, as though we had fallen into some bizarre sort of rut. The only thing missing was Kat to sit in the chair next to Clary and Scott to stand behind her. I usually lingered in the corner with my brother, which was where I went now.

"Get J.J. in here and then shut the door," Ariadne said, not even acknowledging my arrival. We waited in silence until a minute later the fuzzy haired hipster walked in, his dark, heavy-rimmed glasses hanging over the edge of his nose, his flannel shirt and skinny jeans putting him at odds with the appearance of everyone else in the room, except Kappler, who habitually wore skinnier jeans than anyone but Kat would be able to squeeze into. The whole room smelled strongly of shaving gel and masculinity, though neither Eve, Ariadne nor I were the most feminine of specimens to offset the boys, nor were any of us the perfume-wearing sort.

"Good morning, all," J.J. said by way of greeting, surprisingly chipper.

"Stow the sunny optimism and get on with the talking," Eve said, arms folded, drawing an impatient and measured look from Ariadne.

"Righto," J.J. said. "So, I told the Director I found some irregularities in the U.S. Customs systems, some people coming through that we flagged for being part of a batch of passports all issued from the same center on the same day, that contained a few familiar faces." He paused and lifted up the screen of the tablet computer, showing it around to us all in a slow pan. When it came around so I could see it, I bristled. A very familiar face was on the screen—Wolfe. "Oh, yes," he said, "but just like a bad infomercial, wait—there's more." He used his fingers to flip the screen to the next one, revealing another passport photo which he held in position for me to see. A scarred, horrific face was visible on the screen, something that looked familiar, but only slightly so.

"Henderschott?" I asked, drawing a nod from J.J., who flipped to the next screen, pausing for just a second. "James Fries," I said and he flipped to the next one, a dark haired man who was trying his best not to smile. The photograph was color, but something about the eyes was off. He flipped to the next picture, a blond-haired man, and once I saw it, I realized who they were. "Spike and Angel, the vampires they sent after me." I blinked at the pictures. "They didn't look anywhere near that human when I fought them. They had red eyes..."

"Contact lenses," J.J. said. "They were groomed up for the photos." He stole a look at the screen. "Probably had their hair done before travel, kept their mouths shut to keep the fangs from showing. I'm guessing they did that with Wolfe, too, based on the before and after nature of this passport picture compared to the newsreel stuff I've seen from him. But there's actually more still in this batch." His fingers slid along the screen again, and another face appeared. "Look familiar?"

"Bjorn," I said, recognizing the brown hair and blunt face more than anything else about his bearing. "The guy who's sitting down in the cells right now," I said to Reed. "How many of these passports are there?"

"Hundreds in the batch," J.J. said. "It was from one specific facility in the UK over the course of a few weeks. Kinda hard to believe they're all British citizens, but it's possible. Anyway, so we got this whole batch, and I'm sifting through it with the Director for familiar faces, but that's kind of a losing proposition because his sight isn't what it used to be and a lot of these people don't look anything like metas, and some of them don't look like...well...anything."

"Can you track any of them right now?" Reed asked.

"Yeah, and that's kind of the point of this meeting," J.J. said. "We got a good line on one of them, one of them in the batch that just landed in Minneapolis yesterday, came in from London via New York." He held up the pad again, this time showing a female face, a dark-haired, serious woman who looked to be in her forties with a short bob haircut. "Eleanor Madigan," is the name on the passport...but of course Wolfe was in the system under Eugene Dellwood, so..." he looked up and blinked, his twitch magnified by his glasses, "probably an assumed name."

"Now in Minneapolis?" I asked. "So if she's part of this Operation Stanchion, it looks like they're moving pieces into place in the area now."

"Probably more than you think," J.J. said, and tapped away at his tablet for a minute before pushing it toward me to see again, holding it in the air between us. "This is Des Moines Police Department's report on what they found in the house after you finished demolishing it." I cringed, but J.J. paid no mind. "Looks like Bjorn had a Google Map leading him up to a hotel near the airport here in Bloomington."

"He was coming here?" Parks spoke up at last, the voice of wisdom. "If he already had the map, let's assume that he was going to travel within the next day or so after the attack. That puts it about now. You thinking he might be meeting up with Madigan?"

"I don't know for sure," J.J. said, surprisingly smug for a guy who really had nothing to be smug about, looks-wise, "but an Eleanor Madigan checked into that very hotel just last night. Room 1117." He smiled wide, and then it vanished. "That's the eleventh floor, by the way, and it's one of those hotels where the rooms are all centered around a big open-air courtyard, so you might wanna..." he shrugged, "I dunno, use some discretion or something.

Unless you want to do an eleven story plunge in public. Might not hurt you too much—"

"It would kill most of us," Parks corrected him.

"Well, it'd make a hell of a scene for the news, too, y'know." He nodded at me and Reed. "They're still talking about the gangland house crashing down in Iowa."

"That's because it's the most exciting thing to happen in Iowa in six decades," Parks said.

"I want caution," Ariadne said, cutting across all other talk in the room. "Bastian has lead on this, Sienna and Reed, you'll be answering to him. I want everyone working together, no lone ranger BS—got it, Clary?" She waited until Clary picked his head up, gave her a silent nod, and then she continued. "Whoever this Eleanor Madigan is, I think we can expect she's trouble if she's truly with Omega."

"You're going to send all of us?" I asked, throwing looks around the room in return for the ones I got. Questioning orders like this wasn't done. Eve gave me the nastiest look of all. "That leaves nothing to defend the campus with."

"We still have agents," Ariadne said. "We need a unified front. After Des Moines, I want us to be prepared for anything you might encounter, and I doubt they're going to hit us here in the hour or two you're gone."

"You call it being prepared for anything," I said, "but this is Omega we're dealing with and I call it putting all your Faberge eggs in one basket. And then throwing that basket off the top of the IDS Tower." I paused, and wondered where that thought had come from before realizing it had been a subconscious suggestion I hadn't even noticed. "Which I am told is fatal."

Ariadne opened her mouth to respond, eyes looking up as she tried to come up with something. "I can't really do anything with your eggs metaphor, so let's put it this way—we're dealing with an A-rated threat, so I'm sending in my A-Team."

"Or your M-Squad?" I asked with amusement. "If we're going to do this, we need to do it fast and quiet and get back here. With whatever Omega is planning, this is not a fortuitous time to be absent from the campus for long."

"Agreed," Ariadne said. "Kid gloves for the pickup on this one. Take care with her."

"You asking us to give her the benefit of the doubt that she's a civilian?" Bastian asked, his expression almost unreadable.

"Yes," Ariadne said. "Take her peacefully, if possible."

"Omega doesn't do 'peacefully,'" Reed spoke up. "They do bloody, violent and destructive, and that's about it."

"We do that pretty well ourselves," Eve said with a wicked smile.

"And that's fine—if she starts it," Ariadne said, turning to look at Eve. I couldn't see her face, but her tone shifted. "The last thing we need is a civilian casualty for some poor British nanny who picked the wrong time and place to get her passport done before she took her dream vacation to see the Mall of America."

"Wrong season to visit," Eve said, "Christmas shoppers and all that vileness. Horrible idea."

"We will take all precautions not to harm her in any way," Bastian said, ending any debate. "Eve will be at the fore; her nets are second to none for non-lethal containment. Sienna and Reed will follow up, being effective in-fighters, and Clary and Parks will keep overwatch." He looked around at each of us until he saw the nod. "With your permission, ma'am?" He looked to Ariadne, who gave him the subtle nod of approval, and with that he opened the door and walked out first.

"So, yeah," J.J. said as Parks left next, "go get 'em, guys." He looked at me and his cheeks burned crimson. "And girls." He turned and caught an icy glare from Eve (which was probably just her normal expression). "And women." He nodded his head, bobbing it like a jack-in-the-box. "Yeah."

I filed past J.J. Clary didn't even try to rush ahead of me like he normally did, for which I...didn't care, for once. Reed trailed behind me, then spoke as we walked through the cubicle rows. "Good play, you think?"

"Going on the offensive against an Omega agent?" I asked. "Yeah. Leaving the campus stripped of its best guardians? Not so much."

"Scott and Kat are still here," Reed said.

"One's got a hole in her memory the size of the loop on the rollercoaster at Valley Fair and the other is broken into more pieces than that porcelain angel of Ariadne's that Eve stuck under Clary's ass at the Halloween party as a joke." I shook my head. "We just need to hurry, that's all."

"You think they're coming here?" Reed said, and for once he was hard to read.

"I think they're coming for Old Man Winter," I said. "Take him out, you think the Directorate keeps rolling along?"

"Ariadne can keep it going," Reed said. "Why are you worried about this now? He's been around for a good long while, a few millennia. You think he can't take care of himself?"

"No," I said quietly. "I know he can't. He's worried about it, thinks he's at the top of Omega's target list. He's pushing me to step up because...it's like he can feel the axe descending, like he can feel its shadow on the back of his neck. I've never seen him like he is now, and I've known him for almost a year now."

"That's not a very long time to know somebody." Reed kept impassive, casual. "That's about how long you've known me, after all, and I'm way more of an open book than Winter."

"We've had long conversations because we're related," I said, shooting him a half-assed sneer. "Because I wanted to know about our father, and what he was like, and all the things I missed with him being, you know—dead for my entire life. I've worked with Old Man Winter, though, and you get kind of a bead on him after a while. There's emotion under the surface, and for the first time,

I'm seeing worry. He knows bad things are coming, even though he doesn't know exactly what all they are. There are things going on in the meta world that too many people have been warning us about, things we need to take seriously."

"I wonder about that sometimes," Reed said as we walked across the lobby, Parks and Bastian in front of us and Kappler and Clary about twenty paces behind. "Your mom told you something big was coming, and then Zollers said basically the same thing.

Now, it's true Zollers was a psychic—"

"Telepath," I corrected gently.

"Right, a mind reader," Reed said, "so maybe he just fed back to you what your mom said just to mess with you?"

I felt a certain clenching pain in my jaw at the memory of my last conversation with Dr. Zollers. He hadn't just told me that a storm was coming to the world of metas; he'd specifically warned me that no one was looking out for me, which seemed blatantly untrue. If he'd lied about one... "Maybe. Let's put it this way—I wouldn't mind being a telepath myself and being able to dig into Zollers mind to see what was real and what wasn't, because," I blanched as the breath of the cold outside air hit me in the face while Reed held the door open for me and I transitioned to the outside, "he deceived me for six months when he was playing my psychiatrist, so it's kinda hard to tell if he might have slipped a truth in there somewhere."

Reed nodded, and didn't say anything else. We reached the garage and loaded into one of the smaller white utility vans in silence, almost exactly like the one we'd taken down to Iowa.

"No visible powers in the hotel," Bastian said. "The last thing we need is attention on this run. No guns unless the situation gets dire." Bastian's inflection became slightly accented. "If you hear gunfire, you are weapons-free at that point, but keep the bullets contained. No civilian casualties, *verdad*?"

"Righto," I heard Clary say quietly, buried under the verbal affirmations of everyone else on the team.

The ride to Bloomington went quickly; the traffic was minimal at this time of day, and the freeways were clear as we cruised past tall glass buildings and retail spaces. We took an exit a mile from the Mall of America and got off on a frontage road that cut into a parking lot surrounded by small shrubbery and next to a vacant lot. The van doors swung wide and we deployed out the back, probably not looking terribly inconspicuous as we filed toward the hotel entrance. The building was tall, at least fifteen stories, boxy, square with cream-peach coloring that looked vaguely like stucco. The windows separated out every few feet with ornate shutters that added to the effect of making it look like a throwback, or something that might fit better in Italy than in Bloomington, Minnesota.

The lobby doors swung wide, and Clary held one open for me without meeting my eyes. I tried to ignore this, but good manners got the better of me. "Thank you," I said as I passed, and he nodded without looking up.

Eve and Bastian led the way, Parks and Clary trailing behind. There was an open staircase in the corner of the building, and the setup was exactly as J.J. had mentioned. An enormous courtyard lay in the middle of the hotel, the front lobby on one side, kiosks for coffee and muffins and such were scattered around the center of the building. Fifteen floors above us, an enormous skylight ran the length and breadth of the roof, shining daylight down on us through translucent glass that, just for a flash, reminded me of how mother had painted the basement windows in our house.

"Break formation," Bastian said so quietly that no one but a meta would have been able to hear him. "Sienna and Reed, take the far stairwell, Clary and Parks, keep overwatch down here after you tell management what's about to go down. Parks, you do the talking. Clary," Bastian's voice got tight, "don't say a word while he's talking to them."

"And as for exit?" Eve said under her breath.

"We have an escape route," Bastian said, slowing his pace for just a tick. "Hold up our FBI IDs and walk her out the front."

"This is not gonna be subtle," Parks said in a gravelly whisper.

"More subtle than having Eve fly her out a window," Bastian replied. "Let's go."

Reed and I split from them, Clary and Parks making their way to the front desk while Eve and Bastian made for the nearest staircase. I cut across the courtyard, making my way toward open-air stairs built into the far corner.

"Couldn't he have assigned us the elevator?" Reed asked.

"Precautionary," I said. "What if today is the day the elevator breaks down while we're in it? Control is the name of the game, and you want to retain all the control over the situation you can at a moment like this, even if it's avoiding an astronomically small risk like elevator failure."

"What about spraining an ankle taking eleven flights of stairs?" Reed asked with a smile. "What's the risk on that?"

"You know, that's probably not a bad point, if you were a clutz. We're metas. We make Olympic gymnasts look clumsy by comparison."

We took a couple rounds of stairs without speaking. Reed broke the silence. "How come I've never seen Bastian use his power?"

"You see him use his meta strength," I said, trying to outpace my brother but not make it look like I was.

"Yeah, I didn't mean the passive powers," Reed said, "I meant his main one. I don't even know what he is."

"He doesn't use it at all, that I've seen." I let my hand ride the rail as we made our way up, enjoying the tactile feeling of support and the gentle slap of the leather on the metal to coincide with each step. "I've heard the whispers though, that he's a Quetzalcoatl-type, whatever that is."

"Oh," Reed said. "Well, that would explain it."

"Why?" I asked. "I mean, the rumors don't exactly cover that, since I don't think anyone's ever seen it."

"You know who Quetzalcoatl was?"

"Sure," I said, "the feathered serpent. Mesoamerican god."

"Right," Reed said. "Walk among the beasts of the ground, fly among the birds of the air. He can transform."

"Kinda like Parks and his animal forms?"

"No," Reed said with a smile. "I've seen pictures. Think demon-from-hell type stuff. The Mesoamericans who named them feathered serpents might have a talent for understatement."

"Oh," I said. "Probably why he doesn't use it. I asked him once, and he told me he prefers to use weapons—a control thing, of course."

"Of course."

We reached the eleventh floor and emerged into the hallway, separated from the yawning maw of the courtyard by only a high railing. "Majestic," Reed said as he looked down.

Far below, I could see Clary standing next to the coffee stand. "Oh, yeah, it's a great view. Just once, I'd like to fight in a wide open field rather than in a mall, or a house that collapses on my head, or where I could be dropped eleven stories—or fifty—to a splattering end. Somewhere boring."

"How about a basement?" Reed asked with a half-smile.

"Keep it up, wise guy, and I'll throw you off myself."

Eve and Bastian approached from the other side, converging with us upon the door of Eleanor Madigan's hotel room at a very casual pace. We all stopped, wordless, outside, halting on either side of the frame so there wouldn't be any chance for her to see us through the peephole. Bastian held up his hand and gestured to indicate we would be breaking down the door in seconds. I steadied myself and drew the replacement pistol I'd pulled from the quartermaster and took a deep breath, pressing my shoulder to the door next to the frame. Eve stood across from me, Bastian behind her. It was understood that I would be second through the door, and I pulled my gloves off, wiping my hands on my jeans, ridding myself of the excessive sweat on my palms.

I tried to concentrate, tuning out the faint warbling sound of music being piped in over speakers, the scent of lilac pumped into the air conditioners to give the place a nicer smell, the feel of the crosshatching of the gun's grip in my hand and the sight of Eve tensing across from me, her arms bared because she had left her jacket in the car, her pixie-blond haircut almost white because of the lighting.

She moved, rolling herself off the frame and in front of the door, gun drawn, and kicked, breaking it off its hinges. "FBI!" she called and burst into the room, leading with her pistol in one hand and her other hand extended, ready to cast one of the webs of pure energy that her Peri-type meta powers allowed her to command.

I led with my gun, following behind her only a pace or two, watching her blouse ruffle as she slid through the hotel room's entry, past the bathroom without clearing it. I pointed my weapon inside; the lights were off, and I ducked in and flipped them on while Bastian passed behind me to back up Eve. I ripped the shower curtain off the rings to be certain the room was clear, then turned to see Reed pass the bathroom door. I could hear them in my earpiece now that we'd gone active, and Eve's clipped Germanic accent reported, "Clear," both in my ear and also muffled on the other side of the bathroom wall.

"Her clothes and personal effects are still here," Bastian said as I joined them. A simple queen-sized bed sat in the middle of the room, red overtones on everything from the carpet to the bedspread giving the place a warm feeling. The bed was made, the suitcase open but in perfect order. "But this room doesn't look very disturbed. Too clean."

"To you, perhaps," Eve said, unsmiling. "This is how it looks whenever I travel."

"You make your own bed?" Reed asked.

"Yes," she said. "I prefer everything well ordered."

"Sighting," Parks' voice came over the earpiece. "We have eyes on target; she is in the lobby and moving toward the elevator."

"Reed," Bastian said, "make sure the hallway's clear. Let's see if we can set the door back up and lure her in."

"That's a negatory," I said. "That sucker is off the hinges. Even an idiot would bolt if they went to unlock the door and it just fell in."

I saw Bastian's eyes waver as he pondered the options. "Then we take her getting off the elevator."

"You might wanna hurry," Parks voice came in reply, "because she's in."

"Move," Bastian ordered, but we were all in motion already. I kept my pace to the high end of human potential in case anyone was watching, as did the others. We charged along the walkway, the doors of the rooms to our right seeming like a blur of squares shooting by with nothing but open air to our left. We turned the corner and saw the elevator bank; it was built into the walls, with a subtle overreach that had the walkway run under it, like a tunnel, elevators on both sides. The wallpaper took on a browner tone here, protected from the skylights by virtue of being covered over and isolated from the main area. Four elevators, two on each side, serviced the floor. There were potted ferns stuck between each elevator to add some green to the otherwise sterile environment. The yellow lighting on the walls cast the place like a darkened steakhouse at midday, cave-like, with only the suggestion of daylight showing in through the apertures that led back to the open-air walkways on either side of the elevator bank.

I dodged to the side of the elevators, positioning myself in the middle of two of the doors, waiting to hear the ding. If the light lit up on the opposite side, I would have to move fast, but I was ready to do so. I kept one hand free of my gun; the other gripped the pistol tightly. I saw Reed station himself near where we came in, gun in hand. Eve took up position in the far corner, giving her the view of the entire room. Bastian blocked the opposite walkway entrance.

The dinging sounded, and I felt the tension, the sweat back on my palms now, the stress I hadn't even known I was feeling bleeding through me. The triangular light above the door to my left lit up red, and the doors began to open.

Eleanor Madigan emerged, not really looking around as she stepped out of the elevator. Her profile was different than I would have expected from her photo, strong cheekbones but a more pronounced nose than was evident by the front-on passport photo. She wore very casual attire, jeans and a sweatshirt from the Mall of America. She sensed I was there, turning to look at me. I waited to see her reaction, my gun hidden behind me; if she was Omega, she would know me.

A flicker of recognition passed behind her eyes. Her hand came up and I batted it aside with my pistol as I wrapped a hand around her neck. Her eyes widened, this time in outrage, all her teeth displayed in a feral look that was half-grimace, half-snarl. She reached out a hand, past me, toward the elevator and her fingers extended, grasping for something.

I heard the crackle before it hit me; electricity flowed out of the call buttons, snapping across the distance between her fingers and the metal like bolts of lightning. A charge ran up my hand and every muscle in my body seized, clenching, my head exploding in a burst of pain like someone put a thousand knives through me and I contracted in a full-body heave. I held tight to her neck for as long as I could, which felt like a year but was probably more like a second, before I was propelled through the air into a wall as I fell, limply, to the ground.

14.

"Thor-type!" Bastian shouted somewhere in the distance; it felt far off. Another droning hum of electricity filled the air, along with the soft whoosh of Eve's nets striking the wall.

"She moves fast," Reed said, his hand on my shoulder. "You all right?" His voice was practically a shout, but I lifted my head to see him looking at me, lips pursed in concern.

"I'll live," I said as gunfire filled the air. I whipped my head up to see Madigan send a surge of lightning at Eve and Bastian, forked electricity striking the barrels of their pistols. I heard a pop from each of them as their guns flew out of their hands, Eve staggering back into the wall and Bastian ducking behind the arch that led back to the walkway.

I raised my pistol at Madigan and drew a bead on her. I hesitated, though, and she swung around. Reed had just begun to raise his gun when the burst of lightning came for us, arcing toward our weapons, the closest object to the point of contact, and metal to boot. I was already moving my gun to throw it away when the lightning hit and I managed to get clear with only a little stray voltage hitting me. Reed made a similar move and I saw him fall back, out into the uncovered walkway behind me as he recovered from the attack.

"Sienna Nealon," Madigan said, her voice a sort of droll whisper.

"Shocked to see me?" I asked, drawing to my feet. I cringed. "That...was not the witticism I was looking for." A pun. I blame the electricity.

"Not really," Madigan said, her blunt face curving in a slight smile, a British accent barely there. "Perhaps surprised it took you so long to come calling, but not startled to see you here. Not after Bjorn. Not after Fries."

"Yeah, we just keep taking your pieces off the board," I said, circling around to place my back to the elevator door to my right. It was metal, and I had a grand plan to use it as a backstop to catch her next bolt of lightning while I tested my reflexes to see if I could dodge her attacks. The potted fern next to me was going to be my accomplice, whether it wanted to be or not. I could see Eve out of the corner of my eyes, leaning against a wall, breathing heavily, staring at Madigan with glaring eyes but not making any aggressive moves—yet. With Eve, that was sure not to last.

"But a queen has yet to fall," Madigan said with that same eerie half-smile. "And we all know that the game doesn't end until you've trapped the king. So whose pieces are moving faster toward the checkmate? Because everything else is irrelevant. Take all our pawns that you want, because so long as we make the last move, the one you don't see and can't defend against, we still win."

"Aww, that's so sad." I backed against the elevator, felt the steel against my hand to make sure I was positioned right. "You're just a pawn? Give yourself more credit. Maybe you're a knight. Or, like, part of a knight. Maybe the horse's ass."

"You think you're so clever, don't you?" She smiled again. "Because you beat Wolfe. Because you bested Henderschott, and circumvented our spy."

"I also decapitated your vampires, outmaneuvered James Fries and put a bunch of hurt onto your boy Bjorn," I said. "Small victories, but I'll take 'em. What about you? What've you got, Eleanor? And please don't say abs."

Her face twisted in confusion and without warning she sent a bolt at Eve, who dodged behind the archway to hide behind Bastian, who I could see from where I was standing. "You needn't ask what

I've got. I'm a hand of Omega, the oldest and most powerful force in the world. I carry out the will of those who were named gods to the men of old, those who run the world, who wield strength the average man can't comprehend, that every other meta would die to possess. I am one of the chosen, a brandisher of thunder and lightning, and the servant of the—"

I slipped a foot behind the potted plant while she was talking, and sent it at her face with a kick. I heard the crack of thunder, saw the lightning hit the clay and refract as I charged behind it. It shattered inches from her face as her fist intercepted it and I adjusted to keep from colliding with the punch she had intended for the pot. I felt a burst of wind propel me forward, my brother giving me a helpful shove that accelerated me through the clods of dirt, blowing the plant out of my way and allowing me to deliver a punch to Eleanor Madigan's lip. I watched it split with impact, and I followed it with another as I caught my footing, hammering her with a blow that cocked her head to the side.

I heard movement behind me—Eve and Bastian. I dodged to the side as I heard the crackle of electricity shoot through the air I had been occupying only a second earlier. Eve's net didn't miss this time, hitting Madigan in the chest and making a latticework of light from the middle of her thighs to the top of her neck. One hand was caught facing the ground, the other sideways, and I saw the glow as she summoned electricity to her. I stepped forward and cracked her twice on the jaw, watching her eyes roll back, knocking her out cold.

"Tough bitch," Eve said, and whipped another net at her, this one wrapping around her face, setting it aglow and trapping her hair against the lines of it. I could see a closed eye through the gaps.

"Wow," Reed said. "I'd never dealt with a Thor-type before. Crazy. Lightning bolts and everything."

"Yeah," I said, rubbing my knuckles where I had struck her, "but she's no Chris Hemsworth."

The elevator next to us dinged and sent me scrambling. I wondered very briefly if I'd have to take the memory out of a passing civilian when they saw what had happened, but felt a dash of relief when Clary and Parks stepped out.

"What the hell happened here?" Parks asked.

"A clean takedown," Reed answered. "Minus, y'know, the clean part."

"We need to get her out of here," Bastian said. "Clary, you're gonna want to go to rock-form everywhere but your head. Make it look casual, like you're wearing gloves—but keep her away from your flesh. She's a Thor-type, and if you let her touch you, you're gonna wish you hadn't."

Clary nodded, ripping away the netting that Eve had used to restrain Madigan. Madigan didn't even twitch as Clary freed her, the nets blinking out of existence as Clary ripped through each fiber. As he picked her up, I caught a glimpse of rocky skin under his t-shirt collar, and he readjusted her to walk her in front of him in a way that could possibly be described as making her look like she might be conscious and being walked out. If you didn't look too closely. And you were an idiot.

"We need to move,"' Parks said. "Folks in the lobby were asking questions about the noise when we came up. Doubtful this will stay quiet for long."

"FBI IDs out," Bastian said. "Let's not go mugging for the surveillance cameras, though."

We moved toward the nearest stairwell, Bastian at the fore with Eve behind him, Reed at my shoulder. We cleared each floor quickly, passing a few confused hotel guests as we descended, not saying anything. Bastian waved his badge at them as we passed, running interference, saying, "Please stand clear, folks, we have a dangerous fugitive here."

When we hit the lobby, Bastian hurried to the front desk. Dressed as he was, in a suit, he pulled his ID and warned the clerks what was coming.

"I was sure one of us was going to go off the walkway at some point," Reed confided in me as we passed the front desk. "I mean, we fight in an open-air courtyard hotel and no one goes over the balcony?"

"I was sure it'd be you," I said as the first chill of the outside air hit me, wind blowing my hair back. I felt the tickle of static electricity run through my hair and I wondered how long I'd be dealing with the aftershocks (ha ha) of Eleanor's attack.

"Well, at least I'd have been able to pull a soft landing," Reed said as we approached the van. I heard tires squeal as a Cadillac wandered into the wrong lane as it was exiting the parking lot and almost got hit by an airport shuttle. "Geez. Some people shouldn't drive."

"Nice to know you weren't worried about it being me to go over the edge," I said, stepping into the back of the van after Clary.

"I would have cushioned your fall."

"How are we gonna keep her contained on the ride home?" Parks asked. "Have her sit on Clary's lap the whole way?"

There was a moment of perplexed silence that ended as Bastian shut one side of the rear doors. "Yep," he said. "Clary...sit her on your lap and stay in a rubberized form."

"What did the poor woman do to deserve that?" Eve asked, sotto voce. We all heard it anyway and Clary changed his skin to black rubber before any hint of blush or emotion made it to his cheeks.

"Just keep her subdued," Bastian said, and I saw no further movement from Clary. He was still, arms clamped around Madigan's limp body, as the van started up and we pulled out onto the road, the miles ticking by and no one speaking, as though Madigan were not unconscious, electricity still filling the air around us.

15.

Interlude

Bloomington, Minnesota

"Yes, they caught her," the old man said into the phone. He swerved the big Cadillac to avoid a shuttle bus pulling into the parking lot, causing the shuttle to squeal its tires. He looked into the rearview mirror and saw the procession, the four members of M-Squad, the young man from Alpha—and her.

"I have her in sight right now," he said into the phone, watching her dark hair, a little frizzy, bob up and down as she hurried across the parking lot toward the Directorate van. "She is...shorter than I expected." At that moment, she looked up at the car, and he felt almost as though she were looking at him through the rearview mirror, as though a sort of current were between them, and he pressed the pedal, accelerating out of the parking lot. As he turned, his eyes followed her, still making her getaway with her comrades. "Pretty, in her own sort of way. She has a focused air about her, her mind on the things she has to accomplish. Her will is strong, I can tell you that much. I can feel it from here."

He waited as he drove, passing a freeway onramp that was grey, dull, and overdone—just like everything else in America. "I don't know how much of a problem her will presents," he said, answering the question asked on the other end of the phone. "I am merely informing you that she seems to possess a mind of her own, that she is no simple dullard as easily manipulated as the goon in Iowa whom I set upon a different path. He will wake up in twenty years as an electrician and never know that I steered him from his life of crime, because he has all the self-awareness of a microwave dinner. She, on the other hand...her mind is firm in its decisions. All I can do for one such as that is begin to stir the waters of uncertainty."

He pulled the car onto the freeway. "We will be prepared by tomorrow to finish this."

He waited, listening, though he wanted more than anything to interrupt, to assure the man on the other end of the line that, in fact, he was wrong, but one simply did not do that to one's boss, not in Omega. *The fastest way to the gallows*, he thought, and listened to the prattle, waiting for his opportunity to talk. "Yes," he said at last, when the rhetorical question was asked, "but this is simply a choice. I know you had high hopes that they would step aside after we wiped out their human agents." He let a smile split his lips. "No, you know I didn't agree with that operation, and clearly it did not bear the fruit that your advisors told you it would. Because they do not know Erich Winter, his stubborn resolution."

There was a pause in the conversation. "Erich Winter lives up to his name. His coldly analytical nature, his refusal to budge, like a frosted hinge...you were never going to receive the results you were looking for by simply doing things the way they told you to. Anyone who was close to the situation would have said so...and this is the problem with your advisors...they are too young, too unfamiliar with the old ways to deal with the old ones, who are more myth and legend to them than real."

There was a flat pause and the old man looked up at the greying sky, at the impending approach of winter itself, of the trees, now nearly naked on either side of the boulevard he was driving on. "Stanchion is mine, my operation. I will show you. Tomorrow, we move. Tomorrow, everything falls into place. I will call you after it is done, and we will talk. I will fix this intractable mess that your young minds have created for you.

"And after that, Erich Winter will no longer be a problem."

16.

Sienna

"So this is Eleanor Madigan," Old Man Winter said in a low, rumbling tone, the glass between her in the interrogation room and the eight of us watching feeling far too thin for a woman who could cast lightning. She sat on a metal chair, her legs and those of the chair resting in a children's wading pool filled halfway with water.

"I wouldn't advise using ice on her." I said, "I don't think it would end well for you, more like an AC/DC song."

"AC/DC?" Reed asked, turning to me.

"Thunderstruck," Clary said, mumbling. "Good one, Sienna."

"Her talents do not concern me," Old Man Winter said. "Keeping her in a pool of water should nullify her powers."

"Is that an old trick for dealing with Thor-types, sir?" Bastian asked.

"No," Old Man Winter replied, a glint of amusement in his eyes. "I saw it on an episode of *Heroes*." There was a pause, as though someone had thrown a grenade in the middle of us and we were all waiting for it to explode.

"Oh, wow," I said into the tension. "Was that a joke?"

Old Man Winter's voice scratched as he replied. "Yes. Do none of you recognize one when you hear it?"

I looked around; taking the temperature of the room, I felt one thing and one thing only—discomfort. "From you, no."

"What's to stop her from turning the chair over?" Bastian asked.

"Clary will assist in the interrogation," Old Man Winter said; whether he was ignoring Bastian or simply felt that was answer enough was anyone's guess. "While he and I are speaking with Madigan, Parks and Bastian will again have a conversation with Bjorn, and Sienna and Eve will speak to Fries." Old Man Winter turned from facing Madigan to look at all of us, a wintery glow of blue in his frosty eyes. "They will be moving soon. I will have names. I will have times, locations...whatever they know, I want it."

"Did Bjorn talk?" I asked as Old Man Winter began to turn away. "After you broke his arm off, and whatever else you did to him?"

There was a pause, and I got the sense everyone else was waiting, the same as I was, to see if he answered. "No," he said finally. "But that does not mean he will not say more now." He walked out the door, Clary at his heels, and a moment later we saw him enter the chamber that held Madigan.

"He thinks the clock is winding down," Ariadne said after Old Man Winter had begun to speak to Eleanor. "He thinks they'll be getting cocky now, that some unstoppable hammerblow is about to rain down on our heads."

"We've captured three of them now," Eve said, a certain lazy, I-don't-care-ness to her tone. "You'd think they'd be losing some of that arrogance."

I thought for a moment about Eleanor, when we were talking during the fight in the hotel. "Hmm," I said aloud, drawing Reed's eye, and then Ariadne's.

"What?" Ariadne asked.

"When I fought Eleanor," I said, "she didn't seem all that concerned about being blindsided by four Directorate agents. She even sat there and monologued until I attacked her. That's either some deep arrogance or—"

"Or they're playing at something else, something that would instill a serious overconfidence," Reed said. A beep came from his pocket and he pulled his cell phone, looking at the screen. "'Call home.' Be back in a few." He made a move toward the exit and disappeared into the hall.

I watched as Old Man Winter asked Eleanor why she was in Minnesota. The English woman did not answer, did not even deign to acknowledge him, and I watched him gesture for Clary. Clary's skin turned black as rubber, and he stepped into the wading pool and positioned himself behind her, his wrist across her neck, holding her face in place and forcing her to look up at Old Man Winter.

"Enough of these childish games," Eve said, tapping me on the shoulder. "Let us speak with your incubus."

"Excuse me?" I said icily. "He's not 'mine'."

Eve rolled her eyes to the side, as though annoyed at my daring to speak back to her. "Let us speak with this little man whom you almost let into your *scheide* and drag the truth from his lips, all right?"

"Well, when you put it that way..."

As we left, Ariadne was activating the monitor for Fries' chamber. Bastian and Parks followed a few paces behind us, entering the room across the hall from Ariadne's. As near as I could tell, Ariadne was going to be watching three interrogations at once, which I did not envy, especially considering the one involving Clary and Old Man Winter was fairly certain to degenerate into something I wouldn't care to watch.

The door slid open with Eve's key card and we found Fries sitting at a table in the middle of the room. He went from sullen to all smiles, as cheerful a transformation as I'd ever seen a person make in two seconds.

"Who just shot a ray of sunshine up your ass?" I asked as Eve slid into the chair across from him.

"You are such a colorful person," he said. "It makes me glad I didn't kill you in Eagle River."

"Not for lack of trying." I said, "The only reason you didn't is because you got your ass kicked by girls. Twice."

"Yeah, well," he shrugged. "One of them is dead, and the other might as well be. I'd tell you that your aunt is a real piece of work, but you already know that." He laughed, an empty one. "She is seriously damaged goods."

"Said the black hole to the kettle." I folded my arms. "Got anything to tell us, James? Because, otherwise, I've got better things to do, like filing my nails."

"You should try doing your hair," he said with a nod that almost caused me to subconsciously reach up; I'd forgotten that Eleanor had run ten thousand volts through me. I probably looked like Lady Frankenstein.

"Can I beat him unconscious now?" Eve asked me, ignoring Fries completely.

"I have no objection." I really didn't.

"Your hospitality is lacking around here," Fries said as Eve stood and circled around the table toward him.

"Gloves," Eve said to me, and I puzzled at what she meant for a second before nodding, taking off my gloves, and placing them into her outstretched hand. She slid them on, one by one, and I heard the sound of leather stretching. "You have small, girlish hands," she said, but I didn't really hear any judgment in the way she said it.

"Isn't that the way you like them?" Fries asked, smiling sweetly at Eve.

"It is," she said, smiling back, from just over him. "It really is." The first punch didn't so much knock him over as flatten him like a wrecking ball hitting a small building. His chair skittered across the floor and hit the wall, making a gawdawful racket. Fries hit the ground sideways, head bouncing of the tile floor with a terrible crack, his hands still cuffed behind him.

"Oh my," Fries said, his head turning as though he were woozy. "I shouldn't be surprised you're a man-hater, really."

Eve knelt down and got astride him, balancing on one knee, cracking her knuckles. "It isn't that I hate men. I work with some very decent ones." She pulled back her fingers, exposing her leather-covered palm, and then reformed her fist and smashed Fries in the side of the head with it, rattling his head against the floor again. "Bastian, Parks, even Old Man Winter. Decent sorts. Clary... has some rough edges." She hit him again, and I watched him spit out blood. "You, on the other hand, I find no redeeming value in." She pulled back her fist into a palmhand and ran it into his nose, causing it to break. Blood dripped down the sides of his face and, I presume, into the back of his throat, because he started to gag.

"You," she said, rolling him over and placing her weight on his back, "are the worst sort. I know of you, James Fries, and I know what you do to women. How many bodies have you left in dumpsters in the last year? In your lifetime?" She took his face and rammed it into the cold, black floor tiles. "I've been begging Ariadne for months to let me have a shot at you—just one shot, as a personal chance to thank you for how you treat women. It sets me—how do you say?—on edge?"

Fries took a moment to answer, his eyes rolling in and out of focus. He smiled, a terrible, bloody smile. "Yeah. On edge. And I've left some bodies by the wayside, it's true. In alleys, in dumpsters. Tons of them." She snapped him hard in the nose and he gagged, making a glottal-stop noise as he spit blood out. "You gonna beat me to death for them? You didn't even know them."

"I bet," Eve said, wearing the thinnest, most lethal smile, "if I told you that I would kill you if you didn't correctly write down the names of the last five girls you slept with, you'd not only die, you wouldn't remember a single one of them."

Fries smiled again, and I could see the bloody lines tracing between his teeth. "You got me there. I don't even remember one of them. Sandy, maybe? Cindy? Ah, who cares."

Eve nodded slightly, her face tight, then she unloaded another three punches on his face in rapid succession. "You're going to choke on your own blood," she said, turning his head to the side to let him gag it out onto the floor, a slow, steady red spill of liquid rolling its way across the black tile, an ocean of death washing toward me.

I watched, paralyzed, not sure what to say, not sure if I should stop her. My head spun, I felt a pounding sense of guilt, even though it was Fries—the worm—and a murderer of women, and nearly of me. Part of me raged internally and called myself too stupid to live for any remorse I might feel; the other part tried to play up my guilt for not stopping Eve, just as I hadn't stopped Old Man Winter.

"If I tell you something, will you stop beating the hell outta me?" Fries said, causing my head to snap up. His teeth were broken now, and Eve had another fist cocked and ready to unload on him.

"Trying to save your own life now?" Eve asked, and hit him again, snapping his head back. "I think your pleading may be falling on the deafest ears you could have found in the Directorate, Fries." She hit him again, and I saw his eyes unfocus, one of them starting to swell shut, the purpling on his cheek obvious and growing.

"Wait," I said, only just louder than a whisper, but enough for Eve to hear me and halt before her next punch. "What do you think you could say that would convince Eve to stop?" I asked, and Fries turned his head, letting his neck hang slack, looking at me out of his one good eye.

"I'll tell you..." His words came out slurred, his lip split open and bleeding down his neck, "who's running...Operation Stanchion."

"You'll tell us who's running it," I said, taking the two steps to carry me to Fries' side, and kneeling to get closer to him, "and what it's all about, what's happening."

"Don't know...what's happening," Fries said, his head lolling. "Don't even know the objective...they...thought I was a high risk for Directorate capture so they didn't...tell me." His pupil was dilated, he was concussed, and he sounded like he was drunk.

"Give me a name," Eve said, readying her fist. "Give me a name, or so help me, my next punch will sever your serial killing head and end your little perverted reign of impotence forever."

Fries' once-handsome face was twisted, an eye already swollen shut. The strong smell of iron filled the air, and he seemed to have no strength in his neck. Eve had him suspended by the front of his shirt, which she had torn while pounding him into hamburger. He was missing at least eight teeth by my count, and his lips were split in three places, his face swelling so rapidly it looked like he had fallen into a bees' nest. "Okay," he said, now barely audible. "I'll tell you. I'll tell you. I just saw him the other day...Janus. It's Janus. Janus is running Operation Stanchion."

17.

"Who the hell is Janice?" Bastian asked as Eve and I re-entered the observation room to find him waiting with Ariadne and Parks.

"Janus," I said, drawing every eye in the room to me. "Roman god of doorways and transitions. Had two faces, supposedly. Not really sure how that would translate in non-mythological terms."

"He is a liar," Old Man Winter said, squeezing into the room behind us, Clary following him, "so the colloquialism fits for him being two-faced."

"Did no one else manage to return any further information?" Eve asked, slipping off my gloves and handing them casually back to me. They were slick with blood, and I held them at a distance from my body, as though I were too good for them.

"No one got quite as...persuasive," Ariadne said, "as you did. At least not for as long, or as close to the...uh...edge."

"No one else came as close to beating their subject to death is what she means," Parks said with more than a little acrimony.

"My only regret was that I didn't finish," Eve said. "He's slime. He rapes women and kills them with his power, and finishes with their corpses. I bet he couldn't even get it up if a woman wasn't screaming in pain for him. I have never encountered a more loathsome creature in my life, and I wish I could beat him to death over and over."

"This is to the damned edge of the line, Director," Parks said in a low growl that reminded me of the wolf within him. "We don't do this sort of thing, sir. Beating people in interrogations? Freezing someone's arm and breaking it off?" He drew himself up. "We're better than that."

"Not the biggest fan of these aggressive tactics myself, sir," Bastian said. "We let 'em stew, we break 'em traditionally, without laying a finger on them. Not one of them is tough enough to take the isolation forever."

"We do not have forever," Old Man Winter said. "We may not even have a day. Omega is coming, make no mistake. They have marked us as a threat, they desire to eliminate us, and they are operating on a timetable so aggressive we are left with few options." He ran a cold, surveying set of eyes over us, not flinching away from looking anyone in the eyes. I blinked away from his first, though. "This is certain: the damage could be greater than anyone of us can calculate."

"Should we evacuate the campus, sir?" Bastian said, cutting through the air that had suddenly gotten thick in the room. "Get the younger metas out of here, maybe give the admin staff some time off and keep a skeleton crew here for the next couple weeks while we wait for the anvil to drop?"

"Who knows how long it could be?" Ariadne said. "I mean, the Director says soon," she favored him with a submissive nod, "but they've known where we are—where Sienna is—for quite some time. They could have moved against us at any point. It could be tomorrow, it could be the day after, it could be six months from now. Just because they're putting their people into the country doesn't mean it's happening now. For all we know, we just took out their entire strike force."

"You didn't," came Reed's voice from behind Old Man Winter. He shouldered his way into the room. "It's coming, soon. Like... next week or sooner." He looked around at each of us, his long, dark hair disheveled from the wind outside. "My bosses say they're just ratcheting it down right now, dragging the last few pieces into place."

There was a stark silence, one that I finally broke. "Oh, good. Because I hate a long wait before I die."

Reed shook his head. "They don't want you dead. Anything but is the word. They want you alive, just like always."

I let a little scratchiness enter my voice, probably from the fatigue and the fact my head was whirling. "Do your bosses know why Omega is so keen on having me alive that they'd start a war with the Directorate?" I caught a flash from Old Man Winter's eyes as I asked, something that was both subtle and yet obvious; no one else reacted to my question but to turn to Reed to listen for his answer.

"If they do, they're not sharing," he said, "but they barely tell me a fraction of what they know over open lines. I only got this much out of them before they dropped a hammer of their own on me."

I felt a chill unrelated to the Director's presence. "What?"

"I'm to return to Rome immediately," he said, and I could hear nothing but the sour notes as he said it. "Immediate recall. They have me booked on a flight that leaves in three hours."

"You can't be serious," I said, a sick pit in my stomach churning the acids within. "We're looking down the barrel of imminent attack here."

"I know," he said, "and I told them to sit on the pointy end of an umbrella and open it. I'm staying."

"No," Old Man Winter said, "you should go. And you should take Sienna with you."

"Director," Ariadne said, silencing the voices that started to speak around her, "are we certain that sending Sienna to Italy is going to be safer than keeping her here?"

"Europe's in a mess right now," Reed said. "Not something my bosses wanted to get into on the phone, but I get the sense there are some pretty major moves going on over there at present. I'm not sure you'd be protecting her by getting her there. And our headquarters stays mobile by necessity—Europe is Omega's backyard, and our relationship with them isn't exactly peaceful coexistence, if you know what I mean. They're trying to wipe us out, and vice versa."

"Sir," Bastian said, "if we're facing imminent attack, we could really use a meta with her power on the line with us to defend the Directorate. Sending away one of our best fighters might not be the strongest idea."

"Has anybody asked what Sienna actually wants to do?" Clary's voice wavered before it came out.

All heads turned to me. I felt my mouth open and close before I spoke. "I'm not leaving," I said, almost as surprised I said it as the others were hearing it. I saw Parks nod, a slight smile on his lips. "I'm not running from Omega, not ever again." I felt my cheeks redden. "I ran from them once before and a lot of people died. I haven't forgotten, not for one day, what that felt like. I won't do it again. If they want me, they know where to find me, and I'll be right out front kicking the ass off whoever they send to do the job."

"No offense," Reed said, "but that's really dumb."

"Thanks," I said. "But I'm a big girl now, and that means not running from my problems, even when they're pretty big themselves."

"You have no idea," Old Man Winter said, and his voice sounded brittle. "But it is your life, and your choice." He looked down, staring into the distance at Madigan on the other side of the window, before turning back to Reed. "Return to your people. Apprise them of our situation. Ask them for help. Tell them how dire our need becomes. Urge them to hurry."

Reed's eyes were wide, his head snapped back as though from being hit. "You can't be serious. I can't leave now—"

"You must," Old Man Winter said, and he took a step closer to Reed and put a hand upon his arm. "You must. I knew your father, when we were together at the Agency. He was a good man, a noble man."

"Wait, what?" I asked. "You knew our father?"

He turned his head slowly to look at me. "I did." He slid his gaze back to Reed. "He was a man who stayed behind on the day the Agency was destroyed, trying to save as many lives as he could. He was not a man who would abandon his fellows, and I understand your desire to stay, especially for your sister. But—" he cut off Reed's rising protest before the words left my brother's lips, "you remaining here will make little difference now. You returning with the knowledge of what we face and a half dozen more of your people could mean the tide of the battle shifts in our favor."

"I don't know that we'll make it back in time," Reed said in a hushed, almost choked voice, his head bowed. "My bosses—they move slow. I never know what they're going to do, if they're going to listen—"

"You will make them listen this time," Old Man Winter said, and I saw Reed's head come up to meet the Director's piercing gaze. "You know what is at stake. Come back to us with what you know, if nothing else. Come back to us with all you can rally, even if that is only yourself and the knowledge of what we face from this Operation Stanchion."

There was a solemn silence. "I will," Reed said. "I will...be back." He turned to me. "I will. Before you know it."

"I believe you," I said, swallowing the sudden choking fear and trying to replace it with a smile.

"Ariadne," Old Man Winter said, "please have a driver take Mr. Treston to the airport."

She nodded and pulled her cell phone from her pocket, dialing it and speaking quietly into it while Reed made his way over to me. "Are you gonna be all right 'til I get back?" he asked, and I tasted a familiar hint of dry mouth as he said it.

"I managed for seventeen years without you," I said, trying to make it sound as natural as I could. "Somehow I'll muddle on."

"They're coming," he said, and he lowered his voice. Clary and Eve had shuffled away from us, out the door and into the hall, Bastian and Parks were by the window to Madigan's cell, and Old Man Winter watched Reed and I from near the door. "They could be here before I get back."

"They'll get a hell of a fight from me," I said. "I'm not going anywhere quietly with the bastards who sent Wolfe and Fries after me."

"I know you won't," he said, and put a hand on my shoulder. "I...wanted to be here with you..."

"To the end?" I asked, and felt a slight choking sensation in my throat. "It's not over yet."

"Then why does it feel like it?" I heard a quiver in his voice. "Maybe you should come with me."

"I can't," I said, "and please don't ask me to again. I belong here. Before I came here, I was a shell, a prisoner, a nobody. I had no future but four blank walls, and every day was doomed to be the same. Now I'm..." I felt a smile crack my stony facade, "...somebody. Just because Winter is afraid doesn't mean it's over."

"He's lived for thousands of years," Reed said, looking over to see Winter watching us. "If he's scared and telling you to run, maybe you should take a hint from him."

"No," I said, pushing my bravest, most belligerent front forward, determined not to let my brother see me shake. "Because I'm young and stupid," I said with a smile, "and I don't fear anything anymore, not after Wolfe. If the worst comes, maybe I'll just let him out of his kennel to run around and see what happens."

"I can't believe you're joking at a moment like this," he said, shaking his head, grim.

"Gallows humor. It'll be okay. We'll hold 'til you get back." I didn't bite my lip, but I pursed them, holding them stiff to keep the emotion bleeding over from moving them.

"Who's being a jinx now? Should I say, 'I'll be right back'?"

"Only if you want to die in a plane crash."

"I'll hurry," he said, and the levity vanished. "Like Old Man Winter said, I'll get what they know, and I'll come back. I've got a couple friends who owe me favors. If nothing else, we'll come trotting back as fast as I can get a turnaround flight. Two or three days, maybe."

"Hurry back," I said, and I let him start to turn for only a second before I pulled him around, taking care to keep my hands on his coat, not touching his skin. I pulled him close to me, ignoring the cologne that I always hated, and buried my face in his hair, smelled the sweet fragrance of it, hugged him tighter, his broad chest against me. I felt him hug me back, strong arms holding me in them, and I wondered for just a second if this is what it'd be like to be hugged by our father, then I banished the thought from my mind and pulled away, gingerly, giving him a kiss on the cheek as we broke.

"Don't do anything stupid while I'm gone," he said, letting his hand rest on my shoulder for another moment before he started toward the door.

"You mean like fighting off an Omega attack on our campus?" I smiled through the screaming crying in my head. "Wouldn't dream of it."

He paused at the door and gave me a nod. "You know...I wish I'd told you. Earlier, you know. When we first met. I should have trusted you could handle it. We could have had...so much more time...to talk about it, and whatnot."

I made my face a mask, tried to pretend concrete had been poured over it so my cheeks wouldn't move, but even still I felt my eyes get glazed, blurry. "I wouldn't have believed you," I said. "I didn't know what family really felt like until..." I looked around, suddenly a little embarrassed. "I'm glad you waited until I was ready."

He looked like he wanted to say something else, but he rapped his hand against the doorframe, a nervous thing, a few different emotions alternating on his face. I thought he might speak, but he finally just turned and disappeared into the hallway with a last wave—but no last look.

It was just as well. I felt the first drops coming down my cheeks, hot, stinging, and I wondered when or if I'd see my brother again.

18.

The fading shadows of day were growing long when I reached my quarters. The darkening sky reflected the grim sadness closing in on me as I lay on my couch and waited for the sun to set. I felt like I was being swallowed up in the inevitability of the darkness. I thought of Scott, and how I'd seen him earlier, a shell of his former self, and I wallowed in misery like he did. In spite of my brave face for Reed, I worried about when Omega was coming, about what form their attack would take, and who, if anyone, would be taken. I felt my cheek against the soft velvet of the chair I was lying against, and I watched the darkness descend in my room as the shadows rose along the walls with the fall of day, and I felt hopeless, truly hopeless, for the first time in a long time.

A knock woke me from a sleep I didn't even know I was in. I hesitated at the door. "Who is it?"

"No one," came Zack's voice from the other side. "Well, maybe someone. I dunno. What do you think?"

I opened the door to see him standing tall, wearing a sweater that made him look particularly dashing, kind of...homespun, in a way. I pulled him to me, letting the door close. I kissed him full on the lips for as long as I thought I could get away with, and then hugged him tight, felt the fuzz of his sweater against my cheek. "You're somebody to me."

"Whoa, there," he said. "Take it easy on that meta strength." I loosened the grip, not realizing how hard I had been holding him, and he smiled down at me. "What's the matter?" he asked, his smile fading. "What's wrong?"

"Reed left," I said, stifling emotion. "His bosses ordered him home, and he didn't want to go, but Old Man Winter told him to, so...he left."

Zack did not react to this for a moment, almost seeming like he was rocking back on his heels. "Wow. I guess I figured Reed would stick around no matter what."

"He wanted to," I said, leading Zack back to the couch. "He really wanted to, but...he'll be back in a few days." I sat down on the couch and Zack sat on the arm of it. He seemed uncomfortable, and I looked at him quizzically but he waved it off. "I don't know. I think it's gonna get bad."

"I don't get it," Zack said. "We've captured three of their operatives in the last few days, I mean, some tough ones, too, as I understand it. Fries is a pretty nasty incubus from the reports I've read. Bjorn didn't sound like a real picnic; I mean, for strength he had to be top of the scale, and this last one, Madigan—I haven't seen the report yet, but a Thor-type? Nasty. They're throwing their A-listers at you, and you're bouncing them back like they're nothing." He gave me an encouraging smile. "Unless this Operation Stanchion consists of stacking all their people in our jail cells until they burst at the seams, it would appear that they are losing this round so far." He hesitated, and looked to me for approval. "Wouldn't it?"

"Yes," I said. "No. I don't know. The problem is the uncertainty. Yeah, you're right, we've kicked the ass of everything they've sent along so far, with some skill, some luck—but it just feels like... they're in the shadows. They're unknown. We're in the dark, waiting for something bad to happen. You ever have that? Where you're waiting for something you think is gonna be bad, and it comes and it wasn't as bad as what you anticipated?"

"Sure," Zack said. "That's exactly what I'm saying. The fact that you're beating their best, taking down every meta they throw at you...doesn't that give you some confidence that with everything we've got at our disposal, that we can take whatever they push at us and cram it right back down their throat?"

"Maybe. I just know that what they've thrown at us so far hasn't exactly gone down painlessly." I pointed to the wall, on the other side of which lay Scott's quarters. "Look at what happened to Kat. She's never gonna remember a thousand things about her relationship with Scott. And that's pretty mild as far as consequences go, but it's devastated him. What if they kill someone? What if their attack is focused, and determined, and draws a bead on one person and just...takes them out?" I bit my lip. "That's what I'm afraid of. That this time they're not coming to capture me at all, that they're coming to kill Old Man Winter so that they hit the Directorate in a place where it never recovers."

Zack slid off the arm of the couch to sit next to me. "It's sweet that you're more worried about the Director than yourself in all this."

"I worry about you, too, lunkhead," I said, and put my head on his shoulder, letting my hair flow down his chest. "Humans are just disposable foot soldiers to Omega."

"I haven't forgotten," Zack said, and I could hear the tightness in his voice. "A lot of my buddies died when they decided to wipe out our agent ranks, you know."

"I know." I let my hand run along the front of his sweater, coming to rest on his collar. I wasn't wearing my gloves, because I hadn't bothered to replace the ones Eve had sullied with one of the numerous spare sets in my closet yet. I avoided his skin, instead rubbing the soft threads between my thumb and forefinger. "You should get out of here for a few days. Maybe take a vacation."

I felt his head turn more than saw it. I didn't want to read his reaction, but I heard it in his voice. "You know I'm not leaving you."

I felt the weight of my head against his shoulder, and I wondered if it felt like the weight of the world to him. "Yeah. I know."

He took his hand and ran it across my cheek and I realized for the first time he was wearing a glove, a very soft, almost skin-like glove. I glanced down, expecting to see fabric but saw a flesh-toned color in its stead. "You like it?"

I ran my hand across his, felt the ripple of my nerves, my flesh, as we touched for longer than we ever had before. "Did you...?"

"Picked it up this afternoon," he said with a ready smile. "Doc Sessions made it more flesh-colored, said he thought that'd be less...I dunno, odd or something." He pulled his sleeve up and I saw his arm, covered with the material of the suit. I ran a hand up his to his bicep and gave it a squeeze, as though I were touching him, really touching him. "You like?"

"I like." I let my fingers stay on his arm, then ran them further up his sleeve to his shoulder. "And it goes...?"

"Pretty much everywhere," he said, pulling down his turtleneck to reveal the top edge of the suit around his neck. "Hands, feet, toes, and uh..." he hesitated, "everywhere in between. It stretches, too," he said, suddenly looking uncomfortable, "so, you know...it uh...it works uhm...well. And whatnot."

My hands found their way down to the bottom of his sweater, and I lifted the bottom edge of it, sliding my hands along his waist, working the material of the suit between my fingers, feeling it give and stretch as I kneaded it. "And you can feel everything through it? It's not..."

"Oh, yes," he said, nodding. "I can feel everything. It's thin, really thin, and it's almost like touching, no barrier in the way." I leaned in and nuzzled his neck, kissing the area covered by the thin sheen of the suit, and I heard him take a sharp inhalation. "Yep. I can definitely feel that." I broke away and came up after a moment and my eyes met his. "Are you sure you're ready?" His whole face was patient expectation mixed with desire, and I could read it in him as though it were written in letters across his chest, his face.

"I'm ready," I said. "I've been ready for this for...so long. I just...we still have to be careful."

He smiled. "We'll take our time." His hand ran along my arm, taking my hand, his fingers threaded through mine, no glove, as real as if he were truly touching me. I felt the warmth, the pressure of his squeeze, and I closed my eyes. "I love you."

"I love you, too." I tried to return his smile but it faltered.

"You sure?" he asked, and I felt the concern in his touch this time, the way the pressure was different, no leather between my hand and his, no cold cowhide holding back the subtleness of his caress.

I opened my eyes. "I'm sure." I kissed him again, and then stood, taking his hand in mine. "Never been surer of anything."

He ran his hand over my cheek, a caress I'd felt a thousand times briefly. This time it lingered, sweetly. I felt his hand in mine, and I looked in his eyes. I led him toward my bedroom, just as we had a hundred times before. But this time was different, new, unfamiliar, and when we passed through I shut the door behind me, as though I could close out all the distractions, all the worries, all the thoughts of Reed, and Omega, and Old Man Winter, and leave them outside. I closed the door and we went inside, and left everything of the outside world behind until morning.

19.

I awoke to the steady in and out of breath being drawn, and light sliding across the floor from the enormous windows that lined the wall of my room. The sun was streaming in from overhead, already high in the sky, shining bright light on my entire apartment.

I felt Zack close to me; for the first time, I'd tried falling asleep on his shoulder, something that was never truly possible before. I hadn't stayed that way, unfortunately, because I'd discovered after an hour or so that his every breath, every move was jarring, and I had rolled over but remained close. His every movement wasn't quite so distracting this way and he was still so much nearer than he'd ever been before we had the suit.

I watched his face as he slept, the closed eyelids and relaxed look upon his handsome features, the easy comfort. I didn't want to wake him, and I didn't want to leave. I pondered tiptoeing to the bathroom because the need to go was urgently rising, but I held out as long as I could, then used meta strength and agility as well as a tremendous amount of patience to move as slowly as possible to extricate myself from the covers without disturbing him.

I followed the beams of light across the floor to the bathroom, shutting the door before I turned on the light. After I finished taking care of my business, I washed my hands and leaned forward on the marble counter, looked at the mirror above the vanity. The bathroom was spacious, the toilet a solid eight feet from the door and the glass-encased shower just beyond it. There was an independent heating unit that began to run when I turned on the light, cutting the chill in the air as I felt the prickle of cold cause my flesh to goosepimple as I stood there, staring at my face in the mirror.

Little doll, came the voice of Wolfe, just a whisper, in the back of my mind. The image of myself, nude, in the mirror, didn't change, but it was almost as though I could see him looking out from behind my eyes. Once, it would have sent me in a scramble to find clothes. Now, I didn't even move. I just let him stare, because that was all he was good for. Staring and some chatter.

"I'll get to dealing with you in a minute, Wolfe," I said, looking into the darkness of my own eyes. I had heard Wolfe and Gavrikov, the voices in my head, in the past when they had something ridiculously urgent to tell me, but I suspected the effort they had to expend in those instances required cooperation by both of them to be heard. The chloridamide I injected lasted for a good twenty hours and forgetting my dose, which I had last night, was the only way I ever saw them like this. And then, it was only ever one of them. Ironically , it was the one of them I couldn't stand and would never have voluntarily chosen to share my brain with, not in a million billion years.

They're coming for you, little doll.

"This I've heard," I told him, far more casual than I felt. "You want to tell me why?"

Don't know, he said, his voice a rasp. I could feel his eyes using mine to study my curves. Letting him do what he was doing now was my ultimate show of disdain for him. I could feel the disgust somewhere deep inside, but I couldn't tell if it originated from him or me. *Wolfe went where Wolfe was told, didn't ask questions when it came to playing with little dolls like you.*

"Well, I bet they were all just as charmed by you as I was," I said to the mirror, to my image and the one deep behind it. "It's a shame none of them ever had the ability to kill you before I came along, because it would have been worlds better than having you stuck in my head—"

They're coming for you, Wolfe's voice came again, urgent. *Janus isn't like the others they've sent. Vampires? Henderschott? Even that delicate little morsel Fries...they are insignificant compared to the Wolfe. But Janus...* There was almost the sound of a hiss inside my head, as though Wolfe were drawing away at the thought of the name.

"You're afraid of him. He frightens you." I felt the umbrage at my words, the hiss of anger. "Why? Why does he scare you?"

Wolfe fears no man, the words came, *no man and no beast, either. But Janus...is strong. Powerful of body and mind. And he has the ear of those at the top of Omega, he is the loudest voice of their old guard, still at odds with the new regime . The others fail. Henderschott failed, constantly. Wolfe owned a piece of his face after one of his failures. Janus does not fail. Not ever.*

"So now we've progressed from the unkillable man," I said, pointing at Wolfe's image behind mine in the mirror, "to Iron Man, to a guy who tried to get in my pants before smooth talking me into joining Omega, to vamps and a traitor, and more recently the three stooges." I took a deep breath, drawing confidence from the lineup I'd just listed. "Now they're sending me a man who won't fail. Got it. I bet they didn't think any of the others were failures, either."

You've gotten the dregs since me because they're dealing with bigger matters, Wolfe said in a low hiss. *You were always in the back of their minds, always at the side of their focus. Now they turn all their attention on you, and you will feel the strength of Omega descend on you, the power of the gods of old will rain down hell upon your life.*

I tugged the little leather kit from of the drawer by the sink and pulled a needle free from the stock I had, then drew a few milliliters of chloridamide into the syringe and pressed it into my vein, the same one I used every day, because it healed to perfection between doses thanks to my meta powers.

You will break, little doll. The eyes stared at me from behind mine as I looked up to the mirror, those black, soulless eyes, pools of nothing but darkness. *You will look back on this moment and wish that you'd listened to the Wolfe...*

I pushed the plunger and felt the rush of the narcotic as it hit home; it was always a curious sensation, as though the world went slightly muted when I injected, a little feeling of drowsy satisfaction. "I don't think I'll ever be sorry that I don't have to listen to you, Wolfe." I didn't hear a response from him, his voice quieted, and I smiled, my own smile, all the way up to my eyes, visible in the mirror. Nothing of him remained with me now, not even the faintest trace.

I saw movement in the mirror and the door opened as Zack stepped inside, his naked body visible under the thin mesh of the suit he still wore. "Good morning," he said as he wrapped his arms around me and I felt the press of him against my back—in several spots of my back, actually.

"Hi there." I turned to face him, pressing my flesh against him, feeling his warmth even as my feet touched the cold tile floor. I ran a hand down his chest, felt the firmness of his muscles and let out a little sigh of contentment. I gave him a long, sweet kiss and broke just when I heard him gasp slightly. "Sorry."

"It's all right," he said with a smile. "Just in time, it was starting to get that first feeling of ow." He squeezed me in his arms and I lay my head against his chest.

I held there for almost a minute, just enjoying the feeling of being close to him, then a devilish thought lit my mind and I raised my head to look at him. "Do we...have time?"

He looked pained. "Again? I have to tell you...other girls I've talked to, you know, after the first time, they're not really as...um... enthusiastic, let's say. I mean you seem fine and all, I just mean I hope it didn't hurt too much."

"I barely felt it at all," I said, putting my head against his chest. I froze there for a second, and then pulled myself off his chest to look him in the face. "That's not what I meant," I said, watching him raise an eyebrow. "What I meant is that compared to the pain I've experienced in my life, it was fairly small. Pain-wise, I mean." I slapped myself on the forehead. "A small amount of pain! Not that I didn't feel it, because I did, and it felt good, but..." I sighed. "You know what I mean. I hope you know what I mean. It was very good. I liked it a lot. I would like to do it again, as soon as possible."

"I think I got what you mean," he said, with almost a smile. "You were already...prepared... and so the little pain you felt was not that big of a deal compared to the beatings you've experienced in the last year."

"You've got a way with words," I said, pulling close to him again. "I wish I had a way with words right about now. Instead, I'm fumbling, a mess, all that."

"It's all right. But to answer your earlier question, I have to go." He gently pulled from me. "We have a meeting with the other agents, preparations for when this Operation Stanchion lands on us."

"What are you going to do?" I asked.

"Stay out of the way as much as possible if it's a meta assault," he said, taking a slow walk out the bathroom door and back into the bedroom, fishing his boxer shorts out of a pile of clothing next to the bed. He came up with my underwear as well and tossed it to me. I caught it in one hand. "Our job is to effect an evacuation of the campus, not to get into a rumble with Omega's metas. We're assigning out those industrial strength electro cannons like we used on Wolfe, but we've only got a half dozen of them. We've got some dart guns that will put most metas down, but they take a few seconds to work, so pistols and rifles are going to be option one. We've got some shotgun shells that have some extra pop to them, and some slug-throwing shotguns that'll put a hole in an elephant. Other than that..." He shrugged. "Like I said, we're evacuating and trying to make way for you metas to rumble to your heart's content."

"My heart's quite content with no rumbling," I said, and slipped on my panties. "I could use a nice long vacation about now."

Zack smiled. "Like Italy?"

"Somewhere tropical," I said. "Somewhere warm. It's about to get really cold here in Minnesota again, you know."

"Having lived here my whole life, I was dimly aware of that fact."

"I've never been outside the Midwest," I said, looking out the window at the sun, already high in the sky. "I remember thinking when Wolfe was coming for me how much I wanted to be somewhere, anywhere else."

"I remember," he said. "But you knew he'd find you."

"Yeah. I should take those vacation days they gave me, and go somewhere good." I stepped closer to him, rubbed a hand along the smooth covering over his chest as he placed his shirt on and left it unbuttoned. "What do you think? You, me, a sandy beach, warm sun overhead, crystal blue waves—"

"I think that sounds like a vacation that is a little above my pay grade." He smiled. "But I like the sound of it. It sounds like more fun than that time we took a day off and went to Valley Fair."

"I had fun with that," I said, and slapped him on the shoulder. "You remember the list?"

"You mean the list of things you were supposed to do in your life?" he asked. "We did a good number on that list this last summer, you know."

"We did indeed." I stood up on my tiptoes and gave him a peck on the cheek that lasted a fraction of a second. "I had another list, you know."

He turned his head to look at me. "Oh, yeah? What was on it?"

"Well," I said with a nod toward the bed, "this was right up there."

He let out a chuckle. "Mission accomplished, huh? Guess you better start making a new list, or things will start to get boring."

I let a hand slip across his chest again. "I don't think I'll get bored with this for a good, long while."

A flicker of amusement crossed his face as he buttoned his shirt. "That's a relief. If you were tired of it already I'd be a little worried; like maybe I was out of practice or something."

"Oh, yeah?" I let my fingers find the buttons he had just done and unbutton them one by one, pulling his shirt down and trapping his arms. "Well, we can't have that, can we?"

"Sienna..." he said plaintively, "...I'm going to be late..."

"We don't know what's coming or when," I said. "This may be the last breather we get for a while, and I don't think that Omega is going to launch an all—out assault on the Directorate in broad daylight. All I want," I said, unbuttoning his pants, "the only thing on my list now...is repetition." I steered him to the bed and pushed him down, climbing up onto him and staring down. "I think you can handle being late for once in your life." And I brought my head down to kiss his neck.

"Hmmm," Zack said, his voice sounding in my head like the moans he emitted whenever we had been together in my dreams. "Maybe just this once..."

20.

I was late for breakfast, and I knew it as I closed the door to my quarters. Zack had left a half hour earlier, but I needed time to shower and doll myself up (okay, I didn't really do that, but I still liked to feel clean). I paced down the hallway, and stopped at the corner next to the elevator. Scott was waiting there before me, and the elevator dinged, the doors opened, and he started to get in.

I followed him, sneaking in just as the doors began to close. "Morning," I said as he acknowledged me with a nod. He had a suitcase in one hand and a backpack on his back. "Umm...are you..." I tried to find a way to not come out and say it, but failed, "...bailing out before it hits the fan?"

His jaw set, and I could almost hear his teeth grind as the elevator dropped, floor by floor. "I'm leaving, yeah."

"Why?" I felt a sudden deprivation of oxygen, and wondered what the hell had happened to the atmosphere in the elevator car.

"Because I've been ordered to go on medical leave by Dr. Perugini and Ariadne," he snapped at me, turning his head long enough to give me a searing look. "Because when I try to use my power, I think about Kat and this happens—" He held a hand out and a tiny squirt of water came forth, no more than a few droplets that fell immediately to the carpeted floor of the elevator, making little dark spots in the beige carpet. "Because I'm pretty much useless to everybody now, Sienna, so they're sending me home, out of the way, where I won't be a danger to anyone but my parents and my siblings, and not much of one at that."

The elevator doors opened to the lobby and Scott's hand returned to his suitcase, which he dragged along behind him. "Scott, wait," I said, and he slowed. I ran to catch up with him. "I'm sorry," I said. "Sorry for Kat, sorry for everything."

"I told you it wasn't your fault," he said with his lower jaw jutting out, as though he was encouraging me to aim for it, to hit him or something. "And now I'm pretty much out of the fight because I've gone and turned my head into a spaghetti noodle of twisty ties." He waved a hand at me. "Or something. I don't know."

"Have you talked to Kat?" I asked.

"No," he said, sullen. "I tried a couple times...the first, she didn't even recognize me." He adjusted the backpack over his shoulder. "The second time I couldn't even find her to say goodbye. I'm sorry I'm not more use. Sorry I can't..." He shook his head. "I'm just sorry, in every definition of the word." His eyes came up, and met mine. "Get out of here, Sienna."

"Can't do that," I said. "Not after last time. How many people died? You should know."

"I should," he said, "but I guess I don't. I was too hard on you last time." He broke a weak smile. "Kinda hard not to be scared when you don't feel like you have any power to fight with, huh?" He looked at me soberly. "Good luck, Sienna."

"I'll need it," I said, as I watched him wend his way to the exit doors, the suitcase he carried looking like a burden that was almost too much for him, though I knew for a fact it wasn't at all what was causing his shoulders to slump.

When I walked into the cafeteria, they were already starting to clean up the buffet from breakfast, and there was no one else standing in the line. I caught a few dirty looks from the cafeteria ladies, but that wasn't exactly new for me, so I didn't sweat it. I filled my plate with cold eggs, colder toast, and a mug of coffee laden with a ton of cream and sugar, then made my way to one of the countless empty tables. The glass windows that surrounded two sides of the cafeteria provided me with an expansive view of the autumn-laced grounds; leaves were everywhere. Presumably, the gardening crew would normally have dealt with them, but they were now off work for the week. The cafeteria was also emptier than it normally would have been, and I wondered if the administrative staff was also off work because of the pending threat.

"You're not real social, you know that?" I turned at the sound of the voice, unaware that anyone had even noticed me. Standing a couple tables away was the kid whom I had seen staring at me only a couple days earlier. "You don't really talk to anyone but your little group of friends, you know? You kinda put out a... 'get lost' vibe."

"Oh, good," I said, "it's still working. Or, apparently not, since here you are, talking to me."

"I can leave," he said, beginning to turn away.

"What do you want, kid?" I asked. He wasn't really a kid, probably only a year or two younger than me, but if he was gonna make with the fawning puppy eyes, I wanted to start putting some distance between us now, rather than later.

"I'm not a kid," he said, as he turned back around. I disagreed with his assessment, but then, I couldn't fault him for trying. I would have said the same thing at fifteen.

"Sure you're not," I said, laying the patronizing tone on thick. I figured if I gave him enough reasons to leave me alone by being both a smartass and condescending, he couldn't fail to get the message that I wasn't interested in him in any way.

"I'm not." He said it with a decent amount of confidence. "But I don't suppose that matters."

"Not to me. What do you want?"

He gave a subtle nod to the chair directly across from me. "Mind if I...?"

I stared at the chair for a beat before turning back to look at him again, his dark hair, overlarge glasses; he looked as though he were trying devilishly hard to be the biggest geek possible. "Do I mind if you...what? Take that chair, turn it upside down and sit on it? Be my guest, but do it elsewhere." I smiled and took a bite of my eggs.

"Wow," he said, and his face didn't fall from my insult, not even a little bit. "I guess it's true what they say about you?"

"Oh, yeah?" I asked, and turned my head to look down at my food. "What do they say about me? Am I a ball buster? A pain in the ass? A personality wrapped in barbed wire and coated in rubbing alcohol?" I looked back up at him and smiled. "If that's what they say, then yeah, it's true. I'm not the greatest people person you'll ever meet."

He squinted a little bit through his glasses, adjusting them to look at me. "That's the gist, I guess. Some less flattering, more succinct ways it's put, but you captured the common theme there."

"You're not telling me anything I don't already know," I said, and took a bite of my bacon.

He faltered, as though he was going to walk away, but he didn't. "But you've got friends. You've got people who seem to enjoy your presence, so I'm guessing you're not like that all the time, at least not with everybody. I don't see you act like that with your boyfriend."

"You're rapidly entering the territory of being a creepo," I said, looking up, taking my coffee and sipping it while I watched him through half-closed eyes. "Why are you watching me?"

"I'm not stalking you or anything," he said, unabashed. I was a little put off by his self-assurance; it was annoying. "We eat in the same place every day, so it's not like it takes a special effort on my part to look across the cafeteria and notice the difference between how you are when your friends are around, and how you are when I run into you elsewhere on campus." He laughed, mirthless. "I saw you stomp your foot and make a move toward a lower classman a few weeks ago. We all laughed at him, because he almost soiled his pants. People are scared of you, and you want 'em to be scared. Why?"

"Maybe I had a rough childhood," I said, not really believing that was an excuse, but wishing he'd take it and leave me the hell alone.

"Maybe a lot of people did," he said, not moving.

"True," I said, "but I'm not in charge of their lives."

"Do you..." He paused. "Do you really just want to be left alone?"

"Right now? Yes." I sipped my coffee.

"I see." A nod of the head. "Is it because you genuinely always want to be alone, or is it because I'm asking you questions that are making you really uncomfortable?"

I sighed and set my coffee down. My appetite was dwindling from annoyance. "Are you some kind of shrink in training? Did Dr. Zollers have a powerful influence on you before he left? Give you direction for your life? Or are you just incredibly nosy and personally grating?"

"I'm just curious about you," he said, and didn't even bother to blush. "Is that wrong? I watch you, I think you're pretty, the other guys think you're pretty, but everyone but the upper echelon is scared to death of you—all the underclassmen, hell, even the cafeteria workers." He waved a hand around. "And you don't seem to give a damn about your bad reputation."

"What can I say? I was inspired by Joan Jett."

"Why?" He looked at me, and I caught a hint of something in his eyes, some undying curiosity, and in his mousy face there was something else, something unplaceable and yet familiar. And oddly cute, in a deeply annoying way. "Why are you trying so hard to keep everyone at a distance? You're the leader of the second generation M-Squad...you're looked up to and *feared* by every one of the kids at school here. Why don't you care? Why do you want everyone at arms length?"

"Listen, kid..." I put aside my annoyance. "What's your name?"

He looked around, as if afraid someone would hear him. "Joshua. Josh. Harding."

"Nice," I said. "Listen, Josh, Joshua, Mr. Harding, whatever. I'm a prickly person, okay? I've had a few...shall we say...incidents here at the Directorate, some things that might have turned a few people against me. Now, maybe I reacted poorly to those setbacks, maybe I could have used more social skills to smooth things over. But no, I went in a different direction and embraced it. I've got a circle of friends, people I trust. There's only enough room for a few on that ship at any point in time. Understand...it's nothing personal. Forgive me for my limitations, and I'll forgive you for imposing on my personal time and space."

He looked at me, then surveyed the area around us. "Personal space? I'm like ten feet away from you."

"To a succubus," I said, taking another slow, casual sip of my coffee, "that's like an inch. I could take your soul from here."

He cracked a smile. "Now you're just lying. You have to touch a person to use your power."

"Damn. And I was hoping the rumor mill would spread one about me that I could take souls with a look. It'd keep people out of my way."

He shrugged. "You really want people out of your way bad enough that you're okay with them thinking things that aren't true about you?"

I felt my coffee grow cold in front of me, and I struggled to fake a smile. "Look, I'm a soul-taker...being a succubus is kind of a metaphor for my personality, too. It makes my life easier, having everyone think I'm a badass who just doesn't care."

"Huh," he said, and he didn't really let off with the eye contact, which was annoying in a vaguely Old-Man-Winter-Jr. sort of way, "I just thought it made you kind of lonely. But hey," he said, and smiled under the glasses and bushy hair, "I get it. Your boat is full. I'll leave you alone. But..." he smiled. "If you ever maybe get a space open on that limited engagement boat of yours...I might know someone that would clamor to get on it."

"Purely out of concern for my loneliness and well-being, I'm sure."

"Hell, no," he said. "I kinda got a crush on you. Are you blind or something?"

I rolled my eyes. "Kid, my touch kills people. I've been trying politely to tell you to 'spin off' this whole time—"

"That was 'politely'? You need to read *How to Win Friends and Influence People*."

"I've never read that one. But I have seen the movie *Die Hard* a good dozen times," I said with a little sarcasm, "and it strikes me that it might be more useful in my line of work." I waved my hand for him to scram. "I appreciate your well meaning attempts to ingratiate yourself with me, but people who get close to me do so at their own risk. And, as mentioned, I do have a boyfriend. And he is...considerably older than you. No offense. So...yeah." I smiled at him. "Thank you, Josh Harding."

He shrugged like he didn't care. "Don't be a stranger, Sienna Nealon." He walked away, and disappeared out the doors of the cafeteria. I hadn't met a lot of adults who carried themselves with his level of swagger, let alone seen it in someone younger than myself.

I finished my coffee in two swallows and made my way out of the cafeteria a few minutes later, tracing a path across the grounds, ignoring the blustery wind that fought me the whole way. I entered the lobby of the headquarters building to find it quiet, the usual hum of workers absent. I stood by the elevator bank alone, and rode up in the car by myself. When the doors opened on the cubicle farm on the fourth floor, I saw no one; I half expected a lone tumbleweed to blow by as I stepped out. The overhead fluorescent lights weren't even on.

I walked to Ariadne's office, where the door stood open. I saw Ariadne through the viewing window, Eve standing just behind her, Kappler's hands on her shoulders in a familiar way, pushing aside Ariadne's red hair. Eve massaged her neck while Ariadne worked on the computer, her reading glasses perched on her nose.

"Hey, Sienna," I heard a voice call from behind me. I turned to see J.J. cutting through the main aisle of cubicles, heading toward me.

"J.J.," I said calmly. "What, are you too important to be allowed some shore leave?"

"Yeah. This is the problem with being the linchpin of the Directorate's electronic intelligence efforts...no time off."

"At least you're fully appreciated for your efforts," I said, trying to reassure him.

"I think I'd rather have the time off."

I shrugged. "Going to Ariadne's office?"

"I am. I have news," he said, nodding his head, but keeping an even keel, detached under those damned hipster glasses.

"Of the life-shaking and earth-quaking variety or just run-of-the-mill?"

"Maybe somewhere in between?" He held up his hands, either unknowing or uncaring, as we reached Ariadne's office and he rapped his knuckles against the doorframe, causing Ariadne to jump in surprise and knock Eve's hands off her shoulders.

"What can I do for you two?" Ariadne said, trying to casually shuffle papers on her desk, as though she needed some sort of cover for Eve giving her a shoulder rub. J.J. and I exchanged a look, mostly amused, while Eve seemed to glow with a sort of annoying superiority.

"He's here with news of some variety," I said. "I'm just here because I'm wandering aimlessly, not really sure what to do with myself while everyone else is battening down the hatches."

"Oh?" She looked at me over her reading glasses. "You seem

much more relaxed than yesterday. Different, somehow."

I stiffened. "Um. No. Same me."

"You sure?" She cocked her head at me, peering at me, squinting her eyes. "You seem different."

"Nope." I shook my head. Gulp.

She shook her head as though trying to clear it. "Okay. J.J.?"

"Got some minor discrepancies I found here," he said, holding up his tablet computer.

"With the passports?" I asked, before Ariadne could.

"Yeah," he said with a downer tone and looking at the tablet. "We tracked the three coming in, but there's not really been any movement on the others in that batch from the UK. A few of them look like they've been used in the last six months, but not anywhere local. One in Mombasa two weeks ago, one in Kolkata three months ago, another in Shenzen about nine months ago..." He shrugged. "No pattern I can detect."

"Shenzen is in China, isn't it?" I asked.

"Yeah," J.J. said, looking up from the tablet. "Just across the harbor from Hong Kong, I think."

"So it's in China, nine months ago," I said. "Wasn't that when...?"

"When the compound, the meta compound—" Ariadne spoke up, "the one that was run by their government, got destroyed."

"Right," I said. "And Kolkata—err...sorry, the books I've read call it Calcutta—"

"And what fine ethnocentric volumes they must be," J.J. said.

"Wasn't India, three months ago, the site of another massacre?" I watched Eve turn to stone as Ariadne looked thoughtful. "Another few hundred metas killed?"

"Yeah," J.J. murmured. "Hm. Weird pattern, then, huh? You think Omega had anything to do with...?"

"The Director says that extermination is not their game," Ariadne said, a pen in her mouth.

"So why else would they be there at those times?" I asked. "Coincidence?"

"Weird coincidence," J.J. said. "Timing is kinda off, since they don't have anyone there any other times, just during the approximate time when the massacres occurred."

"It could have been an investigator," I said, wondering why I was defending Omega. "They could have been checking things out."

"And I could have been born in Louisville, Kentucky, but strangely enough, I was born in Stuttgart." Eve was all sarcasm. "If it seems unlikely, it probably is."

"Let me see the passport photos," I said to J.J. and he held up his tablet, revealing a face of an older man, in his sixties, grey-haired and with steel-rimmed glasses. He wore the look of a caring grandfather like an old blanket over the shoulders of a bum. "Janos Dichtmann." I looked up at Ariadne and Eve. "Janos sounds awfully close to Janus."

"You think someone decided to get cute with the passport office?" Ariadne looked at me. "Kind of an on-the-nose thing to do, don't you think?"

"Absolutely," I said. "But that doesn't make it any less likely to be accurate."

"If true," Eve said, "and this is the Janus we've been told about, then he's either not in the country or traveling under a different passport batch—since you said this passport hasn't been cleared through U.S. customs?"

"No," J.J. said, flipping back to the data. "This one went to Shenzen, and that's it. I don't even see a return trip, so theoretically he's still in China."

"I don't take that as a positive sign, since he would have been there for about nine months now," Ariadne said. "I think we can assume that he's probably using multiple identities and has at least made it back to the UK by now, if that is in fact where their home base is."

"Which means that your theory of tracking passports is not going to give us a complete picture," I said.

J.J. froze, as though he were running the calculation in his head. "Okay, wait, I got it. We have facial recognition software, right? I'll run it like this—everyone who's gone through customs in the last twenty-four hours, then work backward to a week, then a month, looking for a match to this face." He held up Janos Dichtmann's passport photo. "If I can establish a match, then I've got his current passport, and can trace that; they may have gotten sloppy and done another batch, in which case we've got him, you know?"

"You think they'll have done batches like this more than once?" Ariadne asked, skeptical.

"This isn't the sort of thing most people are going to pick up on," J.J. said. "The Department of Homeland Security doesn't even have the resources to come up with this unless they knew specifically what they were looking for, and this is...it's too good. These are legit passports, and they've probably got legit I.D. to go along with them. They've got people in the UK government getting them into the system the same way we have access to the U.S. systems, and because of it, they're invisible to anyone who's not looking specifically for them."

"Which is pretty much us and no one else," I said, feeling glum again.

"To work, J.J.," Ariadne said with about as much enthusiasm as I had for it. "How long will this take?"

"Depends on how long he's been in the country," J.J. said. "If he's entered in the last twenty-four hours, it'll be fast. If he's been in the country a week or less, I can have this done in a couple hours. Two weeks will take the rest of the day. Longer than a month..." He cringed. "Could be a while."

Ariadne waved her hand. "Get to it." She hesitated. "Can you set it to run and do your work from off-site?"

"Yes ma'am," he said, nodding. "Our servers are pretty much set up for me to do just that, so I can push data wherever it needs to be. I usually use it to work late from the computer in my apartment. Why?"

"Because I want you to do this from the computer in your apartment," Ariadne said, taking off her reading glasses. "Can you do that?"

"Yessum," he said, mostly serious. "And you want me back here when?"

"I'll let you know," she said.

"Shore leave approved," he whispered to me, then turned and vanished out the door. I watched him go and I didn't feel bad about it at all. The campus was no place for humans right now. I felt the tension in my stomach pick up as I pondered that.

Ariadne leaned back in her chair, studiously ignoring Eve, and then looked back to me. "I'm glad you're here. I had something to tell you, anyway."

"Oh?" I said with exaggerated brightness. "You're approving my vacation to Bora Bora, all expenses paid?"

"Hah," she said with no mirth, head resting on the back of her chair as she tossed her glasses onto her desk. "I'd pay for your trip myself right now if I thought you'd go to Bora Bora. No, I wanted you to know I had Scott Byerly sent home."

I felt a tingle of loss I couldn't define. "Yeah, I know. I caught him on his way out."

"Wait, you let the waterboy leave?" Eve looked down at her. "Why?"

"Dr. Perugini said he couldn't form enough water pressure to wet an envelope," Ariadne said. "He's emotionally distressed and completely wrecked at present. Per her recommendation, he is to take two weeks of emotional leave."

"For a breakup?" Eve said with obvious disdain. "If only my employers had been so generous with paid time off every time I had a difficult relationship."

"If only," Ariadne said. "He'll be out until further notice. He's back to his parents' house in Minnetonka. And you," she said, looking to Eve, "could show a little sensitivity to his plight."

Eve snorted. "Teenage romance and heartbreak. He has the emotions of a baby. He doesn't know heartbreak, and even if he did, a real man would continue to work, ignoring the pain. This is courting weakness, inviting it into your sitting room and giving it tea—"

"Noted," Ariadne said, cutting Eve off. "But he still has the time off."

"He's useless to us right now," I said. "Better to get him out of the way."

Ariadne smiled weakly. "That was the idea."

"This is all ridiculous," Eve said, and Ariadne gave her the look again. Exhausted, mixed with exasperated. "I'm due to meet with Bastian and Parks anyway," she said, and with a subtle bend she tried to kiss Ariadne on the lips. Ariadne turned her face to the side and gave her the cheek. Eve shot me a wicked smile and leaned into her neck, causing Ariadne to squirm and curse under her breath, and giggle unintentionally from the tickle of it. I averted my eyes, trying not to pass judgment on what Eve was obviously doing to get a rise out of me. She slid past me a moment later, same cool smile, and pulled the door all the way open before she left.

I waited a moment for Ariadne's embarrassment to fade before I spoke. "Is it my imagination or is she getting more provocative by the day?"

Ariadne averted her eyes from me, focusing instead on her computer monitor. "It's probably not your imagination."

I let that hang for a beat. "She got a buzzsaw in her g-string or what?"

"I don't know," Ariadne said. "And it's not really a conversation I want to have with...well, anyone, actually."

"I'm glad you added that little caveat because otherwise I might feel like I was being excluded or something."

"Have you checked on Kat recently?" Ariadne said, back to business, her eyes on the stacks of papers around her desk, organizing as she went, trying to avoid looking at me.

I grimaced. "No. Kind of um...embarrassing, I guess."

"You're the team lead," she said. "You could at least try and show some concern for her, even if you don't like her."

"I like her fine," I said, folding my arms and leaning against the door. "Why does everyone always say that? I like Kat, she's always been nice to me. I'm just not always sweet in return; it's who I am. It's not like I'd throw her into a pack of wolves if I got the chance. We hang out outside of work, you know. And I would go visit her, but it feels...awkward."

"Awkward?" Ariadne paused what she was doing, and the sun shining through the windows behind her glinting on her red hair. "It's awkward for you...to visit her in the medical unit?"

"It's awkward for me," I said, drawing out my words, "because when Kat woke up, she remembered me, but not her boyfriend. Which is fairly weird, as far as such things go. And a little creepy, you know, forgetting the person you supposedly love and remembering a co-worker? Kind of made me wonder if she might have been harboring a little crush or—" I paused, stricken, watching Ariadne's eyebrow raise, her expression implacable. "It was just an expression. I didn't actually wonder—I mean, I haven't wondered, you know, about anyone else—"

"Whatever," Ariadne said, and turned back to the folder in front of her, opening it.

"'Whatever'?" I stared at her, getting no reaction. "You been cribbing notes from me on how to talk?"

"Just trying to express my disinterest in your mind's wanderings in a way you'll intuitively get," she said, not looking up from what she was studying.

"I take it this conversation is over?" I pushed myself off the doorframe where I was leaning, felt the line of the wood against my back as I did it, felt the weight go back to the balls of my feet, light, agile, ready to move. When she didn't say anything, I turned to go out the door, letting my hand brush the frame. I paused, let myself do a half turn, a question eating at me. "You could have left, you know." She didn't look up, fixated on the folder. "I know it feels like you're essential, but when it's all hands on deck for defense, I don't see you picking up a gun and wading into all hell—"

"I have nowhere else to go," she said, looking up, her tone crisp and impatient, her glasses balanced between her thumb and forefinger. She put them on her face, then broke eye contact with me.

"Bora Bora," I suggested. "Your complexion could use it as much as mine could, and we are heading into another Minnesota winter—"

She didn't interrupt me with words, just a half-snorted laugh of mirth. "I've got work to do," she said, but more gently this time. "Take care of yourself, Sienna. Don't be a hero. You're important. Remember that."

"So when it all comes down, you'll be taking shelter like the assistant director should be, right?" I asked, watching for her reaction.

"Point taken," she said. "Just don't do anything stupid to put your life at risk."

"I won't," I said, and started toward the elevator, leaving the open door behind me. "After all," I said, wending my way across the sunlit rows of cubicles, "odds are real good that with what Omega's gonna throw at us, even if I just stuck to doing smart things, it'll be plenty dangerous enough to kill me."

21.

Interlude
Eden Prairie, Minnesota

The day goes slow, agonizingly so, Janus thought, *even with the unexpected pleasure of company.* "This is how it always was before the big moves, the big operations," he said. "Time slows to a ticking of the second hand, when you want it to speed up. Waiting is interminable, acting is preferable, but patience is all there is at this point. This waiting will be the death of me. Thousands of years of life, and I'll die waiting." The old man's smile crested on his face, then receded. "I suppose that's what we all do, though, isn't it?"

"I wouldn't know," came the soft voice of the female who had slept in his bed last night. "I haven't died yet."

"I've seen enough of it, you know?" He let the words tick out, spill out. "Seen it from humans, seen it from our kind. No one really faces death any differently. No one is ready when it comes, not really. You can go in your sleep, I suppose, and it won't distress you like the other kind does—in your face, obvious, looming. But if you're awake?" He held up his hands. "I've never seen anyone go gracefully awake. Not if they know it's coming, anyway." He turned his head to look at her, the blond curls, her smooth curves and unblemished skin. "How did your brother take it, when he went?"

A shrug. Tanned skin hiding up to the waist under the blanket. "Gracefully. I don't know if he knew what he was in for, at least not at first. Maybe at the end, though."

"He wanted it to be over, didn't he?" Janus stared out the gap in the curtains. "I spoke to him, you know, before he went to the Andes. He was a man slipping, obsessed, trying to get hold of whatever was left for him, focused on one thing and that only." He looked back at her again. He'd seen a million like her in his life, perhaps more, yet had never lost his appetite for them. *Blonds. Brunettes. Redheads. Yes, please. The younger the better, though at a century, this one is older than my usual taste...and yet delicious nonetheless.*

"I'm not all that worried about him now." She shook loose the sheets that gently entangled her, exposing herself to him totally, as she made her way across the dim, cheap, thin carpeting of the motel, away from the comforter and bedspread. "I wasn't then, either."

"That is because you could not remember him before." Janus felt in his pocket for the cigarettes he hadn't carried in over forty years, the things he had quit. "You watched him die and you had no memory of who he was."

"Still don't," the voice came, empty. "I mean, I see it, now, like I see so many other things-like a movie on a screen, but there's no texture, no emotion, no caring." She shrugged her bared shoulders and made a mischievous smile. "I doubt he knew that you had been keeping me as your woman while you were trying to bring back my memory."

Janus shrugged, and felt her hand run across his shoulder, felt the touch of youth and energy in it. "I doubt he would have cared, so long as he got you back. But, oddly, I didn't hear you complain. In fact, I believe it was you who initiated..."

"It was," she said, and kissed him. *What a bawdy old man am I*, Janus thought. *Anyone who saw the two of us in here would know instantly what to think, a thousand judgmental thoughts—and every one would be right. Old man, young girl.* A laugh sounded in his head.

"Careful," he said, and tugged away from her, feeling her touch against the cloth of his suit.

"Still worried about me?" she asked, with a twinkle in her eye that warmed his...well, not his heart, that was for certain.

"Not you," he said. "I believe you, I see the truth and heart of you. Still skeptical, though, if you'll forgive me. Erich Winter is no fool, and although it delights me to see you, dear girl, and overjoys me to have you in my bed once more, I must ask...do you know why you are here?"

"Because you found me," she said, and he saw the coyness. "Because I remember now."

"Oh?" He seated himself in the chair by the window, an old, red one with gold tones in the threads, worn by time and age and people sitting in it. "What do you remember?"

"I remember why," she said, kneeling down and resting her chin on his knee. "Why Omega. Why I was with you. Why I lost my memory. For a good cause , of course," she added.

"Of course." He took a deep breath and reached for the water in the little plastic opaque cup he'd left on the end table by the bed. "I always wondered if the next time you lost your memory, the serum we gave you would work. It was always experimental, you know, but supposed to keep everything there, a layer under the surface, so that when the life drained out of you from overuse of your powers—your good heart, you never could keep from using too much of yourself—it'd be like shuffling your personality to the bottom of the deck. And now, back to the top again." He took a sip of water, felt it roll around on his tongue, cleanse his palate. "Back to yourself."

"I know who I am now," she said.

"Of course you do, my dear," he said, "but you were never in doubt, given the time to come back to us. It's her we need to talk about now." A slight sigh came from the slender girl, and he felt the press of more weight upon his leg. "Now, now, don't be jealous.

I'm only here to help her in her...transition. As I helped you, once."
He looked down into her green eyes. "Come now, Klementina, this
is such an unexpected and fortuitous thing, having you call us as
you did, having you escape the Directorate as you did now, at this
time. Surely, if it is as you say, and you remember why you worked
with us in the past, things have not changed for you...have they?"

She lay her head sideways upon his knee and sighed again.
"No. I haven't forgotten. And I understand she's important, but—"

"No buts," Janus said. "She is important. You need not
understand all of it, but know that she is just as important as
the last one. This whole operation, the entirety of Stanchion, it
was for her." He held up a hand to forestall argument when he
saw the lips purse, the cheeks redden, the whole face turn pouty.
"Listen. Stanchion was first priority, but don't think that it was
my only concern. I would have done right by you. We would have
accomplished our mission," he checked his watch, "which we still
will, and thank you, my dear, for making this interminable wait so
much more bearable by coming back to me. But we would have
done it all—put the Directorate out of the picture, placed Sienna
Nealon just where we wanted her, *and* we would have extracted you
at the same time, brought you back to yourself, dispensed with that
ridiculous identity you've taken on, this—Katrina Forrest that you
had become—"

"Kat," she said, her naked body pressed against the leg of his
pants, almost wrapped around it like a coiled snake, the green in
her eyes flashing with the light of the motel sign. "They called
me Kat."

22.

Sienna

I lay in my bed, alone, as the shadows crept across the floor again. It was quiet. I wouldn't say too quiet, because I knew it was nearing nightfall and the admin staff had been absent all day, but it was definitely not the Directorate I was used to. Any of the meta kids who had tenable home situations had been shuffled back to their parents or relatives. Most of them lived in small towns, dedicated meta communities anyway, so the cloisters would be better protection for them than the campus at this point. It was a calculated risk, but it didn't seem likely that Omega would be interested in tracking down meta kids when the Directorate was their primary enemy. Only the orphans remained here on campus with the rest of us.

A pall had settled over the place; it was starting to look abandoned, the falling leaves taking over the campus in volume and numbers that hadn't been a problem back when we had a grounds crew. The whole place seemed empty without most of the people, even though I didn't associate with almost any of them. It was worse knowing Reed and Scott were gone. I thought about visiting Kat and dismissed the idea as patronizing, as though I were trying to force some sort of empathy out that I didn't really feel.

I waited for sleep to come claim me, wondered if it would. I hadn't heard from Bastian or Parks all day, which I took as a good sign; they were supposed to call if the world started to end around us. Personally, I suspected that would be something I wouldn't need a lot of heads-up about. When Omega came, I kinda thought I'd know the hour and minute it started to happen. It wasn't going to be subtle. Not this time.

My phone lit up and I pulled it off the nightstand at the first beep. The screen lit up when I thumbed the power button, and I swiped my finger across the message icon to bring up a text message. It was from Zack.

All other Directorate campuses evacuated and shuttered except Arizona. Will be by in a little while, finishing up a meeting with Kurt.

I sighed and lay the phone on my chest. I wanted him here with me now, not later. It felt like the next breath stuck in my lungs, caught there, like a stitch in my ribs, a pain I couldn't dispense with. I wanted this over, even if it was going to end badly. When problems came at me, my philosophy was to confront them, because if you fear something and you charge into it anyway, odds were good you wouldn't fear it for very long. Unless "it" was actually something gravely harmful, like a running chainsaw, in which case...yeah, I suppose you'd still fear it even after running into it once.

The stars were starting to come out to play now, and I lay on top of the bedspread, waiting. I looked at the deepening purple of the sky, the first twinkles of light out above the orange fade of the horizon, and I wondered again how long it would be. Wondered why they were coming for me. And then I wondered what Mom was up to. That one was really strange.

I saw the first sparkle of light on the horizon, a red light hanging over the campus like a falling crimson star, and I watched it descend with steady regularity past my window. No surprise attack, no explosions, no metas gone wild streaming across the lawns in attack formation. Just a flare. A simple, red flare, falling onto the south lawn. I watched it go, the very thought prickling my mind—we didn't use flares, didn't need flares, we had freestanding light posts all around the campus to illuminate the whole thing if we wanted it done—

I heard the heater cut out, the lights all died out in the main room. I heard the quiet, reassuring hum of electricity stop all throughout the building, followed by the last few dying sounds of the warm air pushed through the heat exchange. The vent above me quit making the whooshing noise that was incredibly loud to meta ears as it pushed out the last of its warm air.

A moment later, the first explosion rocked the campus.

23.

I was off and running, my feet carrying me down the stairs. I saw no one in the hallway outside my quarters, not Scott, not Kat, and none of M-Squad. I raced across the lobby, the lights casting dark shadows over the faces of people clumped inside, watching out the glass front of the building. As I shoved my way through a (very) small crowd, I saw Kurt Hannegan near the doors. "Keep 'em safe," I said to him as I passed, and got a nod from the big man in return. I paused at the entrance to the lobby, about to go out the front door. "Where's Zack?"

"HQ," he said. "Got a call from Old Man Winter a few minutes ago to run over there; he's in charge of us, now."

"You're in charge here 'til he gets back, right?" I asked, and watched him think about it for a second.

"Yeah." Hannegan nodded, his jowls rocking in the motion. "Explosion sounded like it came from the science building."

"On my way. You might wanna lock the doors behind me."

Hannegan didn't even bother to sneer. "You really think a lock's gonna keep Omega out?"

I ran out the door, the cold night air cutting across me. The skies had turned overcast while I wasn't looking, clouds moving in and darkening the sky further. It was night, blackest , the light of the nearby town shining off the clouds, miles away. I cut around the side of the building and stopped as my eyes beheld the spectacle in front of me.

The science building, the new and shining gem of the

Directorate campus, was in flames—again—fire roaring where it had stood, as though it had been entirely replaced by an inferno. I ran, feet crunching in the leaves, the orange hues cutting through the blackness of the campus night, not sure if I should be afraid or not as I ran toward the destruction.

I slowed as I grew closer, and halted about forty feet from the entrance to the building. I saw a lone body on the ground on the walkway. I ran to it and fell to my knees, rolling the corpse over and smothering the fire that was licking at it. It was scorched up and down it, the flames having had a good bit of time to work.

It was Doctor Sessions, I realized from the half of a face that remained. I had pulled him from the flaming wreckage of the last science building still alive and he had been healed by Kat. This time, I realized, staring into the dead eyes of the doctor, there would be no last-minute healing, no ultimate salvation. I took off my glove and held my fingers to his wrist, trying to feel for a pulse against the burnt and blackened skin; there was none.

I stood, listening over the sound of the crackling fire, my eyes searching the campus for movement and finding none. I flinched as another explosion echoed across the grounds, and realized that this time it was the gymnasium, the brick building consumed in another blast of flame and wreckage. Pieces of brick and flecks of glass and paper rained down around me and I covered my head to shield myself from the falling detritus. A moment later, another explosion came and I watched the training center, the place where I had spent so many hours honing my skills, vanish in an orange-red conflagration that streaked up into the sky under a billowing black cloud.

I stood there, the night air eating at me under my jacket, feeling my hands sweat and chill in my gloves. I tried to gather my thoughts. I had no idea what was causing the explosions, whether it was a meta or some sort of bomb, but so far they seemed to be hitting the most abandoned areas of the campus. Since I hadn't seen motion between the buildings, it seemed most likely that a bomb was responsible, rather than a meta like Gavrikov. I ran a hand through my hair and thought about the quietest buildings on the campus, thought about Zack, and the cold consumed me. I ran for the headquarters building, my feet pounding underneath me as I ran faster than I thought I ever had.

I hit the lobby, throwing open the glass door and dashing into the foyer. The place was quiet, but a single door was open in the distance, emergency lighting washing out of it—the stairs. I cursed and drew my pistol. I ducked into the back stairwell, using my gun to cover the angles as I descended. There was no noise from above me, but below I could hear something, motion, voices. I came down, the eerie floodlights giving me enough light to see by. I pointed my weapon down the long hall as I came to the bottom of the stairs. I could see movement down there, and the conversation was clear now.

"Come down, Sienna Nealon," came the voice of a shadow, standing in the middle of the hallway. "Yes, I know it's you, I can see you in the light. Like a little angel, really."

"So..." I said, and cleared the corners as I entered the hall, waiting to see if someone was going to attack me. I couldn't see ahead very well, and it looked almost like there was only the one figure waiting for me, a man, older, but still just one man. "Are you Janus?"

"Ah, she already knows my name!" He sounded insufferably pleased. "No need for introductions, then, straight to the point. They told me you were clever, and I believed them, but this...this is exceptional, really." His accent was European, but I couldn't quite place it.

"It's still considered polite to introduce yourself."

"Ah, so right," he said, as I closed in on him, stopping about fifteen feet away. "Where are my manners? My name is Janus, and I am here...to help you with a very difficult transition. Now, you need not be afraid, because I'm not here to hurt you, or threaten you or...any of that useless piffle you've experienced from Omega in the past." He waved a hand, as if dismissing those thoughts. "I am merely here to have a conversation with you."

"And then you'll take my gun?" I asked, letting the itch on my trigger finger hold off.

"No one is taking your gun away," Janus said, waving me off again. "At least, no one with me. You keep it, this is only...a conversation. A chance for us to talk, to clear the air."

"And will it be a truthful conversation, Janus of the two faces?"

He smiled, that much I could see in the stark dim light of the hallway. "On my side it will be. On your side...well, that's really up to you. Now, you needn't tell me the truth, because I know it, for that's my gift...my power. But if you feel the need to lie, well, then, that's entirely on you, and keep in mind that you'll be the only one in this hallway that you'll really be lying to." He seemed to take a breath. "And may I point out, that nickname, the one you've heard, about me being two-faced—it's really not accurate. I always tell the truth, to whomever I'm speaking to. The problem is, sometimes I tell them things they don't want to hear. Sometimes I stick to the truths that I know they want. Does that make me two-faced, do you think? Sometimes callous and blunt, others light and dancing around the edges of everything they believe?"

"I guess it kinda makes you selective," I said, not wavering with the gun. "Why don't you stick with the 'whole, unvarnished' version of the truth for me?"

"That's a special kind of truth," he said. "But if you think you can handle it...sure, why not?"

"I've been able to handle everything you've thrown at me so far," I said. "Why should this be any different?"

"Ah, yes, well, let's start with that, the beginning, shall we?" He stretched as though he were looking for a comfortable place to sit, and instead ended up leaning against the wall. "You'll forgive me for leaning, but I am of an...advanced age, for even my type of meta, and it brings with it...certain...unpleasant side effects. I grow weary, especially in moments such as this." The ground shook as something exploded in the distance and I turned to look, then darted my eyes back to him as I realized I didn't want to turn my back on him. "Not to worry, that was just the car garage. We're trying very hard not to kill anyone."

"You're failing," I said, teeth clenched. "I just came from the body of Dr. Ronald Sessions. You blew him up with the science lab."

"Ah," Janus said, and it sounded genuinely pained. "That is a shame. You know, let me get this explanation out before we get any farther, because I feel...truly, bad about it. You see, I'm part of the 'old guard,' you might call it, of Omega. I detest killing, even when necessary. It's such...an...unpleasant expression of powers that most men would crave. We're better people, we should uphold the sanctity of life, even for humans. Now, I explain this because... frankly...you haven't been dealt with in the fashion that I would have chosen had I been in charge of your case this entire time."

"My 'case'?" I almost scoffed.

"Yes," he said. "You see, the...individual who...runs Omega, had gotten some very bad advice from the 'new guard' about how to conduct things. The old ways are fading away, and older metas like me, well, we're not as influential as we used to be. There was a time when I held the ear of the Primus of Omega, when I was first advisor. Now, a chain of failures has elevated me once more, but for a time, I was...persona non grata. And I tell you this because it's so important that you understand that none of what you've seen from Omega came from me. Not Wolfe, not Henderschott, certainly not Fries...none of it."

"Because you wouldn't have unleashed those maniacs, those twits, those sidewinders?" I asked.

"Certainly not," he said with an assured shake of the head. "Because you...you are too important to chance to such...creatures, shall we say."

"But you did send Bjorn," I ticked them off in my head, "and Madigan."

"Of course I did," he said. "Naturally."

"Um...they failed just as miserably as the ones you didn't send."

"Not at all," Janus said with a smile, and there was a beep from the phone in my pocket. "Do you need to get that?"

"It's a..." I frowned and kept one hand covering him with the gun while I pulled the cell phone out of my pocket and thumbed the text message feature. I had three messages and a missed call from Zack. I clicked the messages first, my eyes darting from the phone to Janus. "I have messages."

"I understand," he said. "I'll wait. Personally, I hate those smart phones. Don't get along with them."

"Aren't you supposed to be open to change?"

He sighed, deeply. "There is a difference between helping others with change and embracing it for oneself. Technology may be my bane, but no matter. Read your messages, and then we shall talk."

I flipped through the first, the newest, from Ariadne, to me and all of M-Squad:

Assemble at dormitory. Protect the students at all costs.

"We're not going to attack the dormitory...yet," Janus said, catching my eye as I jerked my head up. "I'm an empath, of sorts. I can't read your mind, exactly, but I get the gist of your emotions, and I know where everyone is. They're safe, for now."

"For now?" I asked, and felt the gnawing sense of fear start to eat away at my confidence.

"Don't worry," he said, and I thought he might be trying to sound reassuring, "they'll be given plenty of opportunity to get out before we destroy the building. If they choose to stay, well, that's on them, not me, but...they'll be warned. You can even tell them yourself, if you'd like, once we're done talking."

"You don't think I'll be going with you?" I looked at his face over the sights of my gun, wondering if I was doing myself any favors by not pulling the trigger.

"No, of course not," he said with a shake of his head, as though it were the most obvious of truths. "Getting you to come with me today was never the purpose of Operation Stanchion."

"That's not what Bjorn said."

"Bjorn is a young bull, charging into everything." Janus bent his head low, as though miming the action of a bull, scuffing his shoe against the tile floor. "He was an excellent distraction for you."

"And Madigan?" I asked, nodding to the room where I had last seen her, up to her ankles in a wading pool. "Was she a distraction, too?"

Janus chortled. "Well, let us put it this way...it would seem that you and your fellows have a taste for herring—in red, at least."

"Wild goose chases?" I asked. "You've been sending me to... what, Iowa? To Bloomington to fight your people? Why? Because they needed their asses kicked and you're too old to do it yourself?"

"Certainly a little humility is good for the soul," he said, with a smile, "but no, I wasn't trying to keep you off balance for that reason. It's a much simpler one. While you were chasing the three metas I dangled in front of your nose to keep you busy, you weren't noticing the fifty I snuck into the country through alternative means." He waved a hand around him. "And now they are all here."

The chill covered me from his words. Fifty metas could level the Directorate campus to the ground. What little army the Directorate had left had zero chance against fifty metas, even if their only power was their super strength, speed, reflexes... "And what are you going to do with your fifty metas?"

Janus smiled again, this one less patronizing, and it faded just as quickly as it came. "I'm going to do exactly what you think I'm going to do with them.

"I'm going to destroy the Directorate. Permanently."

24.

"You said you weren't going to kill anyone." I felt a quiver run through me and down the gunbarrel. I looked over it at Janus, calm, cool, composed, and watched him smile again.

"I'm not going to kill anyone, nor allow anyone to intentionally come to harm, not today," Janus said, cupping his hands one over the other. "I don't need to. Destroying the Directorate isn't a matter of killing someone, or everyone. I'm going to destroy your campus—just as I'm destroying every other Directorate campus in North America, even as we speak—and I'm going to leave your people with a warning that the next time you cross Omega, then," he said, and the smile vanished, leaving me cold, "then I will begin the killing."

"And you made such a point of differentiating yourself from the people who sent Wolfe, and Henderschott, and Fries," I looked at him with a kind of feigned disappointment. "You're not any different."

"Oh, but I am," he said, and the smile returned. "I don't like killing. But that doesn't mean I hesitate to employ it when necessary. The company you keep has thwarted us on several occasions—our Primus would, of course, like you to come with me, but he's been convinced now of the importance of gaining your cooperation, making you understand your importance, your place in things to come. I'm not threatening you. I come to you openhanded— delivering a message by destroying your organization, true, but not out of malice for you, rather for what your organization has done."

His face darkened. "You have no idea what damage you've allowed by letting Andromeda escape, by getting her killed. The new guard was content to give your Directorate a slap on the wrist by wiping your agents out until you did that. Once Andromeda went loose," he said with a quiet shake of his head, "it was...how do you say it? All bets were off."

"What is it about that girl?" I asked. "What is it about her that has you so...has everybody so...edgy?"

"Andromeda was the future," Janus said. "That project was our hope, our weapon, our chance to defeat an enemy monstrous in their application of force. I know you've heard it said that there is a storm coming, that you've heard others tell you of the threat to us, to all of us, and I am here to tell you that it's only partially true. Humans are safe; they have little to fear from what comes. For now, at least. The Directorate is not our enemy, you see, they were but a buzzing fly. And you know what you do to a fly, yes?"

"Please say catch them with honey," I said. "Because I'm getting tired of this manure."

"This is more like vinegar," he said. "The truth always is. I laid the trail for you myself, so you could see I went to Shenzen after the murder of the Chinese metas. They were wiped out, to the last. The government soldiers guarding them were all killed, or rendered so useless of mind and body as to be unwhole human beings for the rest of their lives. India was no different, and even now, across Africa, and the rest of Asia, it continues, the extermination, the destruction of our race—on a smaller scale, one at a time, because there are no cloisters there." He looked grim now, deadly serious, "and it will spread, and grow, across all the continents, until the last of us are dead and in our graves. They who perpetrate this? They...are our enemy. Your Directorate is nothing more than a fly that I have had to take a month out of my schedule to swat. After tomorrow, I won't think of your Directorate again. I will only think of you, and I will be waiting for the day when you join us, as surely you must."

I laughed, at his face, from fifteen feet away. "You think I'll join you? You're talking about destroying my home, threatening my friends with death if we don't disband, and you think I'll...what? Come find you in six months asking if I can join your special club?"

He gave me a noncommittal shrug. "I'd be surprised if it's more than a month. But then, I know things that you don't."

"I.Will. Never. Join. You." I let each word come out with emphasis, and I re-centered my pistol on him, cocking it. "But I'm going to put you in a cell now, then I'm going to get to work checking out how many metas you actually brought with you—"

"Check your phone," he said, with that little bit of a smile, and I forgot I was still holding it. "No tricks, I'm not compelling you to do anything, just suggesting that there might be information that you don't yet have." He smiled enigmatically.

I pulled the phone up after a moment of wrestling with my mind over whether I should. I thumbed the messages and the next came up, this one from J.J.:

Over fifty, REPEAT, over fifty enemy metas presently in continental United States based on analysis of passport batches.

I looked up and saw that smile, and I didn't know whether to scream or put a bullet in him. "The case for letting you live while I've got fifty other metas to deal with is not one based on logic." I faltered. "How did you know about the message?"

"Mmm," Janus said, cringing, "now, you see, this is where the truth is really going to hurt." He held up a hand and slowly put it in his pocket, bringing it out with a cell phone identical to mine.

"Looks like a Directorate phone," I said. "What, did you hack it? Wouldn't be the first time."

"No," he said, shaking his head in amusement. "I'm nowhere near clever enough to manage that. No, it was given to me by one of your own." He flipped it over, and the sight of the pink otter box case gave me a shudder. "Come out," he called, "she knows it's you, now."

The door to his left slid open, the one to the room we had all stood in while watching Clary and Old Man Winter interrogate Madigan. Other doors slid open, too, the one to Bjorn's cell, and Madigan's, and behind Janus, so did Fries'. My eyes weren't on any of them.

My eyes were on Kat Forrest, who strode out of the watchroom in a dark blue jumpsuit, her hair pulled back, and wearing an impish smile that didn't fit the demure, quiet girl I had known for almost the entire time I'd been at the Directorate. "You?" I asked. "You betrayed us, Kat?"

"I'm not Kat," she said with a sour smile, one that truly reminded me of a cheerleader, all sneer and no sweetness. "I'm Klementina—or as near to it as you'll get."

I felt the stir of Aleksandr Gavrikov in the back of my head and ignored him. "You still had a human personality when I saw you a couple days ago," I said, drawing a bead on her as she took position at Janus's side.

"Oh, Sienna," she said with a slight laugh, "don't act so wounded. I don't remember you coming to visit me in the medical unit after you brought me in; unless I missed it, being absent as I was the last day or so. I still remember the things Kat remembered, the things that weren't lost while I was trying to save your life, Reed's life..." she let her voice drop precipitously, "...Scott's life."

I felt a sour taste in my mouth, a bitterness. "We were friends."

"Don't friggin' kid yourself," she said, and there was none of Kat's sweetness there. "We were never friends."

"Klementina, dear," Janus said as she rubbed up against him in a manner that 1) I was sure was meant to make me vomit and 2) would have been really appropriate for ABSOLUTELY NOWHERE, EVER, "would you kindly let James, Bjorn and Eleanor out of their cages?"

"Leave them right where they are, Kat," I said, pulling tighter on the trigger, "or I will spread your treacherous, forgetting brain all over the wall behind you."

"Mmm," Janus said, pondering me. "I think not. You have a gentle heart, and are as yet unsullied by the cruelties of the world. I don't think you'll be killing anyone. We haven't threatened you, we mean you no harm, nor any of your fellows."

"You're destroying the Directorate," I said, "and you've been planning to kill Old Man Winter."

"I could not care less about Erich," Janus said with a wave. "I'm sure he'll continue to live a long and bitter life even after you've joined us."

"I'm not going anywhere with you," I said, as Kat started to move. "Don't push me, Klementina. It's been kind of a rough day."

"It's been a succession of rough days," Janus said, gesturing for her to move on, "but let us not cloud the issue. You are not going to kill anyone."

"I killed Wolfe," I said, almost snarling, trying to reassure myself. "I killed her brother. And your pet vampires."

"Yes, but you didn't know what you were doing when you killed Wolfe," Janus said, "and you killed Aleksandr to save a city. Laudable, I would say. Noble, even. And let us not fool ourselves...those vampires were nothing approaching human, not really, and had not been human for a thousand years or more. You are not a murderer, Sienna." I saw the tilt of his eyes to something approaching sadness. "When it comes down to it...we are not threatening you. We mean you no harm. And you are not willing to do what would be necessary to keep us all here."

"And that is?" I said, my voice cracking as Kat emerged from the cell behind Janus, Fries in tow, his hands freed.

"Kill us all," Janus said as Bjorn emerged from the cell to his left and Kat unlocked the handcuffs that bound his wrists. Then she disappeared into Madigan's cell.

"Nice to see you again, Sienna," Fries said, still a little bruised from his encounter with Eve. "I'm sure we'll meet again."

I felt a cold anger cut through me as Madigan emerged from the cell, freed, leaving wet footprints on the tile with every step she took. I waved the gun at them impotently as Janus took the first steps toward me. "Excuse us," he said gently brushing past me. Bjorn went by next, a glare from on high, his flat face contorted with anger. His arm had returned, though it looked a little smaller than the other. Madigan came next, then Kat, giving me a cool look as she passed, and I knew by looking in her eyes that Kat was gone, that Klementina was all that was left. *No*, a voice whispered deep inside me, *that is not Klementina, either*.

"You know," Fries said, passing by me last, "I always knew you didn't have it in you to hurt me." My gun rested at my side, but I felt it twitch in my hand. "It's the chemistry, you know, between us, the magnetism. You can feel it, can't you? The irresistible pull—"

I raised the gun and fired, the flash lighting the entire hallway, blinding me for a beat as Fries screamed and fell to the ground. "Sorry, gun just went off. Must have been your magnetism that drew the bullet irresistibly to you."

His face was contorted with pain. "You shot me...in the ass!"

"It was tough not to. You're all ass."

He made another little screech and grunt of pain as Janus and the others peered at me from down the hall. "Sienna," Janus said, "that was unnecessary."

"Yeah, well," I said, and stepped back from Fries as Bjorn took a few steps toward the incubus, "it was fun."

Janus gave a half-hearted shake of the head, then motioned for Bjorn to pick up Fries, which he did. "This isn't the end, Sienna," Fries said.

"Well, it was your end," I said. "Next time I see you, though, I think I'll aim for the crotch."

"You bitch," he breathed as Bjorn carried him into the stairwell, "I won't forget this!"

"Neither will I," I promised, "because seeing you writhe in pain has been just about the highlight of my week."

Janus remained as the last of them disappeared up the staircase. "Do not forget—we will be destroying your dormitory in only a few minutes. Do get all your people out in time, all right?" He took a few steps closer to me, but paused, just out of arm's reach. "I know you don't care for what I'm telling you, for what I've done to you, but you'll see in time that you and I have the same goals. I want to protect and save the metas of this world from what comes for them. The only difference between Omega and you is that we are willing to do whatever it takes to achieve our aims." He smiled simply. "And you are not—yet."

"I will never be like you," I said, feeling it all come out at once. "Great intentions, huh? Yeah, I've heard that before. Doing it all for a greater good, for your own good? Heard that before, too. Sounds a lot like my mother...just before she'd slam the door and lock me in a metal sarcophagus."

Janus gave a slight shrug of the shoulders. "Perhaps she did. Perhaps she was protecting you all along from the things that would hunt you, the things that would hurt you, the things that would use you."

"I think she was protecting me from you," I said coldly.

He gave a nod of acknowledgment. "There are worse things than us, though I'm sure you don't see it that way. Again, yet. I wish you well, Sienna Nealon. When next we meet is entirely in your hands."

"How about never?" I asked as he turned to walk away. "Never works well for me."

"Never say never," Janus said, taking hold of the railing of the staircase as he took his first step. He walked up them one by one, taking his time, not looking back. "Never is a very, very long time, and frankly...you don't know what will happen tomorrow that might change your mind."

25.

I ran down the hall, to the other staircase on the opposite side of the building, the darkness at the end of the hallway enveloping me. The thought that Omega wasn't here to kill anyone overwhelmed me, and I shuddered to think under what circumstances he might have convinced me to join him, now or in the future. He seemed so sure, and with every word he had said, my certainty grew less and less, until I was left to defend by anger that which I wasn't sure I even had a defensible position for. I could feel the fury burning inside me, an almost physical reaction, as though I were having heartburn. The still air in the headquarters drove me mad as I dashed up the lighted staircase.

An emergency exit waited on the landing and I pushed through it, felt the resistance against my arms as I opened it and stepped out into the cold. At least five buildings were burning in my field of vision as my feet stepped off the concrete path. The night air was frigid, and I felt it seep through the cracks of my clothing, through the bottom of my jacket to where my shirt had come untucked in all the running, biting at the skin around my belly as I ran off toward the darkened dormitory, the glass and concrete reflecting the fires of the buildings burning all around like some sort of window into hell.

I didn't see Janus or his party, even though they had (I assumed) exited out the front of the building. Perhaps they were lingering in the lobby, perhaps they had other plans. Either way, I ran for the dormitory. I threw open the glass door when I got there, and saw shadowed faces huddled in the entry; Kurt was up front, his electric-shock cannon in his hands. "Time to leave," I said, winded from my run.

"What the hell is happening here?" he asked.

"Omega is destroying the campus," I said, hands on my knees. "You need to get the students out of here. Head for the woods, and don't get near any of the buildings that are still standing." I felt a certain grimness as I said it. "They won't be for long."

Kurt looked around, his fat face turning on his wad of a bullfrog-like chin. He just looked stunned, unbelieving. "Where am I supposed to go after that?"

"Clear the damned campus," I said, "worry about the rest later."

He seemed to freeze like that, and then, haltingly, came back to motion. "All right, everyone," he shouted, turning back to the few metas behind him, "we're getting the hell outta here. Follow me, we're heading to the fence at the edge of campus."

I saw a flash of movement behind me, and heard a shout of warning from a face in the crowd before I saw what was coming. The glass shattered, exploding in a hail, little shards dragging across my cheek and forehead as I hurried to cover my face with my hands. I tried to look out but something dark and shadowed hit me, knocking me through the freestanding directory posted in the middle of the lobby. I burst through it, feeling the plastic break on both sides as I crashed into the cafeteria wall. My arm hurt to even move, though I fought through the pain, trying to get to my feet.

An enormous shadow stepped through the Sienna-sized hole in the sign, breaking it apart and sending it clattering to the ground. "Hello, Cookie," came the voice from the hulking mass of Bjorn, "I was talking to Fries and we don't really like the fact that you're just gonna walk away from this after humiliating both of us the way you did."

I pushed off the wall and tottered on my feet, feeling my balance return, my equilibrium coming back after a world-ending sucker punch. "Oh?" I knew I was dazed, needed to buy a moment of time. A repartee such as "Oh?" was not going to do it. "Well, I don't think your boss is going to be terribly happy with your line of thinking here." I blinked, trying to figure out what to say. "If he ever is. I'm guessing you're not the kind of guy who gets paid to think."

"Always the smart mouth," he said, and started toward me again. "You always have a smart-assed comment, don't you?"

"I've always found it preferable to having some dumb-assed thing to say." I steadied myself, trying to brace as he approached me. "I don't think you've learned that lesson yet, which is sad, because it sounds like you're really old compared to me—"

He moved toward me fast, and I saw a crow in my mind's eye again ,a dark shadow in flight, and it froze me. I felt him hit me, a short, low punch to the gut that rocketed me into the wall, higher up this time, and I fell something like eight feet to the ground in a crunch of pain that left me breathless. "I bet I can beat that sarcasm out of you. I bet I can make you scream it out. Really, all you need to adjust your attitude is a good beating, a few dozen broken bones to set you straight—"

The flash of lightning that hit him was epic. I'd always seen the weapon that Kurt used fired in light or at least semi-light places. In the darkness it was as though Eleanor Madigan had unleashed everything at him, and it took a moment for me to realize it was Kurt, standing behind him, uber-taser cannon firing into Bjorn's back, causing the big man to buck from the fury of it. He didn't fall, though, not completely, instead dropping to one knee as the discharge of lightning halted, leaving Bjorn bathed in a blue glow as the electricity died. "I don't think you're gonna be beating anyone today, you steroid-pumping freak." Kurt's face was lit by the glow of the barrel. "Now back the hell away from her before I light your ass up with another 1.21 gigawatts."

I pushed to my feet again, ignoring the pain in my shoulder.

"Did you just make a movie reference?"

"It was one of my favorites," Kurt said, keeping the weapon trained on Bjorn, who was still on one knee.

"You attack me with lightning?" Bjorn spoke, a low rumbling, and I saw his head shift toward the side to look at Kurt. "Me? The son of Odin? Do you know who my brother was?" He stood, and I swore he was even taller as he stared down at Kurt. "I've been taking hits from lightning bolts since I was no bigger than a foal—"

"Did you say fool?" I asked and launched myself at Bjorn before he could take a step toward Kurt. Fair was fair, after all, and he had just saved my life, even though I knew I was going to pay for this one. "You're still a fool, though you're a bigger one these days than you probably were then—" I tackled him, causing him to slowly begin to tilt over. I brought my working arm up and clobbered Bjorn in the jaw with the hardest punch I had in me, then another as we started to fall to the ground. "And you have to tell me—did your brother look like Chris Hemsworth? Because—"

"Enough!" He hit me with a backhand that caused me to flip off of him. I heard a popping in my jaw as I spun through the air and hit the ground. Another flash drew his attention away, and I saw Kurt fire three times in rapid succession. A red light lit up on Kurt's face, and I knew from experience that the weapon was running out of charge. I threw myself at Bjorn again, more pain overwhelming me than I knew I could honestly take. I grasped at his leg and he kicked me in the head, hard. I faded out for a moment and awoke as I saw Kurt get lifted and thrown through the glass doors, the shadows wrapping around my eyes as I thought about the time limit I had left to get out of the dormitory before it exploded.

Bjorn let out a roar at the kids, the students, the metas that were here to be protected by the Directorate. A stray thought washed through my mind, wondering where M-Squad was when they should be protecting the kids, but that disappeared quickly. A lone figure stepped out of the crowd, interposing himself between

Bjorn and the rest of them, and my eyes, though unfocused, recognized Joshua Harding's glasses even before I saw his face, that still damnably familiar face.

"All the little children of the Directorate," Bjorn said, a tickle of glee in his voice. "Little sheep. You'll all be part of our flock soon." The big man focused on Harding. "It looks like someone needs to be culled from the herd. Our success as metas is predicated on strength. The weak, the stupid, they should not live, polluting our bloodlines to the next generation." He closed on Joshua, shoulder down, as though ready to charge, "They should be killed before infecting us with their—"

"I'm afraid I disagree," I said, leaping onto Bjorn's back, my hands free of their gloves. I jammed my skin against his neck, holding on tight, "though in your case I am sorely tempted to make an exception to that 'no killing' rule I've got going." I felt the throb of blood in his veins as I wrapped my fingers around his throat. He bucked, trying to throw me off his back, his hands prying at mine, trying to wrench them free. I felt the first pull of my power at work, felt the tug of his soul against mine, heard the first grunt of pain from him as his strength began to fail. He screamed, and his legs buckled, and I rode him to the ground, catching it with my feet, holding him in a sleeper hold as he flailed ineffectually against me.

"No," he said in a strained moan, "please...I don't want to...not with you, not my soul..."

"Don't worry," I said, and let him go before punching him in the jaw so hard I heard it break. "I have standards, you know. And frankly, my psycho-mutant quota is filled for five lifetimes." I let his limp body slip from my grasp. "Looks like you'll live to be a moron for another day, Bjorn," I said to his unconscious form. "Bad news for you, worse news for the rest of us."

"Hey," a voice came to me, waking me from the slight trance I seemed to be in, squatted as I was over Bjorn's fallen form. It was Harding. "You said the building was gonna blow up, remember?"

"Yes. Right." I hoisted Bjorn onto my shoulder. "Let's go, people!" I shouted, rallying the half-dozen or so teenagers. They were huddled, frightened after the battle they'd just witnessed, their hushed voices bouncing off the walls. "Last one out gets to die in a horrible explosion." I gestured to Joshua. "Pick up Kurt, will you?"

He raised an eyebrow at me, then looked at the fallen form of Hannegan, lying prostrate in the glass partition between the doors that led out of the dormitory. "He's kind of a big guy."

"What, you haven't manifested yet?" I said, drawing an ire-filled look. "I just saved your life, remember?"

I caught subtlety from him, and saw that confidence again. "Maybe someday I'll repay the favor," he said as he made for Hannegan, stepping gingerly out of the broken glass hole that Hannegan's body had made when Bjorn had thrown it out the window. We fled, Harding and I following the last of the kids out of the dormitory and reaching a safe distance of about a hundred yards away as the building burst into a ball of fire. The force of the explosion threw me off my feet, sending Bjorn to the ground and me ass over teakettle into a bed of leaves.

I looked up at the orange glow all around me, saw the chill of my breath fog the air, felt the pains in my body—shoulder, back, ribs. I could smell the acrid smoke of all the destruction wrought, could almost taste the stench in the air, the oily, chemical flame smell from the campus burning—my home. I tilted my head in time to watch the headquarters go up in a blast of flame and force, the biggest explosion of the night. I felt a quiver in the ground, and I wondered where Zack was, where Old Man Winter and Ariadne were—where M-Squad was.

"You okay?" Harding spoke from above me, still holding Kurt on his shoulders, hands anchored to Hannegan's back and pants leg.

"I'll be fine," I said, forcing myself to sit up and clutching my shoulder to me. "You take Hannegan and the others and get to the woods. Get off campus. Do what I told Hannegan to do and find a way out of here."

He stared back at me through the glasses, and he looked unbowed, cool. More than I felt, that was for sure. "Come with me."

"Can't do that," I said, and I stood, feeling like a zombie coming back to life. I saw the others that were with us, the kids, saw them all recovering from the force of the explosion; it looked like almost every one of them had been knocked off their feet as well. "There's only a few of you; get to safety. Get a headcount, move together, and I'll be along in a little bit, once I finish searching for survivors."

He watched me carefully. "Looking for your boyfriend?"

I sighed. "Among others." I couldn't see much motion through the smoke and shadows that now filled the once-peaceful, tree=lined campus. "Get 'em out of here, Joshua. Keep them safe."

He shrugged, no mean feat with Hannegan on his shoulders. "I'll get 'em out of here. But I'm going my own way once they're clear. I've got things to do."

I shook my head, in no mood to argue. "Fine. Whatever. Thanks for your help."

"So long, Sienna," he said, carrying Kurt on his shoulders and waving to the others as I watched them fall in behind him in a sort of procession, the flickering flames of our campus lighting their passage through the smoke and destruction—their passage through hell. "I'll see you again."

"Why do I not doubt that?" I asked as the last of them disappeared into the smoke being blown from the dormitory fire. I heard a moan from Bjorn and I stomped on his face out of pure pique. The moaning stopped, and I stood there for a long moment, staring at the dormitory—and the wreckage of my life.

26.

I heard footsteps behind me and turned, my hands raised defensively, then I relaxed. "Geez. Give a girl a heart attack."

"Are you all right?" Bastian was at the lead, Clary and Parks a few steps behind him. I caught the glint of light off Eve Kappler's wings as she descended to land nearby. At the rear of the procession, Zack was walking in front of Old Man Winter and Ariadne, who was holding her side, her gray suit darkened by blood coming from her nose and beneath her ribs.

"I'm fine," I said, holding my shoulder. "I sent the kids out of here so I could go look for you all."

"You left them undefended?" Parks said, pushing past Bastian to stand only a foot from me.

"They'll be fine," I said, "Omega wasn't here for them. Nor for any of us, really. Not to kill, anyway."

Bastian looked me over while Parks spoke. "Oh, yeah. And you look like hell because they weren't here to kill anyone."

"They weren't," I said, letting my eyes fall off Zack and back to the fire. The relief coursed through me that he was safe, and I watched the dormitory burn.

"You let them escape," Old Man Winter said in the low rumble, speaking over the crackle of the flames.

"I stopped Bjorn here," I said and gave Bjorn a gentle kick to the trapezoid. I squinted and looked to him. "How did you know I let them go?"

"I saw," Ariadne said, clutching her side. "On the

security monitor."

"Thanks. I didn't need any help or anything," I said acerbically.

"You wouldn't have gotten any from us," Ariadne said, her voice straining. "*I* was watching. The rest of them were fending off about thirty metas that didn't act at all like they weren't here to kill. Pretty damned far from it, I would say."

Old Man Winter walked to where Bjorn lay and lifted him up by the head and neck, Bjorn's unconscious bulk hanging limp in his hands. "Janus deceived you. He likely sent Bjorn back to retrieve you."

"Maybe," I said, and the smoke made my eyes burn as I turned back to them. "I don't think so, though. They're worried about something else, something worse."

"They are right to worry," Old Man Winter said, shaking Bjorn like a puppet in his grasp. "Do you know what this storm is that is coming? Do you know how it will affect us, our people?"

"Since you haven't told us anything about it, no." I folded my arms. "Only what Janus said. It's tied to the exterminations."

"You have no idea because you are not ready," he said, countenance darkening, "because you would not know the enemy if you saw it, this destruction that creeps toward us, wiping out metas continent by continent. If it presented itself to your very face, to you, and you recognized it for what it was, you would still fail to stop it because you are unwilling to do what is necessary—to kill when you confront evil."

I felt myself redden in the heat of the fire. "Maybe you're right," I said, feeling myself fade, as though I could slip into the darkness and away from the ire of Old Man Winter, who was losing his chill rapidly and more obviously than even the time I'd seen him face Wolfe. "Maybe this isn't for me, the fight, the battle; I don't want to kill anybody. I don't want to be responsible—"

"Unfortunately," Old Man Winter said, tugging on Bjorn, letting him hang in front of me, "that is not an option. I know what waits at the head of the organization—they are called *Century*, by the way, since you want to know what I know—and I know that you, and you alone, are the only one that stands a chance—a hope in hell—of stopping them."

"How do you even know that?" I asked, feeling ruthless, cynical, angry. "You didn't know who I was a year ago! You didn't know I existed! You couldn't even figure out what Omega is up to! How do you presume to tell me what some black box organization that sounds like a movie production company is up to a world away?"

"Because I know who heads them," he said, and there was a rattle in his voice, "and I have feared him since he crippled me over a hundred years ago. He is without a doubt the most powerful meta on the face of the earth, and with one hundred followers—some of the strongest metas on the planet—he has assembled an army that is wiping us out, piecemeal. They burned through the compounds in India and China because they were the easiest, but even now they have split, divided their forces and run rampant through Asia and Africa, slaughtering whole cloisters of metas. Next will be Europe, and finally..." His eyes turned grim. "You are the only one who can stop him—and by extension, them. You must be willing to do what it takes—to kill him, because you, yourself, will be the only one with a chance."

"Fine," I said, cowed by the conviction in his eyes. "Fine, I'll...make ready. I just..." I blinked back the feeling. "You know I will, to save lives, to save people." I licked my lips. "I have before. With Gavrikov. I can do it again."

"It will not be enough," he said, glaring at me. "You fear it, your power. I can see it in your eyes; the fear consumes you. You are afraid of it, to unleash yourself—and yet that will be the only thing that will save us all."

"I don't need to unleash anything," I said. "I've got Wolfe in my head, remember? Unleashing has a special meaning with him—"

"Kill Bjorn," he said, and held up the Omega operative, near lifeless. "If you truly mean that you will do whatever it takes, then show me you can do it. Show me you are willing, that you won't hesitate, that you won't falter when we need you most."

"Are you frigging kidding me?" I waved a hand at him. "He's out. I'm not killing a lump of inert matter like that."

"Take his soul," Old Man Winter said. "Show me."

"I want that crawling around in my head," I gestured at Bjorn again, "like I want to take a lit blowtorch and stick it in my ear. No, thank you."

"Kill him," Old Man Winter said, and pushed Bjorn forward, dangling him in front of me.

"No!" I said, and backed away. "I'm not...no."

"Is that your final word on the matter?" There was a dangerous glint in his eyes which I ignored, and I felt the stubbornness come back, like I was talking to Mom.

"I'm not killing an unconscious man, even if he is a monster," I said, backing away. "I'm not a murderer. I'm not like him."

"Clary," Old Man Winter said, jarring the big man out of listening to the conversation, watching all that was taking place, "restrain Sienna, please."

"What?" I recoiled, almost not believing. I saw Zack move in front of Old Man Winter, as if to interpose himself between us, but a net of light hit him, and he spun, dragged to the ground by Eve Kappler's abilities, her hands out as she turned toward me. "What the hell are you doing?"

"Clary," Old Man Winter said again. "Take hold of Sienna, please."

"I, uh..." Clary faltered, unmoving, unsure, his eyes wide.

"*Clary.*" Old Man Winter's voice crackled like thunder, and Clary shook, his skin turning metal as he turned, hesitantly, toward me.

I tensed, ready to dodge him, ready to run, but Eve's net took me to the ground unexpectedly. I struggled against it, fighting the light, writhing hard against the ground, but it held me tight to the dirt. My head hurt from where I'd hit a rock when I went down, my shoulder screamed at me as I railed against it.

Clary's shadow extended over me, a long, dark face cast in metal. "I'm sorry," he whispered as he dragged the net off me and anchored his hands on each of my wrists. He turned me around, pressing my back against him, carrying me, my arms twisted, in front of him. I thought about ramming my head back against his face, trying to knock myself unconscious, but I decided it was pointless.

"Sir," Bastian said, "this is..."

"Not now," Old Man Winter said, dismissing Bastian. "Clary, hold out her hands."

"Are you kidding me?" I said as Clary pried my hands loose and extended them, walking me along like some sort of ragdoll as I tried kicking to free myself, to no avail. "Clary, you douche!"

"I'm sorry," Clary said. "But the man's spoken, Sienna. He knows what he's talking about."

"This is for your own good," Old Man Winter said, advancing on me, Bjorn held in his hands. "For the good of all of us. You can save us, but only if you are prepared."

"I'll prepare," I said, struggling. "I'll train, I'll do whatever you want, please just do not...put this sicko...in my head with the others!"

Old Man Winter pressed Bjorn's shoulders against my palms, held open by Clary's grip. I felt the drain of the soul begin, the cumulative effect of touching Bjorn earlier drawing the process faster, as my head started to spin. I whimpered, and closed my eyes tight as the burning began, like the joints of my fingers were on fire where I was touching him. Blissfully, Bjorn made not even a sound, though I could clearly hear him screaming in my head as the last of him left his body and joined me in my own, a searing, joyous, agonizing, pleasurable experience as my body reacted and I felt myself shake from all my nerves tingling.

I heard my breath, falling, rising, felt the slow smile creep onto my face that I had to wipe off by sheer force of will; Charlie was right, it was better than anything, better than the sex—

"I am sorry," Old Man Winter said, staring down at me. "But you left me no choice."

"Okay," I said, trying to regain my breath, pragmatic, wondering how long it would be before I could get away from him, from everybody, torn between what had just happened that made me feel so dirty and violated and yet tingly and warm —I wanted to simultaneously shower and cast myself into the fire of the dormitory, feel it scream across my skin, searing all the yuck off of me along with this horrible feeling of being used, lied to, betrayed—

"I very much doubt that it is 'okay'," Old Man Winter said, withdrawing. "You are still unready, unwilling to do what it will take. You will hesitate and it will be the death of you. And with you, all our hopes." He snapped his fingers at Parks and Bastian in turn. "Free Zack from the net...and bring him here."

It took about two seconds for my mind to register what he had said, and another one or two before I realized what he was intending. "No," I said, nauseous, disbelieving.

"Sir..." Bastian said under his breath.

"That's not right," Parks said, a little louder.

"You're beyond the line here, Director," Ariadne said, stepping up next to him.

Old Man Winter was quiet for a long moment. "When our entire species is in danger of being wiped out...there are no lines I am not willing to cross." He turned calmly back to Bastian. "Bring him."

"NO!" I shrieked and fought against Clary's rock-like grip, flailing and kicking. I felt him wrap his arm around my midsection, snugging me tight to him while leaving my arms extended, holding them tight enough to numb them. "No!"

"You can't do this, sir—" I heard Ariadne say.

"Kappler," Old Man Winter said, "take her away."

Eve grabbed hold of Ariadne, who screamed as Eve bent her backwards, causing Ariadne to hold her side in pain. I watched Eve wrap an arm tightly around her and drag her away, even as Ariadne tried to fight back. They disappeared into the smoke.

"Roberto...Glen..." Old Man Winter spoke again, warning. "This is the moment to decide whether you are willing to do what it will take to preserve our world...or whether you are content to die with the others."

"I..." Parks mouth opened and shut, no words coming out.

"Come on," Bastian said, landing a hand on Parks' shoulder and pointing him toward Zack, who lay watching the whole exchange under the net, strangely quiet. "You know why we have to."

"No, please..." I wasn't even ashamed that the begging came from me. I could see Zack watching me. "Please, please, please don't...Clary...Parks...Bastian...Please...."

They had Zack up on his feet, by the arms, and brought him forward, toward me, toward death. I looked up, away, tried to pretend I was anywhere but here, in the ruins of the only place I'd ever really thought of as a home, surrounded by the people I trusted with my life, with my future.

"Look at me," Old Man Winter said, and I did, even though he was blurry and I had to strain to see him. "You will hate me for this. And that is the way of things. You will never need to thank me, when you realize what I have done to save us all here, today. But you will know, the day will come, and you will realize that I have done what I have done...for the good of all of us...and for your own good."

"Please..." I pleaded. "Please don't do this. I will kill whoever you tell me to."

"You are not a killer," he said, quiet. "Not yet, anyway."

I didn't look at Parks or Bastian, holding Zack by the shoulders and using their meta strength to carry him, struggling, toward me. He stopped struggling when he got within a couple feet, stopped kicking, probably for fear of hitting me. I looked into his eyes, and I was more afraid than I'd ever been in my entire life, than when I'd been locked in the box, than when Wolfe threw me into a wall in my basement, than when I thought Gavrikov was going to nuke me or Fries was going to gut me—

"I'm sorry," I said to Zack as Clary pressed my numb hands against his face, as Bastian and Parks held him there and I felt his skin against mine, the cool touch of the night air revealing the perspiration on my palms, the slick feeling of fear that was all that stood between my lover and I.

"It's okay," he said, and he rubbed his cheek against my hand, as though he were stroking me. "It's okay. Just...be yourself, Sienna. Please." He smiled, a glorious, genuine smile that lasted only a second or two before the first waver came, as I felt the burning in my hands, felt the swimming in my head, the flicker of those coffee-brown eyes that I loved, and I saw the tensing of the muscles, the clenching of his teeth, that beautiful smile wiped away, now, aghast with horror and anguish—

"I'm sorry," I said, and I screamed it, "I'm sorry!" The swirling picked up in my mind as my brain made way for him, and he started to shout on his own, to scream, to cry, jerking in the grip of Parks and Bastian, and I fought back against Clary again, but it was impossible, he was immovable, and I hated them hated them hated them ALL...

"Be...yourself..." Zack said, the only discernible sound in the hurricane around me, the gale-force wind in my mind, the tempest rocking my body and his in a tornado of combination, as he screamed, louder and louder, the pain a driving agony now and tearing him apart—

And then he was still, the brown eyes dull, empty; the soul

gone from them.

I felt the nausea double, triple, mix with something else, a kind of reckless joy and rush of euphoria that was a hundred times more powerful than what the chloridamide did to me when it hit the vein, and a kind of weak drowsiness settled over me, the emotion blown, and now I wanted more than ever to throw myself into the fire.

"Let her go," Old Man Winter said, and Clary dropped me to the ground, where I lay huddled, my head overwhelmed, too many thoughts and minds, even behind the wall of chloridamide that remained. "You will remember this day, and look back, and know that I was right."

"I will look back on this day, and remember..." I said, "...and I will kill you...the next time I see you..." I looked up at him with all the hatred, all the venom, everything I felt down to the last inch of my soul.

Old Man Winter was above me, Bastian and Parks flanking him, and Clary sidling into line behind them. The old man's face was indecipherable; there wasn't any expression. It was like it was when I'd first met him, as though I'd never known him at all.

With that, he turned, and strode off through the carnage, the grass and leaves of the dead summer crunching underfoot. Bastian followed first, then Clary, and finally Parks, though he waited a moment. I didn't look at them, not at any of them. I didn't want to dignify them with so much as a glance. I clutched my shoulder tight to me, rubbed my arms, which I could not even feel, and lay on my back, looking up to the sky. I didn't want to look at the body; I knew they had laid me next to him. I reached out for a hand and found it, his bare skin on mine, but his was cold, and lifeless... and mine was not, no matter how much I wished it were. I curled my face against his chest, and it wasn't moving now, not like last night or this morning, and I knew I could sleep here next to him, undisturbed by his breath because now there was none.

I stared into the black sky overhead, the smoke and darkness lit only by the fires of the burning Directorate, and I felt a touch of something on my forehead. Another followed, and another, and I opened my eyes. Snowflakes fell in little flurries, wending their way toward the earth, falling down around me, around the chaos of the destroyed campus, the destruction of my life, the end of my world, and I lay there, Zack's cold hand in mine, as they fell.

27.

Interlude

Chanhassen, Minnesota

The Cadillac's wheel was tight against his hands; the ache was in them, *from the weather*, he told himself, the first flakes of snow hitting the windshield, illuminated by the headlights as he drove down the darkened highway.

"I can't believe you left Bjorn behind," Fries said from the backseat. "How could you do that?"

"He disobeyed my order," Janus said, and gave a reassuring smile to Klementina in the passenger seat, "and he paid the price for it."

"You let him remain a prisoner of Old Man Winter—" Fries said.

"Hardly," Janus said. "He's quite dead, now."

"Dead?" Fries said into the silence. Madigan, for her part, did not question, did not say a word. She knew. He had worked with her many times before, and she understood the way of things. "You let them kill him?"

"I did not let them do anything," Janus said. "But I believe Erich Winter has hit his breaking point. You see, Winter is afraid, and Bjorn will suffer the rather unfortunate consequences of that. It's all part of the plan, you see. All expected."

"You manipulated him?" Klementina asked, a look of awe on her face. "Old Man Winter and Bjorn?"

"Only Bjorn," Janus said. "Erich Winter needed no

manipulation. Over a hundred years ago, in Peshtigo, Wisconsin, he saw the truth of what we now face, the leader of Century. He knows now how critical Sienna is to the survival of our people, and he will not hesitate to...push her in the right direction." Janus smiled. "Which, coincidentally, is our direction, though I doubt he fully realizes that right now." The smile evaporated. "Not that he would care, even if he knew. Meta survival is somewhat higher on his list of concerns than our petty disputes, after all."

"What is he?" Klementina asked, and even Fries fell silent. "The leader of Century, I mean. I'd heard—well, Kat had—from Old Man Winter that Sienna was important, was vital, but no one seems to want to explain why."

Janus felt the cold chill run through him too, the remembrance, of a meeting long ago. "So you want to know about the most powerful meta on the planet, do you?"

He could see the hunger in her eyes. "I do."

"I can only tell you so much; his abilities are beyond that of any class of meta you have ever heard of," Janus said, with a smile that he didn't feel. "He is...adaptable. He has powers that no meta should have, abilities you have seen before but in combinations never before possessed by anyone else."

"Does he have a name?" Klementina asked.

"A thousand of them, Sweetness," Janus said. "A million perhaps. Excuse me for a moment." He lifted the disposable cell phone to his ear, and waited to hear the receptionist on the other end. "Message for Alastor. Stanchion went as planned. One casualty, Bjorn Odin-son. All other operatives returning to duty stations. Mission was a success, and Sienna—code-name Savior— will join us within a month." He halted. "Did you get all that, dear?" The voice repeated it back to him and he listened carefully. "Very good." He hung up the phone and tossed it back into the center console before closing it.

"'Savior'?" Fries said from the back seat. "She's the same kind of meta I am, you know."

Janus shrugged. "She has something you don't."

"What's that?"

"A soul of her own to start with, I would think," Janus said, and smiled at Kat. "Enough. Our plans are our own. You will remain in Minneapolis and wait for her to make contact."

"Are you kidding?" Fries said, dull astonishment from the back seat. "She shot me! What's going to stop her from killing me if she comes after me again?"

"Human restraint and little else," Janus replied, "but your life is a sacrifice I'm well prepared to make. Remain here until she makes contact, then we'll work out some sort of arrangement to her satisfaction."

"You really think she's gonna come to me, after everything we've been through?" Fries asked in disbelief. "That she'll be willing to deal? That she won't shoot me again?"

"Yes to the first," Janus said, "yes to the second, maybe to the third, but I'm indifferent on the outcome of that one."

There was a lengthy pause. "What makes you so sure she'll come to us?"

"Because," Janus said, and there was little satisfaction in it, "she has nowhere else to go."

28.

Sienna

I stole a car out of the Directorate employees' lot. It was Zack's car. I doubted he'd miss it. It rattled a little—the transmission, a small voice told me, one that I didn't want to think about yet. It carried me down the road though, the old windshield wipers shrugging off the slowly accumulating snow as I drove down U.S. Highway 212 in the middle of the night, the headlights illuminating the snow that was falling ever faster now, little dots of white that flurried past the beams.

It was well after midnight by the time I had managed to peel myself off the snowy ground and get going. Not a single police siren was to be heard, nothing, nada, and no one was around when I came to. No one but him, his body. I didn't know whether I had fallen asleep or passed out, and I didn't much care, either. The car smelled like him, and I wanted to burn it, burn me, make one giant funeral pyre and be done with it. But I couldn't. Not now.

Not yet.

The freeways were starting to get slushy when I hit Eden Prairie and Interstate 494. I followed the road I'd driven a million times in the last year, took Minnesota Highway 62 toward the south side of Minneapolis, then headed up Interstate 35W. I could see the skyline in the distance as I drove, getting closer and closer. The houses grew older as I went, and when I exited in my old neighborhood, I rolled down the window, felt the flash of cold rush into the car, and realized that the cold was like home to me. The snow was insignificant. It covered the ground the first day I left my house, and for the longest time it was my whole world, a snow-covered, frozen-over hell. Let it snow, I thought, let it come down in volume enough to bury me.

I pulled onto my old street, the trees catching the headlights and casting twisted shadows on the walls of the houses as I drove past. Like the shadows from the flames of the campus, they seemed to take on a life of their own, as though they would reach out for me, take hold of me, shake every bit of decency and life out of me until there was nothing left...

Well, they were welcome to try. I suspected there wasn't much of either remaining, anyway.

I pulled into my driveway and killed the engine, leaving the keys where they were. I didn't care if someone stole the car. I almost hoped they did, because it smelled like him, and I could hear the engine the way he heard it, could almost taste his kiss again, as I sat in it.

My feet crunched in the first accumulation of snow, one step at a time as I made my way up the walk. I opened the door to the porch and it swung wide, closing behind me. I felt the handle of the door to the interior of the house, remembered my keys had burned in my dorm room, and twisted the lock until I heard it break. I pulled out the guts and used my finger to twist it. It broke the skin, but I didn't care. A bleeding finger was insignificant compared to the other things that were on my mind.

I opened the door and stood silhouetted in the darkness of the living room. I felt a flash of memory, a thought of his, not mine—of him and Kurt, making their way across this room. Kurt hit the coffee table with his leg, making a noise. I could hear their breathing, steady, the motion, the smell of the outside—my memory now, intersecting with the other. I shook my head, tried to forget it, to put it out of my mind. I closed the door behind me, shrouding the room in darkness.

Darkness. Peace. Quiet. Nothing moved, there was no sound. Bliss.

I looked to the hallway, and I could see my old bedroom from here, remembered I had been lying there when—

I put it out of my mind again, tried to quiet it, to shut it up. "I don't want to think about that now," I said to the empty room. "I don't want to think about it." My eyes went back to my bedroom door, and in the midst of the familiar sights and smells of my childhood, I smelled another.

Zack's cologne.

I walked to the bedroom door and looked at the bed where I had lain when he woke me up the first time. My prince. Not with a kiss, but his very presence, jarring me awake. And I'd hit him for it. In the groin. I pulled the door closed, put my back against it. "No," I whispered. "No— no— no..."

I drew a deep breath, the ghosts of memory plaguing me. I tried to separate myself from it, from the smells, from the sounds, the phantom thoughts and memories that wouldn't stop. "Fine," I said, "just fine, be that way." I walked ahead, to the old, wooden door, and turned the handle. The steps led down, turning on a wooden landing below, though I couldn't see it. I knew every step by memory, having walked it a thousand times, and I closed my eyes and felt for the handrail. I heard the creak of the floorboards and the rattle of the water heater over in the far corner of the basement, but I didn't care. All these sounds were familiar, but they weren't intimidating. I didn't fear them.

I didn't have much left to fear.

When I reached the bottom step, I took a few more forward. The neighbor's porch light shone in through the window I'd had replaced almost a year ago after Reed broke through it while making an escape. I could see the light through the snow, the definition gone but the light remained, just a little bit, almost like moonlight shining through the glass. It caught my face, and I turned, looking toward the corner for it, for the shadow.

It was there, pushed against the wall, not in the same place it had stood for all my life, but near enough. The box stretched to a foot over my head, forbidding, dark, the door hanging slightly ajar and open, still bent from the last time I had been in it, when I had broken my way out. It was only a few hours before the memory, the one I wanted to forget, desperately, to believe had never happened—because if it hadn't, if he hadn't come, then I wouldn't have met him and we wouldn't have—and he would still be alive, and not dead and—

I ran my hand across the pitted metal surface. I tugged on the door and it opened with a squeal, still hanging off its hinges at a broken angle, twisted. "I never should have left you," I whispered to the darkness within, and it felt like the darkness answered me, like it moved inside, welcoming me back. I took a step in, and turned, facing my back to the open door, then grasped hold of it and pulled, dragging the door shut behind me. It fought me only a little, then I heard it creak into place, and the darkness surrounded me once more, only the faintest lines showing around the door where the lamplight came in from outside the window.

I stood there, alone again, in the dark, the quiet, the peace, the solitude. Just stood. Breathe in, breathe out. I liked the dark. The quiet. The solitude. I didn't mind alone at all. Breathe in, breathe out. It smelled like home. My legs gave out a moment later, and I slumped, my back sliding down the back wall of the box. I folded in on myself, pulling my knees close as I dissolved, finally, the emotion coming now, here, in the darkness. This was where I belonged, where I deserved to be. Where I never should have left. Back in the box.

And I resolved I would never leave again.

An Apology For The Agony I Just Caused You, The Reader

Yeah, I know that hurt. A lot. It hurt me too, honestly. I finished writing that scene - yeah, that one scene, you know which one if you finished reading it, and yes, it broke me. Killing characters like that is painful for the author, too, I promise, and I didn't just do it to be cruel. This is book 5 of a 10-book series. We're now at the midway point, and things had to take a turn to get us where we're going. I promise it's all for good reasons, that it's all part of the story. There's always been a bigger plan, a thread that stretches through the entire series, and I hope it's all going to be worth it for you, the reader, in the end. I even thought about ways I might be able to soften what just happened here in this book, but there really isn't, not without fundamentally changing the story. I hope I've built enough trust with you by this point that you know I didn't do what I did capriciously and for no purpose. Things were always going to get worse for Sienna before they got better.

I hope we see you for the next book (full preview of Book Six on the next page!) and if you want to know as soon as it comes out, go to robertJcrane.com and sign up for our mailing list. I promise I won't spam you (I only send an email when I have a new book released) and I'll never sell your info. You can also unsubscribe at any time - like maybe now, in some of your cases, after I just killed one of your favorite characters in a horrible way. I hope you don't feel that way, but I understand if you do. If you want to talk about it, feel free to send me an email (please don't yell

at me) at cyrusdavidon@gmail.com, stop by my Facebook page
(Robert J. Crane (Author)), send me a tweet (@robertJcrane) or
stop by my blog, which will have a dedicated discussion post where
you can talk with other fans about this book (compain about how
insensitive the author is - ZOMG what a jerk!!1!1!). If you don't
want to talk to me, you could always send Sienna a tweet of support
- @SiennaNealon.

I hope to see you again next time.

Robert J. Crane

About the Author

Robert J. Crane was born and raised on Florida's Space Coast before moving to the upper midwest in search of cooler climates and more palatable beer. He graduated from the University of Central Florida with a degree in English Creative Writing. He worked for a year as a substitute teacher and worked in the financial services field for seven years while writing in his spare time. He makes his home in the Twin Cities area of Minnesota.

He can be contacted in several ways:

Via **email** at cyrusdavidon@gmail.com

Follow him on **Twitter** – @robertJcrane

Connect on **Facebook** – robertJcrane (Author)

Website – http://www.robertJcrane.com

Blog – http://robertJcrane.blogspot.com

Become a fan on **Goodreads**
http://www.goodreads.com/RobertJCrane

Sienna Nealon will return in

BROKEN

THE GIRL IN THE BOX, BOOK SIX

Sienna Nealon is a broken human being. Her lover is dead, her closest friends have deserted her, and her employers have betrayed her. From the ashes of her desperation, she must master the metahuman powers at her command and finally tame the souls that share her body for one ultimate purpose - revenge against the ones who destroyed her life.

Coming Summer 2013

The Sanctuary Series
Epic Fantasy by Robert J. Crane

The world of Arkaria is a dangerous place, filled with dragons, titans, goblins and other dangers. Those who live in this world are faced with two choices: live an ordinary life or become an adventurer and seek the extraordinary.

Defender
The Sanctuary Series, Volume One

Cyrus Davidon leads a small guild in the human capital of Reikonos. Caught in an untenable situation, facing death in the den of a dragon, they are saved by the brave fighters of Sanctuary who offer an invitation filled with the promise of greater adventure. Soon Cyrus is embroiled in a mystery - someone is stealing weapons of nearly unlimited power for an unknown purpose, and Sanctuary may be the only thing that stands between the world of Arkaria and total destruction.

Available Now!

Avenger
The Sanctuary Series, Volume Two

When a series of attacks on convoys draws suspicion that Sanctuary is involved, Cyrus Davidon must put aside his personal struggles and try to find the raiders. As the attacks worsen, Cyrus and his comrades find themselves abandoned by their allies, surrounded by enemies, facing the end of Sanctuary and a war that will consume their world.

Available Now!

Champion
The Sanctuary Series, Volume Three

As the war heats up in Arkaria, Vara is forced to flee after an ancient order of skilled assassins infiltrates Sanctuary and targets her. Cyrus Davidon accompanies her home to the elven city of Termina and the two of them become embroiled in a mystery that will shake the very foundations of the Elven Kingdom – and Arkaria.

Available Now!

Crusader
The Sanctuary Series, Volume Four

Cyrus Davidon finds himself far from his home in Sanctuary, in the land of Luukessia, a place divided and deep in turmoil. With his allies at his side, Cyrus finds himself facing off against an implacable foe in a war that will challenge all his convictions – and one he may not be able to win.

Coming Early 2013!

Savages
A Sanctuary Short Story

Twenty years before Cyrus Davidon joined Sanctuary, his father was killed in a war with the trolls and he has never forgiven them. Enter Vaste, a troll unlike most; courageous, loyal and an outcast. When Cyrus and Vaste become trapped in a far distant land, they are forced to overcome their suspicions and work together to get home.

Available Now!

A Familiar Face
A Sanctuary Short Story

Cyrus Davidon gets more than he bargained for when he takes a day away from Sanctuary to visit the busy markets of his hometown, Reikonos. While there, he meets a woman who seems very familiar, and appears to know him, but that he can't place.

Available Now!

The Girl in the Box
Contemporary Urban Fantasy by Robert J. Crane

Alone
The Girl in the Box, Book 1

Sienna Nealon was a 17 year-old girl who had been held prisoner in her own house by her mother for twelve years. Then one day her mother vanished, and Sienna woke up to find two strange men in her home. On the run, unsure of who to turn to and discovering she possesses mysterious powers, Sienna finds herself pursued by a shadowy agency known as the Directorate and hunted by a vicious, bloodthirsty psychopath named Wolfe, each of which is determined to capture her for their own purposes...

Available Now!

Untouched
The Girl in the Box, Book 2

Still haunted by her last encounter with Wolfe and searching for her mother, Sienna Nealon must put aside her personal struggles when a new threat emerges – Aleksandr Gavrikov, a metahuman so powerful, he could destroy entire cities – and he's focused on bringing the Directorate to its knees.

Available Now!

Soulless
The Girl in the Box, Book 3

After six months of intense training with the Directorate, Sienna Nealon finds herself on her first assignment – tracking a dangerous meta across the upper midwest. With Scott Byerly and Kat Forrest at her side, she'll face new enemies and receive help from unlikely allies as she stumbles across the truth behind the shadowy organization known only as Omega.

Available Now!

Family
The Girl in the Box, Book 4

After six months of intense training with the Directorate, Sienna Nealon finds herself on her first assignment – tracking a dangerous meta across the upper midwest. With Scott Byerly and Kat Forrest at her side, she'll face new enemies and receive help from unlikely allies as she stumbles across the truth behind the shadowy organization known only as Omega.

Available Now!

CPSIA information can be obtained
at www.ICGtesting.com
Printed in the USA
LVHW011556170119
604290LV00017B/589

9 781482 393392